Day Terrors

The Harrow Press™

The Harrow Press
365 E. Avenida de los Arboles #230
Thousand Oaks, CA 91360
www.theharrowpress.com

First publication: February 2011

Editors: Kfir Luzzatto & Dru Pagliassotti

Published by arrangement with the authors.

ISBN-10 0615406408

ISBN-13 9780615406404

Cover Art © 2010 Michal Luzzatto

Table of Contents

Introduction

A nything can be scary at night.

Floorboards cooling and creaking. A shadow cast by a piece of furniture. A raccoon in the trash.

When we can't see something, our imagination goes into overtime, with the inevitable result that the threats we conjure in our mind's eye are much more frightening than the reality we see with our physical eyes once we flip on that lightswitch.

Darkness acts as a sort of Pandora's box — Schrödinger's steel chamber — Nietzsche's abyss —the psychological black box of the mind. That is, we know that something unpleasant could be lurking where we can't see it, but as long as the box remains closed, we are frightened but unharmed.

As long as we close our eyes and pull the covers over our head, we tremble but feel safe. We are comforted by our superstitious belief that what we can't see can't hurt us.

As long as we don't see them, the world's evils will remain confined; the cat will be alive; the trauma will be nothing but a bad dream; and the monster out there will be nothing more than the wind rattling the windows, after all.

Ignorance might be frightening, but it offers plausible denial.

It's only after we open our eyes — turn on the light, peek inside the box, gaze into the abyss — that the damage is done. Evil escapes, the cat's fate is sealed, the repressed trauma returns —

— the monster turns and meets our eyes.

In Sigmund Freud's 1919 essay on "The Uncanny," he quotes Schelling's definition "of the uncanny as something which ought to have remained hidden but has come to light," or, in Freud's psychoanalytic understanding of the world, something once known but repressed is pushing its way back into our consciousness again, bringing with it feelings of fear and anxiety.

In other words, the moment we experience as being uncanny is that moment in which we see that which should not have been seen or we realize that which should not have been realized.

It is that moment in which our reality turns upside-down as we're forced to reinterpret everything we thought we understood about reality or ourselves in the light — and of course there *must* be light — of our horrible, gut-wrenching new knowledge.

Every horror story revolves around such an unfortunate revelation: seeing the contents of the ancient tomb that shouldn't have been opened; comprehending the lore in the forbidden tome that shouldn't have been read; discerning the origin of the mysterious noise that shouldn't have been investigated; comprehending the truth about the mysterious stranger who shouldn't have been approached; remembering the childhood event that should have stayed forgotten.

It isn't the darkness you should fear; it's the light. Because you can keep denying the monster exists until that dire moment that you finally see it.

And when you see it, it is all too likely to see you, too.

To see, to name, to know, is to become vulnerable. If you keep the lights off, the door closed, the box shut, you'll be safe. At least, you'll be safe up until that final, dreadful moment in which your curiosity or fear becomes so great that you finally peek.

And there the monster is, right before your eyes, sending a hopeless shiver down your spine as your mind rebels against the dreadful truth.

And in that moment, your world is changed forever.

In myth, the price of knowledge is often the loss of the sight that won it. Oedipus, confronted with the horrible truth of his actions, tears out his eyes; Tiresias, privy to forbidden knowledge, loses his sight; Wotan, to gain wisdom, sacrifices an eye; Rapunzel's prince, seeing the witch, falls backward and is blinded by the thorns at the bottom of the tower.

Of course, those are the lucky ones. The unlucky ones lost their life: The heroes who sought to defeat Medusa; the hunter Acteon who gazed at naked Artemis; Lot's wife who turned back to watch Sodom's destruction.

They should have kept their eyes closed and stayed huddled up safely in the dark, hoping that dawn never came.

Maybe, just maybe, they would have been safe.

Just as, maybe, just maybe, *you'd* be safe if you stopped reading now.

Because if you continue to read, you'll be opening yourself up to the same perils they faced. You'll watch dark pacts made and broken, witness terrible crimes committed and punished, learn about malevolent forces natural and monstrous, and see humans' deepest fears, regrets, and obsessions return to destroy them.

All taking place in the unrelenting, unforgiving, undeniable, unavoidable light of day.

What follows are *Day Terrors*.

Don't say you weren't warned.

Dru Pagliassotti – Thousand Oaks, February 2011

Ataraxia
Scott Brendel

When I shot the child in the head, his mother wept, her tears of grief—and gratitude—like rain on a hot summer's day.

There was a time when such an act would have made me a monster. But those days are behind us now. The world has changed.

The boy—a wispy nine or ten year old—stood in front of my desk, jaw slack, a string of drool descending from his mouth, his milky eyes as empty as the wind-blown desert west of town. He had the fragile substance of a kite. Had I poked him, he would have fallen to the floor. His mother sat in a chair beside him, waiting, her chin trembling. All this I took in at a glance as Terry and I entered the office.

Terry took up his post beside the door while I sat down behind the desk and opened the file.

"How long has he been like this?"

"Nine months."

"*Nine*?" I was incredulous. The disease usually ran its course in less than four. "Why did you wait so long?"

"I hoped..." She stopped, her throat convulsing silently.

They all hoped—that the catatonia would pass, that the person they loved would awaken as if from a dream and rejoin the family they'd left behind. But such awakenings were rare—and some were deadly.

Catching Terry's eye, I gave him the signal. The big man

slipped through the door to fetch the woman a glass of water.

"You know the odds?" I asked gently after he'd gone.

She looked across the room, past the steel bars bolted to the window, and nodded.

Five hundred to one that he would live another month, a thousand to one he would awaken as the loving son he'd been before the sickness claimed him.

"Are you aware of the options?" I asked, knowing from the threadbare condition of her clothes that there weren't any. "There's private care ... or Ataraxia."

Just naming the place made my skin crawl. Because I'd been there. But she hadn't; she wouldn't know. A blessing that she didn't.

"Tell me about it."

I hesitated, trying to think of something that would give her some modicum of comfort about what lay ahead for her boy, trying to imagine what I'd want to know if I were in her position.

In the silence, a sound—a rasp like a zipper. Then a smell so foul I recoiled. The boy had urinated on the carpet and his sphincter had let go, his body finally giving in to the inevitable. Which meant—

When I glanced at his face, he stared back, the glazed look gone, his eyes wide and riddled with veins, a feral smile pulling at the corners of his mouth.

"Get away from him," I screamed, diving for the phone.

Before the mother could move, the boy backhanded her across the room, then launched himself at me over the desk.

The stench of shit made me gag and I felt my own bowels loosen as I tried to call for help, but he was too quick. Although he couldn't have weighed more than fifty pounds, I was off balance when he hit me. He drove me into the desk chair and we both went over backward.

Struggling to my feet, I tried to channel the Krav Maga martial arts training they taught us for just such a situation. But my suit jacket hampered my ability to move and fear fed my frenzy.

The boy tore at my face and eyes like a cyclone filled with razor blades, and even though I outweighed him by more than a hundred pounds, he drove me to my knees.

That may have saved me, because it put me within reach of the underside of the desk. I threw him clear—he was as light as a feather—and grabbed at the holster strapped beneath the middle drawer. I raised the gun as the kid flew at me one last time.

Terry's black face paled as he helped me to my feet.

"You all right?"

I nodded, avoiding his eyes as I set the handgun down on the desk.

Designed for close quarters, it looked like an over-and-under double-barreled flare gun and took shotgun shells. If your first shot missed, you had a second. If that one missed, you'd probably never get a chance at a third.

"Let me check you," Terry said.

"I'm fine!" I snapped, raising my hands to keep him away.

He backed off, clearly unhappy at the breach of protocol. Behind him, the mother crouched on the floor and cried, her hand on the boy's leg, her eyes averted from his body.

"Get Mrs. ..." I couldn't remember her name, wasn't sure I had ever known it. "Take her down to the discharge area."

He nodded.

"And clean up this mess," I said, waving at the wall coated with the remains of the boy's head.

Rain fell in tangled, wind-blown sheets beyond the window of my office as I left for the day. But weather had little effect on my trip home, since I stayed within the secured confines of the tunnels that connected the city's buildings.

No one walked the streets anymore. Hadn't since the blight. Like the white mice I'd raised as a child, we scurried from point to point through tunnels and tubes we hoped would protect us from the decaying world around us.

My footsteps echoed in the empty space as I made my way to the subway platform. Years ago, it would have been a hive of activity at this time of day. Rush hour, they called it, when the millions who lived and worked in the city left their jobs at the end of the day. But now it was deserted, silent except for the distant rumble of the driverless trains.

From behind me came a rustle and a glassy clink. I whirled and dropped into a crouch, the gun out of its holster and in my hand. Then I relaxed as an old wino—one of the few nimble enough to escape the predators that sometimes found their way into the tunnels—picked up the bottle he'd dropped and farted a windy greeting.

My hand shook as I slid the gun back into its holster. I could have killed him. An innocent man. But what made me tremble was the look I'd seen in the boy's eyes.

By the time I got to my apartment, it was late.

"Honey, I'm home," I called, hanging my coat in the closet beside the door. "Sorry I'm late. A problem at work."

I didn't elaborate; no sense in darkening the mood. I needed a drink. But it would have to wait. Stepping into the bedroom, I turned on the light.

Theresa stood in the corner where I'd left her that morning, a glazed look of indifference on her face. The look that had taken up residence there six weeks before. The suffocating sense of loss I'd managed to ignore all day hoisted itself back into my heart.

"Miss me?" I asked, kissing her gently on the cheek.

After fixing myself supper, I bathed her.

I undressed her, then slipped out of my own clothes and led her to the shower stall. Stepping in beside her, I lifted the showerhead from its bracket, ran the water until it was warm and sprayed her body.

"Not too hot, is it?" I asked, knowing I'd get no response. It was important—at least to me—to talk to her, reassure her, just in case she was still in there, listening.

"Let's do your hair, too." I tilted her head back and wet her hair, then lathered it with shampoo and rinsed it, careful to keep the suds out of her eyes. Thick and lustrous, her hair fell halfway to her waist and would take hours to dry. But tonight we had no plans; there'd be plenty of time to brush it.

"I picked up a new body wash," I said, holding it beneath her nose so she could smell it. "What do you think?" Opening it, I squeezed some into my hand and lathered her shoulders and back. "It's got aloe and papaya. Good for your skin."

After rinsing her back, I returned the showerhead to its bracket and squeezed more body wash into my hands.

"Lift your arms," I said, slipping behind her and raising them for her. Obediently, she held the pose while I soaped her sides and moved my hands around to her stomach.

Her skin felt smooth and taut; it hadn't yet begun to sag with atrophy. An athlete, she'd been proud of her body and always kept fit. My hands slowed as they moved up her torso and soaped her breasts. Leaning into her from behind, I embraced her and closed my eyes, wishing for her back, the loneliness and sorrow overwhelming.

Then my breathing grew ragged and I felt myself grow hard.

"Oh, God!" I backpedaled. Crashing into the shower wall, I slid to the floor, repulsed by my need and desire. Revulsion and self-loathing filled me.

Theresa stood in the rising mist of the falling water, arms held out from her sides, unmoved.

They stood until they died, leaving their loved ones to watch their slow but steady deterioration. Most expired after a few months, skeletal reminders of the laughing and loving people they once were. Some lingered, twisting the knife of patience and love in the hearts of those they'd left behind. In rare cases—at the moment of death—some turned into raving creatures driven to murder and dismember, unspeakable things that haunted the darkest places of the city and beyond.

Public reaction had been predictable. Law-and-order types insisted on detention and lethal injection, applying the same logic that had once been used at animal shelters. Liberals, on the other hand, demanded that the civil rights of the poor souls be protected—until a catatonic woman woke one day during her court hearing and tore the head off her attorney. The religious right opposed euthanasia but demanded incarceration, at least until nature could run its course.

The debate brought us Ataraxia: a vast military reservation already used for the storage of nuclear waste, newly repurposed for the storage of the empty shells that once were people.

Would I have told the boy's mother all this had we had a chance to talk? No, my job—to counsel people on such end-of-life issues—prevented me from doing so. But for six weeks, I had faced the same paralyzing dilemma about what to do.

The woman I loved stood beside the fireplace where I'd placed her, dowdy now in an oversized cotton nightgown. How much longer would I agonize over it?

I turned back to my computer screen and to the image on the web page for Ataraxia. Tranquility for the patient and peace of mind for the caregiver, it promised, over photos of rolling meadows and a quiet stream winding its way through a cloistered forest.

Something—a change in the light?—made me look up and across the room. Had Theresa moved? I felt a moment of irrational hope. Then the hairs on the back of my neck prickled as I remembered the boy flying across the desk at me.

Lifting the gun from the desk beside me, I rose and crept slowly to where she stood.

"Did you say something?"

I watched her, looking for signs of awareness, but saw nothing, just the milky glaze that coated her eyes. The same look that had been in the kid's eyes until the moment he had turned.

"Come with me, sweetheart," I said, leading her to the back bedroom. "Just for tonight. Until we get this figured out."

I closed the door and locked it. Set the key beside the gun on the nightstand next to the bed.

Just in case.

Sleep eluded me that night. I tossed and turned, then, just as I drifted off, I shuddered awake and reached for the gun, convinced that Theresa and the boy stood over me, their eyes glinting with malice.

When the filthy light of morning finally pushed past the curtains, I sat up and stared out at the bleak promise of another day. Nothing had changed since I'd tried to find solace in sleep the night before, but perhaps that was what I needed to accept. Pushing aside the covers, I walked to the back bedroom and unlocked the door.

Theresa stood there, waiting patiently, as beautiful as the day I'd met her.

A lump formed in my throat as I embraced her, rocked her gently in my arms. But her arms hung at her sides as if I didn't exist.

"It's time to go," I whispered.

The train to Ataraxia crossed the country through its center, past decaying cities, fenced-in farms, suburban neighborhoods collapsing from neglect, and private compounds protected by armed security forces. In an irony lost on all but those who'd been around long enough to remember, prisons had become the most sought-after places of refuge.

With Theresa and the rest of the "cargo" safely secured in lockers on the last car of the train, I stared out the window of the dining car at the passing landscape. It was oddly verdant, rejuvenated by the absent transgressions of man. A pack of coyotes ran alongside the train as if trying to keep up.

"Excuse me." A woman's voice.

I looked up.

"May I join you?"

She was middle-aged, maybe five to ten years older than I, attractive in a weary sort of way. And in desperate need of company. I nodded, and if she noticed my reluctance, she gave no sign.

"Would you care for something to eat?" My own meal had been largely ignored.

"A drink is all. May I buy you one?"

We placed our order on the table-top menu and tipped the waiter—a burly man with a sidearm discreetly strapped beneath his jacket—when he delivered the drinks.

Her name was Joanne. She taught elementary school on a farming compound in Iowa. Childless herself, she spoke about the kids in her class as if they were her own and in this way avoided the one topic we had in common. I let her talk, knowing she needed to. We spent the evening that way, watching as the light fell from the sky and darkness took its place, until we ran out of things to say.

"Who is it you're taking?" she asked, after the silence had grown unbearable. Her face, illuminated by the glow of the candle between us, looked haunted.

"My fiancé," I said, forcing a smile. The lie was a minor one, for on the day I had planned to propose, I'd awakened to a vacant look on a lost woman.

"Your first?" Meaning, 'the first person you've brought to Ataraxia?'

The question caught me by surprise. I fought to keep the smile stitched to my face.

"Yes," I said, this lie significant. For Theresa had saved me when I thought all was lost. A light had come into my life when I'd thought the sun had set for the last time. "You?"

"My husband. Thomas." She scratched gently at the linen tablecloth, then looked up. "Twenty-one years. The only man I ever slept with. Never apart, until..."

Until the sickness left her a widow with a husband she couldn't bury. Her face looked ashen, even in the warm glow of the candle.

"Are you all right?" I asked, fearing she was about to faint.

"No, I'm not." A hand pressed to her mouth. Then, "Would you walk me to my cabin?"

I took her arm gently as she stood and steadied her as we left the dining car; the rocking of the train wasn't helping her balance. We made our way through several cars, past empty compartments, until we got to hers. Pulling the key from her pocket, she unlocked the door and opened it.

"Thank you," she said. "You've been most kind." Her eyes began to fill with tears—or was it loneliness?—until she had to look away.

I cleared my throat and shuffled my feet, no longer sure what to do, a condition I'd suffered from all my life.

Releasing me, she crossed the threshold, began to turn, and then she paused as if uncertain. Finally, she raised her eyes to mine. "One more thing..."

"What's that?" I asked.

She took my hand and drew me inside.

Our act provided release but no relief, though we searched for it all night, trying to separate anger from grief. Daylight brought exhaustion, along with the realization that what we searched for couldn't be found.

"What will happen after I leave him there?" Joanne asked.

Our bodies touched beneath the sheets as we stared past the window at a landscape now empty and harsh.

"He'll die."

"How?"

"Lack of water, most likely. Starvation. Exposure. The elements." I thought of the coyotes pacing the train, of those just like him who would turn and wreak havoc until they themselves befell a similar fate.

She curled into a ball, pulling away.

"You should go now."

I watched from the train as Joanne led her husband to a sheltered place not far from where we'd stopped. With the help of the waiter with the sidearm, she erected a small canvas shelter and led Thomas inside. There, she anointed him with sun block and placed a hat on his head as if this were just another day at the beach.

A year from now, the spot would be marked by faded fragments of cloth and a scattered pile of bones, and the hat would be long lost to the playful desert winds. Just one of the things they didn't tell you about Ataraxia.

After returning to the train, Joanne locked herself in her cabin as I knew she would, so I never saw her again. Never saw her to thank her for helping me pass the endless hours of that final trip.

Sitting beneath the beach umbrella, I reach into the cooler at my side and pull out another beer, pop the tab, and suck at the frothy brew as it foams over the sides of the can. In another hour or so, I'll fire up the grill while considering the biggest decision of the day: hot dogs or steak?

Not that it's all fun in the sun. The ice in the cooler has all but melted. The radio reception could be better. And there's that seeping wound on my leg where the boy bit me.

"But that's okay," I say.

Theresa stands fifty yards away, where I put her four days ago when we got off the train. Staring off into the distance, she ignores me.

I look at the sky's heartbreaking blue. Then back at the woman I love.

"I'm a patient man ... willing to wait..."

Theresa suddenly turns her head to look at me and that feral smile pulls at her lips.

"...a man who's got everything he needs."

She breaks into a run, chewing up the distance between us in long, athletic strides.

One for her, I think, cocking the gun.

And one for me.

Sea of Green, Sea of Gold
Aaron Polson

"Pile the bodies high...
Shovel them under and let me work—
I am the grass; I cover all."
– Carl Sandburg, The Grass

A hawk pulled Ben's focus from the trail, or something dark and swift *like* a hawk flying through the clear sky. As he looked up, his left foot snagged on the trail and his ankle crumpled, sending him to the dirt. A grunt slipped out of his mouth when he struck. There had been a tiny pop as he went down.

"Ben?" Barry pulled the straps tighter on his hiking pack and jogged forward, already sweating under the Kansas sun. He stumbled to a stop next to Ben, slipped out of the pack, and dropped it to the ground with a dull thud. "Damn, man...you all right?"

Ben's face twisted. He glowered at Barry. "Do I look all right?"

"Sorry." Barry dropped to his haunches.

"Sprained ... I think." Ben pulled off the boot and delicately rolled back the grey-brown sock. His long face was red with the effort and his ankle had already puffed to twice its normal size, red and bulging. Pain shot over his knee, across his back, and to the base of his skull with each throb of his heart. "Must've tripped on a rock," he said, but his mouth hung open as he searched for the offender. "I had to have tripped on..."

Barry mopped his fat, round face with a handkerchief and allowed his eyes to wander away. Surrounding them on every side were the Flint Hills. Limestone formations cut into deep valleys and folds in the earth by glaciers 10,000 years before encroached in every direction. Tall strands of razor-thin Switch Grass and the fat-headed Bluestem, both native to the prairie in the Konza Preserve, covered the hills, some taller than a grown man's waist. It was a golden-green blanket covering crumpled stone; alive and holding the hills together.

The rocky nature of those hills had protected the Konza from pioneers and farmers, and now the government had guaranteed its protection by making it a national preserve, a piece of land lost in time. It was land that remembered a time before roads and houses and the interference of humans.

"God … it's like we could drown in the grass." Barry flipped open his phone. "No trees."

Ben squinted at Barry. "What?"

"No trees nearby … you know, for a splint. No trees means no limbs. No sticks. Nothing but grass. Not even cell phone reception. Shit."

"I can use your hiking pole."

Barry looked at the aluminum rod in his hands with an expression of surprise. "My pole?"

"Like a crutch. I don't need a splint. Here," Ben said. He tore a section of his pants from the right leg, starting at the cuff and ripping until he removed a strip. He began to wrap it around his swollen ankle.

"What are you doing?"

Ben winced as he tightened the makeshift wrap.

"Trying to keep the swelling down, at least until we get back to the car."

They'd been friends for a long time, ever since Ben's parents had moved next to Barry's. Since that day in third grade when

Barry's sister, Lane, had joked that his butt was made of donuts. Ben had laughed, and Barry had chased him with a pocketknife for five blocks, only to slip on a garden hose and collapse face-down with a mouthful of grass. The pocketknife had rattled into the street where Ben had picked it up. It had been open to a nail file.

Ben smiled at the memory. "I expected you to be the one to sprain—"

A shadow cut across the sky again, and Ben glanced up from his ankle. He expected to see Barry standing between him and the sun, but he wasn't.

"Those birds." Barry pointed to the sky. "What are those birds?"

"Dunno. Vultures?"

"Grandpa called them turkey-buzzards. Scavengers." Barry shivered. A breeze cut across the rolling hills, and the grass bowed, its hushed voice praying in a strange whisper. "Let's get you back to the car."

Barry helped Ben to his feet, picked up his own pack, and the two men turned and staggered the way they'd come, straining up an incline. Ben struggled with his lame ankle and the makeshift crutch. Barry crested the hill in front, stopped, and waved to his friend.

"Can you see the car?"

Barry shook his head.

"No. No that's not it. It's those god-damned birds, man."

The air filled with the scratch-clunk of Ben's awkward gait until he joined his friend and leaned, panting, on the walking pole.

"Where's the car? We … should be able to see the car … from here. The road at least." He sheltered his eyes with one hand and squinted. "Nothing."

"Ben." Barry patted his friend's shoulder. "Ben—that's a dude down there."

Below them, at the bottom of the fold between two hills, a black shape twisted in the grass. He—it looked like a man—was only a few feet from the trail, on his back, waving his hands in the air. From a distance, he could have been a black beetle, its legs kicking the sky in death throes.

"It's like he's wrestling something." Barry brushed his arm against the sweat on his face. "Looks like he's trying to get to his feet."

"Barry … those birds are right over that guy." Ben gave his friend a shove. "We should help."

The bigger man lurched and began an awkward, teeter-tottering jog down the hill. Ben followed as quickly as he could, almost hopping exclusively on his good leg. His head wobbled uncomfortably as he tumbled down the last few yards of incline. Ahead on the path, Barry stopped short and held out his hand a few yards from the stranger.

When Ben caught up to him, he understood why. The man's clothes hung about him in ragged tatters and loose strips, filthy with mud and spatters of something darker; likely dried blood. Tiny cuts criss-crossed his face, making a network of red lines like the burnt image of a net. He wore at least a week's worth of beard, short and patchy, with plenty of smudges on his exposed skin. As he struggled, he let out a few raw grunts.

"Don't just stand there—" His wild eyes circled to Barry and Ben. "I need some help, goddammit—"

Barry didn't move. Ben took another step forward. The man's mouth clenched in a half-grimace, half-smile as his arms seemed to be stuck below the surface of the prairie.

"Huh…." The man's arms flopped to one side then dropped on the packed dirt of the trail. His eyes rolled into his head and closed.

Ben and Barry exchanged a look.

"Hey, buddy … are you okay?" Ben leaned forward, resting his left knee on the ground with the injured ankle behind him. From that distance, Ben received a faceful of the stranger's body odor, an ammonia stench that indicated he hadn't washed in days.

"Unnnnh," the man groaned. "Just lost my balance—fell into some of that devil grass."

"We've got a car—"

The man's arm shot out and snatched the hiking pole from Ben's hand. Before Barry could move, the stranger knocked Ben to the ground and perched on his chest, holding the aluminum bar across Ben's throat while his knees pinned Ben's arms to the ground on the trail.

"Who the hell are you?" White, foamy spittle trailed out of the stranger's mouth.

Barry stepped away with his hands in front, palms forward.

"Hey—I don't want any trouble."

Ben's face swelled red like a steamed beet. He kicked his legs and tried to free his arms from under the stranger's weight.

"Who the hell are you?" the man repeated.

Hoarse, choking sounds slipped out of Ben's mouth.

"Just a couple of hikers … checking out the trails…." Barry's eyes darted between the stranger's face and Ben's. "You're killing him."

"Fucked." The stranger leaned back, releasing the pressure from Ben's throat. "You bastards are fucked, too."

Now free, Ben rolled away, grasping at his neck. He coughed, and the color of his face gradually returned to normal.

"What … the … hell … was … that about?" he rasped.

The man's eyes narrowed. "Can't be too careful." He scratched his beard. "Out here."

"Look, man, we're just tying to get back to the car, get Ben here some help." Barry knelt next to Ben and helped his friend to his feet. "Sprained his ankle."

"Huh. That's how it got Andrea."

"Who?" Ben asked, leaning on his knees as he panted for breath.

"My girlfriend. Six days ago." The stranger stood, glancing to his left and right. "It got her ankle, then … she tried to cut across a open patch … get back to the car faster…." His chest shuddered and he covered his face with one hand. "God. God … it took her."

"Took her?"

"The grass." He reached out, grabbed the loose collar of Barry's shirt, and tugged him closer. "It devoured her. Smothered her." The stranger looked at his hand, then Barry's shirt and face, and released his grip. "The birds got what was left. Sorry … sorry … oh, God. Do you have some water? I'm dying…."

Barry slipped off his pack and rummaged around until he found an aluminum bottle. He passed it to the stranger.

"What's your name?" Ben asked.

"Nick. My name's Nick. Andrea and I … we were just gone for an afternoon." Nick tilted his head back and poured the water into his open mouth; droplets meandered through his stubble to the tip of his chin. He swallowed and pulled back one shirtsleeve. "I know you think I'm nuts. I'd think I was fucking crazy, too, but look." His voice shook as he extended his arm toward the others. Tiny scars marred his flesh, each puffed and pink.

"How'd you get all those cuts?"

Nick glared at Barry. "It's hungry again."

Ben shifted the hiking pole to his other hand, allowing his weight to shift.

"We better get to the car."

Nick wheeled, his eyes blazing. His tongue seeped out of his mouth, past chapped and peeling lips. "That's just it, isn't it? There is no more car. When are you—" He broke off, his eyes open and alert. "Listen."

The grass answered with a *swish-swish*.

"That sound?" Ben turned and looked behind him. "What is it?"

The waist-high blades to the south bent toward them. The swishing grew louder. Closer.

"It's coming again. For fuck's sake, run!" Nick pushed Barry out of the way, and the big man tumbled into the grass toward the oncoming mystery, dropping his heavy pack next to the trail.

Ben lifted the pole in his fist, raising it above his head like a club despite the pain in his left ankle. The action was instinctive, without thought. He limped toward the matted grass where Barry went down. Barry howled and groaned. Green-gold stems folded across his body.

"Barry?"

Barry shot up, shaking like a seizure, with fresh wounds oozing on his face and one arm. He roared and flung his arms. The grass waved in the distance, a game of pantomime working against the breeze.

"Jesus," he cried. "It fucking cut me. Bit me." He stumbled backward, found the path, and turned to follow Nick's flight up the hill toward the highway.

Pole held aloft, Ben watched in disbelief as the stand of Switch Grass near the path stretched toward him. Barry's staggering footfalls sounded up the hill, but the sound of whispering blades swallowed the world. The grass moved. *Swish-swish*. Its roots wove into the dark soil of the trail. The sun caught a glint from the aluminum pole as Ben swung like a reaper with a scythe, striking at the advancing blades. The pole *whooshed* through the grass, but still the roots crept toward him.

Ben turned and started toward the hill, staggering as well as he could against the incline. Ahead, Barry and Nick squatted near a rocky outcropping, both facing away from the trail.

"What the hell was that—what's going on?" Ben felt the fear in his stomach, cold and heavy.

"The grass. It's alive," Nick muttered. "And hungry."

Ben rubbed his face with his free hand.

"Bullshit … grass doesn't eat people." He said it aloud as much to cool his own fear as he did because he believed it to be true.

"God, Ben. What got me?" Barry's face was ashen, drawn. He lifted his right arm, blood oozing from fresh wounds, and pointed in the direction of the road; only there wasn't a road. "Something fucking cut me. And ... and we're lost."

Nick coughed and spat a dark mix of blood and mucus on the ground.

"You aren't lost. You're trapped."

Ben shook his head.

"Bullshit. Barry, try your phone again."

A moment passed in which none of the men moved. The air sagged around them, humid and thick, the sun waiting directly overhead. Barry slowly pushed his hand into a pocket and fished out the phone. He flipped it open.

"Nothing. Still nothing."

"It'll come back, you know." Nick nodded in the direction they'd fled. "It will keep coming until we're all dead."

Ben turned and started down the opposite slope. He did so without a word, without warning, with only the broken rhythm of his shuffling gait in his ears. There was something in the valley below, something dark, shaped like a car, obscured by a mound of grass.

"Wait!"

Ben stopped and turned to see Barry waving his arms above his head.

Barry cupped his hand to the side of his mouth.

"I'll come with you. I have to grab my pack. I dropped it. I'll run. Make it quick." His voice trembled as he spoke. He vanished over the crest of the hill. Nick melted into a black lump at the top of the ridge.

"Jesus, Barry," Ben muttered. He forced himself back toward the rocks. Clouds, fluffy like stretched bits of polyfill from a torn teddy bear, encroached on the western horizon. Ben allowed his eyes to circle the rim of the sky in all directions. Nothing but hills, grass, and the distant dark blot of a cluster of trees. He pulled in a breath of hot air. Barry was below, jogging down the slope along the path.

"You coming with me, too?" Ben asked Nick.

"Strength in numbers?"

Ben shook his head. "No, to get out of here."

"I told you, man. There isn't any 'getting out.' It's a trap."

The word 'trap' resonated in Ben's ears as he watched the scene unfold in the valley below. A breeze sent the waves rippling from the southwest, but a large cluster of prairie grass defied the wind. Ben's throat tightened.

"It's coming for him … the tops of the hills are the safest bet … too rocky up here for it to have a good foothold."

As they watched, the grass swallowed the trail. Barry shouted, his words muffled and indistinct. Lithe shadows crossed overhead, swooping down toward the path.

"Vultures…." Ben clenched the hiking pole and shifted his weight to climb down the hill.

Nick's hand wrapped Ben's left arm.

"Don't. He's done. They always stay near the grass … the thicker grass down below. They know how to get an easy meal." Another howl of pain echoed from below.

Ben wheeled on Nick, striking him with the pole across the left shoulder. He swung a second time, this blow cracking against ribs after Nick raised his hand in defense.

"Shit … uhff." Nick tumbled backward, landing on his bottom.

"That's my goddamned friend down there."

"He's … dead," Nick panted. "That's how it got Andrea…."

Ben drew the pole back a third time but hesitated.

"But you were down there when we found you—you were

fighting. You got out." The pole lowered.

Nick's head shook back and forth.

"I ... don't know how ... the grass is a monster." He sank to all fours. "Too late for us all ... only a matter of time." His chest began to heave, laughs and sobs coming together. "You'll either starve or...."

With the pole still clenched in one fist, Ben turned. He took a tentative, limping step down the slope toward his friend, but his friend was gone. The trail was empty. The grass waved in the wind, long, sweeping ripples like waves cresting across the ocean.

"Barry?" He leaned his weight on the pole and cupped a hand to his mouth. "Barry!"

The vultures flapped their great dark wings and alighted near the path.

"Jesus...."

Nick, still on his hands and knees behind Ben, coughed.

"You ... and me ... trapped. It likes to toy with you ... fuck with you."

Turning away from the trail, Ben limped past the prostrate man and started down the other side. "I saw a car earlier. In the distance. I think it was a car. It couldn't be ours, but..."

He staggered down the slope, pain still radiating from the ruined ankle. His head throbbed, his eyes blurred with tears, and his mouth was dry and hot in the sun. Nick cried out, but Ben was deaf, focused, driven despite the burning pain.

As he approached the meter-high Bluestem, he slowed. He glanced back toward the top of the hill. No sign of Nick. His eyes circled around front again. There, nearly buried in the thick grass, was a car. A silver Honda—just like Barry's, but *wrong*. The front windshield was spider-webbed from several punctures and scratches marred the paint.

He ignored the pain and half-ran in a limping, ungainly fashion, closing the distance to the car, sure to stay on what path was left. Nick's warning, 'trap,' echoed in his head. He peered into the window and found his cell phone lying on the console, snapped in two. The steering wheel was pulled from the column, wires hanging loose like a disemboweled pig. Dirt and glass fragments littered the seats and dash.

"Fuck," he pounded a fist against the door with a hollow thunk. The impact shot through his arm. "Barry's car … it's Barry's car…." His mutterings faded to a whisper as the grass rattled in the distance. It was coming, heading toward him, bringing blades like sharp, biting teeth. The roots scratched a foothold on the open path. He tightened his grip on the metal pole and pressed his back against the car.

Trapped.

The Wish Man and the Worm
J. M. Heluk

A child named Georgia sat on a concrete stoop watching lines of summer traffic creep past. She sniffed at the air: garbage baking, the tang of gasoline mingling with the aroma of boiled chicken and rice. It was pleasant enough, she thought, glancing across the street at them, the noisy collection of children playing on the sidewalk outside of the bodega. They ate ice cream sandwiches and laughed too loudly, shouting out words from stupid songs only they knew.

Georgia looked at the naked, choppy-haired dolls littering the ground near their feet, then glanced at her own doll, a broken-limbed autopsy of pink plastic warming in the sun. She huffed, kicking it, and the doll skidded away. Coppery hair snagged nubs of concrete, separating the head from its body. She kicked once more and the rubber head rolled to the curb, then off, disappearing out of sight somewhere on the street below. Georgia frowned. Dolls, she'd decided when she'd turned eight, were stupid, as stupid as her brother's friends across the way, as stupid as her brother, Miles. She'd only dragged the doll outside so she'd look normal, like them.

Georgia smiled at a handsome, brown-skinned man sauntering by, sweat glistening on his hard-muscled shoulders. Dark-eyed women swept past, bundles of paper bags in their arms overflowing with plantains, oranges, and other sweet fruits. A bus choked by. The sun felt too hot against her pale skin. She got up, moved back a step into the protective shade of the awning, and plopped down again. Somewhere in the distance, a Spanish melody cascaded from an open window, flowing into the street like liquid.

Georgia looked down to find a worm twisting on the heated pavement near her foot. With a child's intensity, she watched its blind, rolling squirm as it attempted to escape the sun by slipping itself toward the shadow cast by her shoe.

She bent and plucked it off the ground between her tender thumb and forefinger. It felt cool in her grasp, rubbery even, as it coiled around her pinkie. Georgia laughed and then blew on it. The worm went limp, dangling from her hand like a dead thing.

But it pulsed in her pinch. See, it wasn't dead, it was just pretending. Georgia understood that—she pretended things were dead all the time. The kids across the street started up a game of kickball, her older brother yelling something about rules or boundaries. When no one was looking, she popped the worm in her mouth.

A man approached quickly, his big boots pounding the concrete with psychotic intensity, his oily-black eyes darting between the child on the step and the group playing ball across the street. He slowed when he got near Georgia, and then, looking pathetically sweet, he leaned over and said to her, "You're a good little girl, aren't you?"

Georgia looked him up and down; she saw a square jaw, neat black buzz cut, and clean clothes. His eyes were round, glassy and dark. A pleasant howdy-do smile cut across his pale face.

"Yes," she replied, a bit muffled. "I'm good."

"And what have you got in there?" The man grinned, pointing to her mouth.

Feeling slightly more comfortable, Georgia opened up to show off her worm. It draped across her molars, flat and stunned. The man's eyes sparked with an odd curiosity.

"I *am* a good girl," she stated, more enthusiastically. The worm flopped toward the tip of her tongue before dropping into the moist pocket between her lower teeth and gums. For a moment, Georgia feared it would slip out. She returned a tight-lipped smile as the man squatted down on the steps beside her. The worm turned warm in her mouth, squirming against the seal of her compressed lips.

The pair quietly sat. The man stared ahead at the boys across the street. Georgia ignored them as usual, her head down, swishing saliva around her mouth to force the worm into another, more tolerable position. It now rode the swell of her tongue with every swallow, but Georgia was very careful with it.

The man, obviously pleased with how tenderly the girl was treating her guest, asked, "And why, might I ask, have you got that worm in your mouth?"

Her gaze settled on the noisy clan across the street, her inky eyes narrowing into slivers.

"I'm pretending," she huffed. The worm struggled against the hot bed of her cheek. "I'm pretending it's one of them … those stupid boys over there. See the one in the red shirt?"

The man nodded.

"Yes. I see him."

"That's my brother, Miles. He's always mean to me."

She stared at the boy and, with each breath, grew angrier. Her lips shrunk together, turning milky along the seams from pressure.

"He hates me you know," Georgia continued. "So I want him to die."

The man flashed a plastic grin. "But why the worm?"

Georgia's eyes crinkled at the edges, and her voice grew prickly.

"Cuz," she whined. Air whistled through her piggy nostrils. "I'm gonna make believe this worm is Miles, and when I believe it is with all my heart, I'm gonna bite it and swallow it dead. Just pretend of course. They make fun of me for being skinny, especially my brother."

"Ahhh." The man's face tightened down on itself, his dark pupils shrinking into nailheads beneath his brow. He scooted closer, reached out, and grabbed Georgia by the chin. His fingers were cold; the pads, hard as a shell as they sunk into her flesh. Georgia tried to wriggle free, but he leaned into it and a slow pressure assault began; he, hoisting up her face by his finger hooks in degrees, and she struggling a bit, but not too much. He was stronger.

"If that's the case, my sweet little diddles, a worm won't do. No, not at all," he said, squeezing her chin entirely too tightly. She already felt bruises forming, the muscles under her skin sliding across bone in all the wrong directions, so she popped her mouth open for him to see. The worm tumbled out, hit the top of his hand, and then, like magic, it wriggled into the pasty webbing between his thumb and index finger. Georgia watched the creature disappear in segments, burrowing inch by inch until it coiled beneath the pale sheath of his skin.

"Worms are too soft. Soft and passive. Is your brother soft and passive?"

The worm bulged at the top of his hand like the rest of his veins and just as black. She frowned when the tip of it vanished into his thumb with a slurp. The stranger let go of her chin. Georgia rubbed her jaw and winced.

The man leaned in close, puffing earthy breaths in her face. To Georgia, he smelled like an old basement, or wet dirt under a rock.

"I must have something better in here for such a special girl to wish upon. Something nasty and sharp ... like your brother. Ah! A bee, perhaps?" To Georgia's delight, he hooked his pinkie beneath his eyelid, then shimmied closer until his cold knees struck hers. With his chin compressed and his bottom lip hanging, the man fished around under his eyelid and was up to the knuckle when he finally got out what he wanted. Smiling too much, he presented her an insect.

"Ooh! I love magic!" she said, clapping her hands together.

The man bowed, fluttering his eyelids in a way that made Georgia forget about how badly he'd hurt her. "Hey, Mister, is it alive?"

The insect flapped its wet wings dry on the perch of his fingertip. She giggled. Yes, this was much better.

The man's voice turned greasy; something awful glittered behind his obsidian stare.

"Oh, yes, I love magic, too. But this isn't magic. Think of it more like … a very special wish."

His finger hovered near Georgia's face. The bee buzzed and jittered, its legs kicking as it tried to unglue itself from the damp tip. With one light breath, the man dried it.

"A bee is better than some stinky old worm. Why don't you play with this, instead? It'll be fun." He extended his finger.

Frowning, Georgia inspected the bee.

"Go on now, show me what little girls like you can do when they're angry and full of bugs." He snickered. "Open your mouth, baby."

Georgia hesitated. Her lips turned down in protest. "I am not filled with bugs."

"Yes, you are; now, open up."

"No, I'm…."

He screwed up his face and thrust the bee at her.

"I said you are filled with bugs; you are! Fat, squirmy ones, too! Great stag beetles and a bushel's worth of roaches, knots of silverfish as big as softballs swimming in your belly, budding spider eggs, whole armies of ants, and everything else that crawls, wiggles and flies, and I should know, so … open your mouth *now*!"

And Georgia did.

"Wider, oops, uh-huh, W I D E R," he cooed, his fingers at her chin again, coaxing her head to tilt back. She closed her eyes, let her mouth unhinge. "Oh, good girl. Now, make your wish."

The bee dropped to her tongue like piece of hard candy, struggled a moment, and rolled over. She didn't like it in there. It wasn't at all silky and warm like the worm. This moved too much and made noises that frightened her. It struggled and beat against the inside of her cheeks, trapped and crazy. Then it stung her.

Her mouth flopped open. Her eyes watered as its stinger punctured her palate and then stabbed its way toward the back of her tender throat.

"It hurts!" Georgia cried, gagging. She bolted up and gasped; wrung her fists around her neck, stumbling toward the railing. "It hurts so bad!"

The man grabbed the crusty hem of her shirt and yanked her back down to the step. Georgia doubled over, her head wedged between her knees. She thrust out her tongue. It was swollen and blue. The man took a quick look then shook his head.

"You think that hurts?" He laughed, gesturing across the street. "Now look what a special girl you are. Bet I can guess what your wish was."

The swarm came instantly, rising like a demonic vapor, swirling apart and connecting again to form an angry, rolling chain. Georgia tried to swallow as she watched the black cloud stream up from the storm drain near the bodega and buzz ahead with epileptic fury toward the playing children. Her throat disobeyed her, its walls swelling together so tight that air just whistled through. Her jowls watered as much as her eyes. She tried swallowing again and again. It was useless.

The man slapped a clammy hand over her knee; clicked his crooked teeth at her.

"We eat our wishes, love. Let it go."

Georgia winced.

"I said, *let it go*." She did and the bee tumbled down.

It was the screaming she remembered most; the flailing arms, young eyes flashing in horror, little fists flowering open and dropping ice cream bars to the curb as their bodies crumpled over, folding into themselves like strips of wet cardboard, and the operatic shrieking as the swarm covered their flesh with painful kisses.

Winter days were wet and dark. Rain fell, lots of it, but there was hardly any snow. Georgia crouched on the stoop, knees drawn to her chest, arms wrapped tightly around her shins. A few cars slipped past. All that dampness reduced her hair into something spongy. She smoothed it behind her ears and sighed. Water flowed off the awning in dirty gray sheets. No one important came by.

She stared toward the bodega across the street. Five tiny wood crosses perched on the railing near the steps. Below them, armfuls of stuffed animals sat, plastic flowers and heart-shaped candles and photographs, all drinking the rain. Sympathy cards turned to pulp, sliding off the steps like snot.

Why were the adults still doing that? It had been months since … since what exactly? Since they'd died. She looked to the storm drain remembering the song her brother made up about her, but she quickly abandoned those thoughts. He was gone and they were a nasty bunch anyway, but still, she'd never wished *that*.

Georgia stood, wiped the damp from her palms on her jeans, and started toward the curb. She stepped over puddles collecting at the lip of the street, dodged rotten fruit peels and trash, and then crossed, heading toward the storm basin. *That was not my wish*, she tried to convince herself as she stood above the drain, sleet pelting her head. A small rubber sphere dotted with stubble laid against a pile of wet newspapers near the maw of the grate. Georgia bent down to inspect it. A car rolled past spraying her back with cold water. It was a doll's head. Her doll's head. She picked it up.

The man had such eyes, she remembered, palming the doll's moldy face. Pulsing like engorged leeches when she swallowed her wish as they sat together on the porch; her pretending the jeers sailing from across the street didn't sting and him pretending, well, him pretending something else. He was nice, she'd thought at the time. He was kind to her in an odd sort of way. Plus, he'd said she was a good girl. No one said that much. She had liked him the way she liked Santa Claus or Jesus. She'd been curious.

But why did he have to go and say that awful thing, that nonsense about her being filled with bugs? She popped the doll head in her coat pocket and wiped her hand on her knee. Little boys were supposed to be filled with bugs, not girls. Girls were made of sugar and spice and everything nice. Everyone knew that. But ever since he'd said that nasty thing about her she'd looked, standing in front of her dressing mirror before bed, her mouth open as wide as it could go, staring down her throat, waiting. She never saw a thing in there, not once, not ever. He'd lied to her, just like he'd lied when he'd said it was *her* wish that came true. She hadn't wanted them to die like that, not really, anyway. It was supposed to be a game of pretend. And she wasn't filled with bugs at all. He was.

Georgia stood and kicked the pile of newspaper onto the drain catch. It bunched up on the tip of her boot and stuck. She lifted her foot and shook it. The newspaper clung like an all-too-friendly uncle. She bent to pull it off and caught sight of what hid beneath on the grate. A fleshy mass about the size of a softball wiggled against the rush of rain water. A knot of milky tubes, blanched extra white at their centers, slapped weakly on the rusted iron. Worms, the exact color her fingertips turned when she sat in the tub too long.

Georgia looked around. The street was deserted. There was no one to call for. She'd made it that way, too.

Rain crept under the collar of her coat, sliding beneath her shirt in icy tendrils. She knelt back down to study the pile.

They were dying. Georgia hunched in the empty street, the cold teeth of winter chewing her face raw. It was all so ruined. The unused steps of empty storefronts, the gray expanse of pavement, as flat and as lifeless as the worms at her heel, the joylessness of it all, the horrible darkness she'd unleashed and piles of uncollected trash rotting into slime all around her.

No one was looking so Georgia teased one of the worms from the center of the mass. She tugged and it stretched from the rest like taffy but didn't break when it snapped free. The elongated creature just flopped in her clutches, cold and hardly pink anymore. Georgia felt tears chilling along the edges of her eyelids. She wasn't a good girl at all. She was as bad as little girls got.

Georgia closed her eyes, grimaced, and popped the dying worm in her mouth.

She heard him this time. Boots dropping like bombs on the watery pavement, the clicking of his jaw, the drone in his throat, and the raspy curses tossed under his breath as he slammed down the deserted sidewalk at her. Georgia tried to stand, but it was too late. He was already by her, kneeling on the street by the gutter with his horribly long fingers clamping down on the top of her skull like a mitt of tentacles.

She recognized the smell now. It *was* wet earth and mud and damp winter basements. The smell of things crawling behind baseboards and hiding beneath moldy skins of wallpaper. She crinkled her nose at him.

His fingers groped along the breadth of her head, slid behind her ears, coiled up around them and weaved back down through her nappy hair. He was buzzing, clicking something unseen deep in his throat. His black leather coat dragged along the mucky water flooding the storm drain like torn dragonfly wings. Without a word, he twisted her face around toward his.

It was an awful face now, his underground face, his hibernation face, the one that hid from the rain in dark deathly places. A living curtain of centipedes twisted across his forehead, migrating in spastic movements toward his eyes—eyes that bulged, two black-gloss spheres rolling in deep sockets. When he opened his mouth to smile at her, there were no teeth, just the bloated bodies of slugs pasted to his jaw line where gums were supposed to be.

"Problem, is there?" he asked, hissing and glancing at the pile of worms drowning by the gutter.

Georgia fixed her lips tight. She shook her head *no*.

"What is it this time? Has Mommy been mean to you? Someone call you a nasty name again?" His head jerked left, then right. Up, then down, grunting, clicking. "Is there anyone *left*?"

Georgia almost screamed, and when she tried to crawl away from him, the man shot up, lifting her off the pavement by the scruff of her neck.

He dangled her there, inspecting Georgia as one would a bug. The skin of her throat grew tighter in his grasp and she felt the half-moon impressions left by his nails already filling with blood at the rear of her neck. She brought her hands up, slapped at his squirmy face. Her feet skimmed over the storm drain, connected with the knot of worms, and kicked them free. The mass rolled over the lip of the grate, disappearing with a thud when they hit the watery bottom.

"I am not filled with bugs!" she insisted, sipping breaths through her nose and staring at the grotesquery she hung from. "I am ... a good girl."

"Oh?" The man titled his head. Spider legs poked from each nostril then coiled back, folding neatly into the dim passages. "Good girl? Ha!" His eyes glinted from the silverfish gliding beneath them. His jaw dropped open and when his tongue rolled out, Georgia screamed. It was a crawling black carpet of flies.

"Open your mouth again and I'll have a look for myself." His free hand folded over her jaw. "Open wide so I can see all those horrible things clawing up the back of your throat!" he shrieked, his tongue flapping and exciting the flies. "You know they're in there. You know what's rolling deep in your gut. You're a dirty little thing, with dirty little wishes. Now, open up!"

The worm in Georgia's mouth slipped when he yanked her head back. It tumbled down her tongue toward the sucking, pink folds of her throat.

She whimpered, twirling off his hand like bait. The man laughed, his locust eyes squeezing into slits, pinching in the corners. Streams of carpenter ants leached from his lids, crawled down each cheek as living tears.

"You disappoint me, squiggly wiggly," he moaned. A shiny brown beetle crawled from his ear and shimmied under his centipede bangs to escape the rain. "I thought we were friends, and friends tell other friends their secrets. Now, come on, sweetie, what will it be today? Make another wish upon me."

She pressed her lips together as tight as she could; so tight, they went numb.

An understanding of what she was wishing for slipped over the man's face and Georgia knew he knew. *We eat our wishes for a reason, love, because if you tell, they'll never come true*, she remembered him saying that awful summer afternoon. His lips chattered hungrily as he squeezed the pockets of her cheeks inward.

"OPEN!"

Georgia whimpered. Her mouth was buckling.

"You open that mouth; you open up wide so I can see!"

But then, to the man's horror, she didn't, and in one quick gulp, Georgia made her wish.

It was the screaming she remembered most, the insidious, collective drone as the billions of monstrous things he really was scrambled in waves toward the safety of the awning, and the mind-shattering fear they felt as the tower of worms rising from the storm drain swept down in a furious rush to smash every squirming part of him.

The summer sun beat a constant rhythm on her face. Georgia basked in the pleasant heat, sniffing sweet summer air. She pulled her new doll close to her chest and hugged it tight. She liked dolls now. She'd better. "I am a good girl," she mumbled, her eyes settling on the chatty bunch gathering on the steps of the bodega.

Across the street, children bounced, their faces twisting as they shouted out words to a song Georgia knew all too well. They jumped in place, naked dolls clamped in their dirty little fists and ice cream sandwiches turning into black-and-white puddles on the concrete around them. They giggled and laughed, leaping over the wiggly chalk lines of their hopscotch board. Her brother, Miles, was there again and instigating as usual. He was calling her names and now the rest were, too.

You'd think he'd have learned his lesson by now, especially since she'd killed him so many times. Name-calling was impolite, so rude. It hurt people's feelings. How could he still be doing that after what she'd done to him? But maybe he didn't remember any of it.

Sometimes she thought he'd be better off dead. Sometimes, she missed him.

This was one of those days, she decided. Georgia smiled. Yes, she was glad he was there. Summer was boring without him, without them. Traffic crept down the street. Couples glided past. Music floated from the open windows of buildings around her. Her wish had come true. The street was alive again. Darkness had lifted.

Georgia glanced toward her feet. A corpulent wasp flapped helplessly near the tip of her sandal. She bent over to pick it up but stopped herself when she heard her brother calling for her to come over and play.

Why was he being so sweet now? Maybe it was a trick. Maybe she'd get over there and they'd taunt her as usual. Or worse, maybe they'd be swallowing their own worms and making wishes.

She eyeballed the bug and its long, long stinger. *Give it time*, she thought, dropping her doll next to it. *He'll learn one way or another*. The wasp scurried into the doll's hair for protection. Georgia stood, her neck craned, and peered suspiciously across the street. They weren't making fun of her at all. They were playing

"Mother May I" again. Still, Georgia hesitated near the curb.

But all five of them? That might be unfair. She turned, bent down, and quickly dragged the wasp away from her doll. Then she ran across the street with it buzzing against the prison of her palm. There was always tomorrow, she thought, slipping the bug into her pocket for safety. If he made fun of her again, then she could. Sure. Making wishes was easy. Georgia grinned.

Let it be, *for now.*

The Woman in the Ditch
Scott Lininger

I spin this memory from my sleepless cell. I can't know if I'll see the dawn, for there's a familiar buzzin' in my head suggestin' that death won't skip me again. Though I do imagine this story would give the law and others who've judged me some pause, it ain't confession or excuse. I've done some dark badness, and I think the trial laid clear enough what I perpetrated on Ms. Ester Jackson, but those acts are nothin' when stacked against the worst thing I ever saw.

When people from my hometown of Sterling, Colorado, talk about 1957, they talk about the blizzard. Snow was deep enough that even the coal trains stopped runnin'. For two whole weeks everybody was a shut in from work and school, includin' me and my three brothers out on the farm.

To set the picture proper, it's needed to say that I've only two brothers left today, which is somethin' that everybody back home knows but never talks about. I wonder all the time what little Bill would have made of his self, and I suspect that everyone else does, too. He grew up playin' with short wave radios and talkin' about rocketin' to the moon. In 1957, Sputnik had just gone up, see, and I guess all of us wanted to be astronauts, but Bill was the kind of bright kid who coulda done it. People don't like to remember him 'cause of all that potential.

But I'm gettin ahead of myself and have nearly lost my thread. As I said, people tend to recall the blizzard, but to me '57 will forever be remembered for the day we found the woman in the ditch.

The only reason that we did was because of the blizzard, of course. Bill and I had been sent out by Father to see if we could make it the three miles over to town to get him some cigarettes, of which he'd run clean dry. Bill had argued well that the store would be closed, though really he just didn't want to go out in the bitter cold. Father didn't give a shit about what we wanted; never did. He came close to givin' us a right painful reason to obey when Mother stepped in and suggested a halfway track, tellin' me and Bill that if the store were open we'd each be able to buy a piece of candy. And so with my sweet tooth and Father's threat of the belt all weighin' in on the side of the snowy trek, Bill gave up and we donned our warmest things.

We smelled the woman afore we saw her. We was just crossin' the little bridge over the inlet ditch to the reservoir, more'n halfway to the store, havin' already come through blowin' snow for well over an hour. We were tired and angry with Father by that point, and even I was no longer wantin' the candy. Bill'd traded my knit gloves for his warmer mittens just to get me to shut up about my hands bein' cold, which at first had been a triumph over my little brother but soon turned sour as I imagined bein' blamed for the need of amputatin' his frostbit fingers.

"Shit, you smell that?" Bill grabbed my coat to make me stop walkin'.

"Can't smell nothin'," I said. "Damn snot is frozen." But I had no sooner finished my bitchin' when I did smell somethin' odd. I knew right away what it was because Father always let me gas the Ford. "Goddamn, that's fuel," I said.

Suddenly there was a drop in the wind, and in the big quiet we both heard a voice. It was a tuckered moan, somewhere between pain and givin' up. Like chalkboard fingernails or the bleatin' of a calf bein' pulled from its mother to slaughter, it lashed my heart to a gallop. It weren't human.

"It's comin' from down there," hissed Bill.

"Bullshit," I said, mostly because the last thing I wanted to do was know any more, but Bill was a curious type. He'd be there 'til he cornered that sound.

He walked up to the west lip of the bridge and leaned over. A shelf of snow broke free at his feet and whumped down into the fall. At the noise the moanin' stopped, and Bill met the woman in the ditch.

"Help!" she cried. "Oh Lord, help us, please. We crashed."

I ran over, and I saw that indeed she had. At the very bottom of the thirty feet of ditch there was a fancy car, completely upside-down, with its hood smashed through the ice that covered the creek. It was at such an angle that the engine was full underwater. The snow near its rear was yellowed with spilled gasoline, and there was a sizable spot near the driver's window that was red with blood.

We couldn't actually see the woman, but she was clearly trapped inside the cab. Her voice was stronger now that she'd heard us. "Hello? Are you there? Anybody ... please..."

The car rocked slightly and we heard the woman hiss in pain. My young mind was filled with horrible images of her legs bein' chopped off, or of bloody, broken ribs protrudin' from a ruined Sunday dress. Lookin back on it today, I believe that I thought of her in church clothes because her voice, even in her distress, was unaccented. Educated.

Just like I imagine yours to be.

Bill looked at me hard, a dare. He wanted to go down there and see all the gore for himself.

"Bill Hettimer," I whispered, not wantin' her to hear, "if we try to climb down there, we're likely to drown or worse."

"You're a coward," he said. "If we don't go down there she might die before we even make it to town."

We glared at each other, a battle of wills.

"I hear you, boys," called the woman. There were tears 'midst her words. "Please, you must hurry. Summon the fire department, or the sheriff."

Both of our eyebrows rose at the mention of the sheriff. Even at that age, I'd had some run-ins with the law, so neither one of us wanted to see him for a hundred years, at least.

"Could you please talk to me?" she asked. "I think my husband ... I think he's..." She trailed off.

"You hurt, ma'am?" called Bill loudly. I frowned at him.

"Yes. I think my leg is broken, and I'm pinned. My husband isn't awake anymore. He is injured quite badly."

I was feelin' cold and nauseous. All I could think about was crushed bones and leakin' wounds. I'd not yet developed a taste for that sort of thing.

"I'm gonna go see," Bill said, bitin' his lower lip. He walked to the far end of the bridge and climbed, ladder-like, over the barbed wire between the road and the ditch. He jumped off the top of the fence pole and landed in a drift clear up to his waist, and then he knee-stepped the yard or so to the lip of the incline.

"I'm comin down," he called.

He moved fast, lettin' the slope do the work. The snow made easier effort of it than I'd imagined, since it provided a kind of stair once smashed under his boots. Soon he'd edged out onto the ice and bent down to see inside the driver's elbow window, right where all the blood was. When he saw whatever he saw, he jumped back with a yelp.

There was a loud crackin' sound. The ice groaned like a bull and Bill skittered toward shore. The car sunk another six inches into the water, which sloshed up around the front tires. The woman screamed. Bill put his hands on his head, overwhelmed.

"Oh!" cried the woman. "My husband! Oh Lord, his face is in the water! I can't reach him. Oh Lord, we need help!" She continued on in some hysterics. She kept sayin' "Bill! Bill!" over and over again, which knocked my brother to his knees, even though she clearly was sayin' the name of her husband.

There was another loud crackin' in the ice, and a sense of family duty overwhelmed my lack of confidence. I hopped the fence and slid down the furrow to the bottom. I reached the little bank where Bill knelt and pulled him away from the ice, but as I did so my left boot sank through some mud and I felt water soak into my sock. I think I may have been cryin'. Bill certainly was. The woman screamed again and then inhaled as if holdin' her breath.

The sounds in the ice stopped as the car quit its sinkin'. Bill and I clung to each other, which I believe was the first and last moment that we exchanged a hug. After what seemed like a very long time, the woman's quick breathin' became audible again.

Bill was speechless. I leaned down to try and see into the cab, which was much underwater.

"Ma'am, can you reach out of the car at all?"

There was a splashin' sound, and then a thin and tremblin' hand extended from the broken passenger window. It was mottled with blood. She gave us a pathetic little wave, and the gold of her wedding band glinted in the snowy light. The ring stood out more than usual because the hand of the woman, much to our surprise, was a rich chocolate brown in color.

Cold betrayal uncoiled itself inside my chest.

"Shit, Bill," I whispered. "She's black." In fact, neither of us had ever seen a black person in the flesh, but we knew plenty about them from Father, who'd served in the Army and been as far as Atlanta.

Bill shook his head, still lookin' like a deer in the headlights. I was angry now and dangerously chilled. My soppin' foot was grown numb. Random images of bein' punished by Father for not fetchin' his cigarettes spilled into my brain. There was a hummin' sound in my skull.

"She knew my name," whispered Bill.

The woman spoke, but quietly.

"Please, little boys. You want something, I can tell. If you just help me get out of here, I can repay you."

"Let's go, Bill," I said. "She's a goddamn Negro and none of our concern! Father'll kill us if we don't get his cigarettes."

"Her husband weren't no Negro," said Bill. "I saw him..."

"Damnit, Bill, that's even worse!" Hummin'. Somethin' was wrong here. I felt panic creepin' up from my belly.

Her hand emerged from the window again and weakly tossed a packet of cigarettes our direction. "That's what you want, yes? Please ... I cannot die in this place."

I snatched up the cigarettes. Winston Salem in the green box, exactly Father's brand. It even had the price sticker from Starr's. Confused, I stuffed it in my pocket. I grabbed Bill forcefully by his neck scarf like you'd lead a donkey.

"We gotta go."

"No! She's gonna die! Nobody else will come this way."

"We don't know that."

"Please," whimpered the woman, "I can't feel my legs..."

Bill was lookin at me like I'd made him spit on the Bible. The woman's chatterin' breath was mixed with coughs. Bill's eyes cast around as he tried to think of somethin'. Then he flapped his arms and pointed.

"She's got a diamond ring," he said. "Think how much that's

worth."

My fear was slightly pushed aside. I glanced to her hand clutchin' the edge of the window, and its treasure all gleamed at me. That one rock'd fix the tractor; buy the whole seed stock come spring. I imagined Father's grateful response if I was to bring back such a prize to the farm.

I set my jaw.

"Fine, but I'm not goin'. You're lighter than me, so lie down and scoot out onto the ice. I'll hold your feet 'til you get ahold of her hand."

He nodded and took off my gloves, shoving them in his pockets. I reached into my coat and pulled out my pocketknife. It was my most prized possession. I kept it razor sharp.

"You might need this." I flipped it open and slapped it into his hand.

My brother nodded and sleeve-wiped some snot from his red nose. He bent down and started to crawl onto the ice, pushin' the snow ahead of his knees. The smell of gasoline was strong as I knelt to hold his boots.

"We're comin', ma'am," he called. The ice groaned but did not crack as his tiny pink fingers reached, spread, and then clasped shakily 'tween hers. She squeezed back.

"Thank you," said the woman. Her voice was growin' weaker by the moment.

"Okay!" called Bill. "Try to pull us back!"

"Slide off her ring, Bill. Then pass it back to me."

"Damn it! Pull us back!"

"Shut up, Bill!" I yelled. "You hear that ice snappin'? If it breaks then it's all over anyway. Get the damn ring first!"

"I don't care," said the woman quietly to Bill. "Take the ring ... just be quick." Pathetically, she spread her fingers wide. Bent as I was, I could see her features now in the shadows and watery reflections of the car's cab. She was sideways, only her head and one shoulder out of the water. There was the body of a man floatin' behind her, face down. She made eye contact with me, and I saw a malice as deep as I've ever seen, all directed at me, almost as if she knew my every sin. The hummin' in my head grew louder, like a buzz of flies over road kill. I scowled at her.

Bill reached forward with his other hand and tried to slide the ring off of her bloody finger, but it wouldn't budge.

"It's stuck!"

I'd seen that comin'. I spoke slow and low, the way Father did when he really wanted us to obey.

"Listen, Bill. Use the *knife*."

What happened next is somethin' that I've spent my life tryin' to understand. Surely, the car shifted. The woman started to howl, but in as much anger as fear. The ice cracked like a barrage of rifle shots, and I pulled hard on Bill's boots. But he didn't slide, for the woman had hold of his hand, and she put a death grip on it. With a roar like hell's great flames, the ice folded around Bill with a splash, the car and my little brother sucked rapidly into the depths. The last detail I saw was that murderous bitch sneerin' at me before she went clean under.

Both of Bill's boots were in my hands.

I heard a voice sayin' the word "no" over and over again, atop death's buzzin' breath, and I realized that the voice was mine. I threw the boots and dove forward, determined to swim down and get my little brother free. But my cheek struck hard mud just some inches under the surface, and I came up blubbin'. I flailed about in the shallows, screamin', the snow swirlin' above a black mirror of open water, its bubbles all comin' up and soundin' in a way like laughter, for there weren't enough water in that ditch to drown a baby, much less a whole goddamned car.

Bill was gone, and I was certain somehow that the woman knew me.

"Move," I said out loud to myself, shakin' my head violently in the splash. "If you don't, you'll for sure die out here. Now stop your goddamn cryin' and let's get home before we freeze."

I struggled to top the incline all drippin' and shakin', confused and doubting the world. I scrambled over the barbed wire and realized that if a car had crashed through it'a taken the fence out with it. There weren't even tire tracks from the road. The only marks left a't all were that black pool of unfrozen water and the blood of that woman's husband—or whoever Bill had seen—a stark gash of red in the white.

I stumbled the lonely miles back to the farm. Father got his cigarettes and didn't ask me where Bill was 'til the next day. I made up some story about him headin' back halfway 'cause his hands was cold. I buried his mittens in the barn.

They never found Bill nor any car at the bottom of that ditch, of course. But I knew what'd happened, and that gave the weight of it. Fractured me, you could say. Despite all of the horrors I've seen and made since, the worst was that woman's eyes as her face pulled under the water, the same look that I more recently seen in Ester Jackson's shiny black face as I held my blade to her throat, still red with her husband's blood, summer'a last year.

But of course you already knew that.

"May the Devil punish you for this," she spat, and I recognized that educated voice, oh yes, filled with that same malice. For the woman lyin' 'neath me on that dark and sweaty night was none other than the woman in the ditch. I knew, somehow, impossibly, that you was grantin' me my wish for revenge even as she wished her own, so I made sure to use mine good. That night, the bitch lost way more than her finger.

Now, I've precious little time before the executioner comes. I don't care to argue with your unholy cycle of sin and revenge across all that chain of years. You can do as you please. I did not craft this story to plead for me, or for her. We both deserve what awaits us.

But Bill?

Bill deserved none of it.

So please, if the Devil has ears for a sinner's last wish, let loose of little Bill's soul if you still have it, and let him see the Gates of Heaven.

And the Crowd Goes Wild
John Jasper Owens

We stood on the roof of the Plangient Hotel, looking down at the crowd below. They filled the lot, grounds, and access road, surrounding the building like an amoeba curling around a snack. They clogged the highway beyond, and no cop was even trying to clear them out. For all I knew, they stretched back to the airport.

At least the National Guard was keeping the airspace clear. But occasionally one of their hybrid wasp-copters arced a little too close, the soldiers staring out, vid-feeds running.

Has it spread to the military?

This will not be a good day.

"Geneticists should've taken a cue from climatologists," I said.

"I don't know what you mean, Boss," said Bellows. I caught some nervousness in his voice, and Bellows is a man who is never, ever, nervous.

"What I mean," I shouted over the noise, "is that for centuries people believed that the global climate changed at a geological pace. Then the little ice age was mapped out and scientists realized that the world's weather could shift in just fifty years or so." I blinked my glasses to the lobby view—barricades holding nicely—blinked again to the office outside Alyssa's room—everyone on-task—and blinked again to the corporate satellite, which should've given me a nice, tight shot of the hotel from about a mile overhead.

Corporate's offline. Static.

Nope. Not a good day.

"But then, ice cores drilled from pristine fields in Greenland proved that global climate change can take place inside a year. Maybe inside a month."

Bellows shook his head. From far below we heard that same chant crank up: "A-*lysss*-a, A-*lysss*-a, A-*lysss*-a ...." The screams of maybe a quarter million people reaching us up here like the edge of a soap bubble.

"I still don't get it," he said.

"I believe," I told Bellows, "we are witnessing the end times."

Bellows shrugged. "That's gonna play hell with residuals."

He had dark patches under his eyes and a bright scrape on his forehead—trouble securing the perimeter last night.

Behind us, our C-80 Aerodyne Luxury Defense Copter roared down toward the pad. Bellows yelled over the racket.

"Six riots last night. All contained." The chopper wind shoved our hair and flapped our jackets forward.

"Tokyo?"

"Burning."

Tokyo was our first stop on the Rise from Grace world tour. They projected Alyssa's hologram a hundred stories tall. I hadn't been able to access a vid-feed from there since we fled.

The Japanese fans had rushed the copter and lost arms and heads to the whirring blades. And they had been overjoyed to do it.

I blinked through my views again.

Everything steady but corporate.

"Let's go down," I said.

Inside the levelator I felt the oppressive emptiness of the hotel beneath us, like we were in the attic of the world's biggest haunted house. I wasn't with Team Alyssa back when they just rented a floor; I came on about the time we rented the whole hotel. Now we just buy the damn thing. And guests are happy, *happy*, to get kicked out in the street. "Anything for Alyssa Germane," they say. "Can I get a slice? A holo? Can I buy something she touched?"

In Dubai they projected her videos on the ocean, and water sculptures of Alyssa's teen years rose ten feet along the shoreline. That was our second stop.

I think the fans have completely destroyed Dubai. News reports are inconclusive.

I used to play this holo-game, and in one of the stages the hero was expected to jump from island to island, picking up vital items, leaping away just as the ground exploded beneath him. That's how this tour feels. I rewatched LOTR on Classic Movie Transmit the other night, turning up the sound to drown out the crowd outside, and jacked the scene where The Fellowship rushes across a bridge that is disintegrating right behind their heels. That's it, too.

The levelator took us right outside the office.

Everyone shouted questions, comments, whatever, when we strode through. The place was semi-controlled chaos, dealing with a million different arrangements, and Rose French's problem, not mine.

Alyssa's door.

I stopped for a long breath. I had to every time I met with Alyssa, and that was about a dozen times a day, more on show days.

The first second is an assault by sheer beauty; the perfection of her.

The next is a fall into the deeper awe of her presence as she turns her attention, like a prison searchlight, on what I have to say. There is always that flash of humility that she could find anything I have to tell her worth listening to.

By the third second, I'm usually okay.

I knocked and waited for permission.

She was on her exercise bike, head bobbing to some internal music, watching a news channel with the sound off. She eased off the pedaling and mopped her face with a towel when she saw us come in. No makeup, just tumbled out of bed, dressed in a tracksuit, still the most beautiful human being ever born. And maybe the most talented. Number-one movie star in the world and number-one music performer, with at least five songs in the top ten every week for the last four years.

"Did you hear about Jakarta?" she asked. Of course I had, but I let her talk. "They're building temples, man!" She pointed at the screen. "Statues of me." She laughed. "The goddess Alyssa Germane, dude. Fear my wrath." She winked at me, and I felt it down to my knees.

She wasn't even twenty-three.

Her hometown, a flyspeck in southern Arkansas, no longer existed. They'd come for her girlhood home first, carting it away, every brick, board, and nail, and then her elementary school, down to chunks of the pavement. The park where she said she'd had her first real kiss was sealed off by private security, a shrine now, attended by the occupying army of her fans, who danced along Main Street and communed in the old restaurants and garages.

"Mr. Bellows?" she asked. The big man snapped to like the ex-soldier he was. "I think we need to get rid of Jenny Beauchamp out there, if you don't mind. She's getting strange on me."

That was another problem altogether. Even people used to being around Alyssa sometimes couldn't help themselves. One moment she had an employee who could fetch coffee and make reservations and otherwise leave her the hell alone, and the next moment that person was staring at her wide-eyed, hands shaking.

And their faces changed. Was I the only one who noticed that?

I've been a celebrity wrangler since I was a kid, and I've seen them put up with a lot—stand here, say this, and who's that new man on your arm?—but one thing they will not abide is discomfort in their private spaces. It's a particular problem with publicists. Working directly with the fans infects them, I think.

So Beauchamp was out on her ass, and it wasn't going to be pretty. Being cast down from paradise never is.

Plus, Bellows was sleeping with her.

He went out to ruin the woman's life.

"I want rehearsals closed today," Alyssa told me. I nodded. Closing rehearsals on two hours' notice was next to impossible.

"Feeling crowded?"

She blew a bit of hair out of eyes. "I was signing headshots for the *other performers* yesterday. The staff down there is a mob. Can't do it again." She slid off the bike and reached for her drink, which I knew had damn well better be an iced skinny half-caff sugar-free hazelnut latte.

"Have you seen the overnights?" I asked. She shook her head. "You'll open number one this weekend in the E.U. You beat your own record—five in a row."

"Go, team!" she said, throwing a fist up. Then, "Listen, may I ask you a question?" She had to know perfectly well that if she told Bellows and me to play leapfrog around the room, we'd do it until she got bored, but Alyssa was authentically polite.

Even through the thick door and shag carpet, we could hear the wails of Jenny Beauchamp.

"Am I handling all this right?"

"I believe we are witnessing the end times," I said. *What? What the hell? I would never talk to Alyssa like that.* My hand flew up to check my face, but I stopped it.

"No joke." She laughed. "Six more dates and we're back in the studio, thank God. Or one of my Jakarta statues. *B-u-u-u-t* seriously, folks—you're the pro. Am I being a good superstar?" She held me with big, earnest eyes.

"At your level? No one knows. We're in uncharted territory."

"Gee, thanks, John. You're a *huge* help. Elvis was more famous than me." Alyssa idolized The King.

"Elvis was *bigger* than you, so were The Beatles. We're not talking about adoration, we're talking about celebrity. Celebrity is an ancient concept."

She crossed her arms. "Here we go. You've been talking to

Hana again." Hana Nakada was our tech, an internet theory grad from Harvard, and yes, I had.

My glasses alerted. Alyssa noticed.

"Bellows," I said, and she waved for me to take it. I half-turned and activated ear-feed.

"She's in the hotel," Bellows panted. "Jenny's gone nuts. I shut down the levelators. We can't catch her."

Alyssa was watching me, smiling softly. I smiled back.

"Well, we need to correct that," I said.

"There she is!" Bellows shouted to someone beside him. I could hear the echo of the stairwell before the connection dropped.

I returned my full attention to my boss, who went on with her train of thought.

"My freaking fourth cousins can't go out on the street without protection. I'm going to have to ship the whole family to the Boca compound. I just feel like I'm not handling all this too well."

Alyssa Germane, former child star, famous since she was a baby, really, on some wretched sit-com, then pre-teen sensation, then tween idol, then her teen years, and explosion into the adult consciousness, and now biggest celebrity by any estimation—ticket sales, vid sales, cash accrued, any factor of measurement you can come up with, of all time, without question, is now asking *me* if she's handling her fame okay.

Just another day at the office.

Kim, Hana's assistant, ducked in with a stack of papers, left them on the table, and ran out. Nothing focuses the staff like someone getting fired.

"When humans evolved," I said, "fame was a way a man could distinguish himself within the pack, even though he wasn't the leader. Best hunter, fastest runner; these people were *celebrated*."

Alyssa wandered over to the closet and started looking at shoes. She was never much of a student.

"And celebrity increased as the ability to spread fame

increased," she said, absently. "I talk to Hana too, you know."

My glasses alerted again. Alyssa was glancing at the mirror as I picked up.

"Oh, *Christ*," yelled Bellows. "She jumped. Christ, man, she *jumped* off the *roof*." I could hear the wind behind him.

"Would that be the front or back of the hotel?"

"Oh, *Christ*, I'm gonna hurl." Bellows threw up.

"I'm going to need an answer," I said.

He was still retching. "The front."

"I'll be right there. Oh! Tell Terrence we'll be taking the bird to rehearsal earlier than expected. There's a heli-pad on St. Mark's Hospital—we'll sneak her down through there. And have someone unlock the levelator."

He didn't answer for so long, I thought he was about to quit. I watched Alyssa stare at a row of sneakers, doing little dance steps on the carpet.

"Heard and understood," said Bellows.

I closed the connection.

"History lesson over," I told Alyssa. "Some of us around here have to work."

She waved me away.

I felt the usual half-second refusal as I walked away from her, a deep and resounding "No!" from my brain telling me I must not leave her presence.

Then it passed, as always.

In the outer suite I bent down next to Rose French, Alyssa's personal secretary and the woman in charge of our office. I whispered to her about Beauchamp, and when I drew back, her eyes were wide and wet.

"So you're going to have to handle that on this end and keep her calm until after the show. Are we clear?"

Rose glanced at Brent and Lizzy, the remaining two publicists.

"Yes," she said.

I used my time on the levelator trying to make the first few arrangements to close rehearsal. Stadium offline. Corporate still offline. I wondered if the moon project was screwed up.

Thirty-six floors straight down, the lobby was nearly as empty as the rest of the place, with a handpicked skeleton crew of hotel staff and a world of security. I noticed the glass wall was boarded up—someone had driven an ATV through it, right over the barriers, sometime last night.

I snapped my fingers and pointed ("You, you, you, you!") and four of our biggest guys followed me out.

I used the men as blockers and shoved into the crowd. A woman just hit the pavement out here—they'll be horrified, backing off. I know crowd dynamics. I'll be pushing off journalists and waving in police.

But everyone seemed to be milling around where I assumed—I couldn't see yet—the body landed.

A woman grabbed my hair and one of the guys decked her. On the sidewalk, she looked at the few strands caught in her fingers and grinned through a bloody mouth. A mouth that looked just like Alyssa's.

Ahead of us, a roar went up. Someone held aloft a high-heeled shoe.

Jenny Beauchamp's foot was still in it.

A bigger man lunged for it, and a fight broke out. A boy, maybe thirteen, rushed by me, chunks of scalp and skull in each hand. I only caught a glimpse of his face, but he could've been Alyssa's brother.

Someone tapped me on the shoulder and I looked down into studious eyes—fortyish, glasses. She held out her palm. In it was Jenny's finger, her Duke class ring still set below the knuckle.

"Excuse me," she said. "Can you tell me what this person's position was under," she sighed, "Alyssa Germane?"

One of my guys turned my shoulders and pushed me back

toward the hotel.

I glanced back. The woman popped the finger in her mouth and chewed.

I ran.

We locked the hotel doors and watched them carry away pieces of Jenny Beauchamp.

Bellows arranged the helicopter seats lounge-style at a speed just under panic, and Terrence took us over the city. Alyssa was used to being hustled here and there for security reasons—she settled with her feet folded under her bottom and flipped through one of the fanzines devoted entirely to all things Alyssa Germane.

"Fat," she said, pointing at a picture of her rushing out of Sardi's. She turned the page. "Fat." She pointed again, kept going through the photos. "Fat. Not bad. Fat. I like that one." She flipped another page. "My ass is *not* that big. Is it?"

"They use a trick lens," said Rose French. By rights she should be back in the suite, running the office, but her presence had a calming effect on Alyssa. Like a goat in the stables soothes a thoroughbred.

Bellows, pale and sweaty, sat across from me, and Hana Nakada—tiny little thing—perched between Alyssa and me, reading her neuro-feed and scrolling along on her laptop.

"Did you know," she asked, "that scientists at the Brookside Institute discovered that a chimp will forgo sips of fruit juice for an opportunity to stare at images of alpha males and females? True."

I barely heard her. Dear God, they had carried away pieces of Jenny Beauchamp.

"Instead of ten sips of juice," Hana Nakada said, "eight sips and a few seconds looking at The Big Guy, or the lady chimp is all the young boys crave. It's the primate equivalent of putting back a few candy bars and throwing a copy of *Germane Magazine* in the bag."

"I have the thighs of a washerwoman," said Alyssa, as if she weren't flawless. Rose cooed at her.

The copter banked hard left. We have internal stabilizers—Alyssa didn't notice. But Bellows and I did.

Terrance sounded in my ear-feed, asked me to please move forward into the cockpit.

"I believe the current analogous fan behavior is the confluence of two factors, actually," Hana Nakada said.

Alyssa and Rose weren't even listening.

"One, evolution. The knock on Darwinian evolution has always been that there doesn't seem to be enough time, epoch-to-epoch, to produce the higher organisms through natural selection and mutation alone. Higher evolution seems to occur suddenly, in batches, and in times of stress." She was staring at her eye lens as her fingers darted over her laptop. I don't think even Hana was listening to Hana.

I made my way to the cockpit and dropped in the empty copilot's seat. Terrance pointed at vid-feeds displayed on a wall of screens around us. No transparent anything on this sucker—we were all reinforced bio-steel.

"We were three minutes and I had to pull up," he said. He tapped a monitor.

Below us the hospital roof, heli-pad included, was jammed with nurses, orderlies, patients and doctors, hoisting signs and carrying banners, watching our approach as if we were Jesus Himself descending. Some of the patients were swaying, IVs still attached, and there was fresh blood everywhere—on hospital gowns, surgical scrubs—red and glistening in the sunlight. What? Did they rush out of surgery?

Or….

I had an image of the floors beneath them jammed with bodies trampled, suffocating, those on the roof the ones who had managed to claw their way up.

"We'll set down somewhere else," I told Terrence.

"They'll move," he said.

He hadn't been with us in Tokyo; hadn't seen them decapitate themselves.

If we dropped close enough, they would leap up and drag us down.

"I don't want to crowd our girl," I said, "so hold tight." I stuck my head back out to the cabin, where Hana Nakada was still going on.

"… because you can really trace this back to the printing press, but the Internet allows one section of the brain, intelligence, to far outstrip the other brain functions on an evolutionary—yes, sir?"

"Get up front with your neurolinks and find Terrence another place to land us."

Hana moved liked she was paid to do.

"Something wrong?" asked Alyssa. When I sat beside her (but not too near) she leaned over and palmed my arm. I saw it coming, so I managed not to tense up.

Alyssa's touch burns me, something I've been not thinking about. That's weird enough—she's the Goddess Alyssa, right?—so of course her touch burns. But why does it burn when I don't know it's her? Once she came up behind me at a party and put her hands over my eyes, and I screamed in real agony. She thought I was just on edge and apologized all over—as I said before, she's authentically polite. But how did I know it was Alyssa?

"Word got out," I told her. Stuff like that she understood. "If we can't find a pad nearby, we'll just put it down in the stadium."

She tossed the 'zine she had been reading across the aisle.

"Explain the jumping gene to me."

The shock on my face must've been obvious.

"I've been trying this weird new thing called reading actual books," she said. "Stuff Hana leaves me. You know what? Some of them aren't even about me."

I didn't know what to say.

"That's a joke. You can laugh."

I did, dutifully, then said, "So, what's Hana been giving you?"

"Mostly stuff I don't care about. *Loved* the Elvis bio. This one book she gave me was totally fascinating, but too hard to get through. Too many science words. She highlighted the part about the jumping gene, but that was just after Tokyo, so I got distracted."

The copter banked hard again, dropped maybe two hundred feet. Bellows, stood, acting casual, and went up to the cockpit.

"Way back in the 1950s," I said—

"Elvis!" said Alyssa.

"A scientist named Barbara McClintock first developed evidence that corn can mutate rapidly under stress, due to a tiny bit of DNA that jumps up and down the double helix, turning other genes off and on. Heresy back then, but she won the Nobel prize when she was in her eighties."

"What kind of stress can *corn* possibly be under? And why did Hana want me to read about it?"

My ear feed activated. Bellows. "Get up here!"

I stood. "Stress means all sorts of things."

The copter lurched so hard even the stabilizers couldn't hide it, and Alyssa, precious Alyssa, was thrown to the floor like a sack of garbage.

"John?" She was terrified.

"Give me a second."

I had to jam my palms against the walls to push myself up into the cockpit and the brawl inside. Terrence was pressed against the control panel by Bellow's back, trying to keep Hana off him. The tiny woman snarled and snapped and hurled herself into Bellows.

"The Wasps are driving us down," yelled Terrence. I remembered wondering if it had spread to the military. In one of the monitors I watched the hybrid copters crowding us, using stun cannons to concuss us toward earth.

I absorbed problem number one and focused my attention on problem number two.

Hana had turned.

Evolved.

Stamped across her Asiatic face was a semblance of Alyssa's features. She lunged again at Bellows and I shoved her back, pinning her in the copilot chair. She bit at me, her eyes filled with disgust.

Homo sapiens looking at Cro-Magnon.

"She's *ours*," she said.

I shoved my knee against her chest and strangled her in her seat.

The stun cannons hit us again. I fell over Hana's corpse, panting, and Bellows pulled me to my feet.

"They want us to land at the stadium," he said.

"They can blast us out of the sky any time they want," said Terrence.

"Evasive?"

"Military. Not a chance."

Bellows pointed at Hana's face, her blank, bulging eyes gone from brown to Alyssa's blue-green. "What? *How*?"

"I'd imagine it's kind of like cancer," I told him. "One second you don't have it, the next you do." I grabbed his lapels. Both our suits were ripped and pulled, our gun straps showing. "Do *not* let Alyssa up here, no matter *what*."

He nodded.

Back in the cabin, Alyssa took one look at me and started crying, rocking in her seat. "Oh God, oh, God, oh, God...." Rose sat mute.

I sat beside the goddess and patted her shoulder, feeling the burn up my arm. "It's going to be okay," I said. "We're landing at the stadium."

"What about everyone back at the hotel?" asked Rose in a dry whisper.

I blinked over my vid feed. Brent, Lizzy, everyone we left behind was dead. The fans had stormed the penthouse, ripped them to pieces. They packed our offices, snatching any token or memento they could. My view wouldn't reach into Alyssa's bedroom.

Probably just as well.

"They're fine," I said.

"You're bleeding," said Alyssa. She reached and rubbed a slash mark Hana had left, smearing blood down my cheek.

"Times of stress."

Moments later Terrence, remarkably calm, instructed us to strap in for landing. "And we've got company."

Until the disembark dropped open, I assumed he meant the Wasps.

Terrence had dropped us near the stage.

We straggled out, the five of us, Terrence and Bellows up front, the goddess on my shoulder, burning into me, and Rose last, wondering what the hell she'd gotten herself into. We all froze when our feet hit the grass, when we looked forward, up, around.

Nope. Not a good day.

The stadium, a hundred-and-forty-thousand-seat monstrosity, was filled, packed with fans, all stamped with the mark of Alyssa. They overflowed the aisles, the stairs, perched on railings and crammed back through the exits. They swung like monkeys from the crossbeams.

All silent. All watching.

From high above, the Wasps painted us with searchlight.

Rose French fainted.

Alyssa pressed harder against me.

"I guess you weren't able to close rehearsal," she said. When I looked down at her I saw she was laughing and crying at the same time. "You're fired."

I hugged her. "Just give me some time to clear my office."

I took her by the hand and led her up onstage, two, maybe three hundred thousand watching us live, and however many billions more on vid-feed.

In the sky, far above the copters, a daytime moon appeared. This was something corporate had been working on for some time, acres of orbiting mirrors that would keep the moon illuminated, the side perpetually facing Earth carved with Alyssa's face.

The howl of two hundred thousand voices.

I felt it then, the charge in my spine. I felt it in my nose and cheekbones. I saw Bellows and Terrence charging me, and my gun was out, two quick, sure shots to their chests.

The goddess screamed and tried to twist away. Where she planned to run, I have no idea.

I held her against me, reveling in the exquisite burn of her body.

I yanked her head back by her hair and sank my teeth in her neck, crunching through her esophagus, and again, and again, chewing, swallowing, her blood washing hot over my face, my neck, feeling her spasm and die, sacrificed to the new race she had created.

I dropped her corpse, a gravestone over what humanity had been.

I raised my bloody fists to the sky, to the future, and roared.

And the crowd went wild.

No Sin Remains a Secret
Jack Bowdren

In the dark coolness of the church hall basement it had appeared quite ordinary, but once I had lugged it up into the light, I could see that it wasn't like any other statue of Christ I'd known. It was hewn roughly, to my mind almost angrily, into a shape representing rather than mirroring a human being. A wash of pale blue paint over His robe must surely have been added years after the statue was created, unless it was a trick played by the sweat in my eyes. My goodness, I wished Terry had been there to help me carry it.

Of course, Terry was the reason I'd had to navigate the beastly thing out of the basement in the first place. He was my church warden, and in that capacity he often took it upon himself to enact minor repairs. The original statue of Our Lord had stood in an alcove next to the doors for longer than I could tell you. In the course of attempting to correct the balance of a wobbly hymnal stand, Terry had managed to drop his hammer on his foot, hop backward, and topple it. The resonant crack as it broke in two had been so loud that I heard it in the vicarage.

I didn't blame Terry, of course: it could have happened to any of us. But the timing certainly left me in a peculiar pickle. As the vicar of St. Stephen's-on-the-Wold, it was my duty, every year, to lead the procession on a traditional walk around the parish to bless the harvest. The procession always formed up with me in the lead, followed by the statue of Our Lord borne on a pannier by four sturdy farmers. Here, of course, lay the predicament. Personally, I considered the hauling of holy statues across acres of farm land rather unnecessary and—though I never dared say it—somewhat pagan. My previous appointment had been in a small town and the harvest, usually consisting of a lettuce and five cans of Spam, had been blessed during the usual Sunday service. Here in St. Stephen's my predecessor had turned the harvest procession into an important community event, and out of respect for both the community and his efforts I felt obliged to follow suit.

Strangely, it was only due to my predecessor that I'd known of the statue in the basement at all. The Reverend Bartholomew Thurrock was not an overly talkative man, and he already seemed to have one foot in his retirement when I met him, but in the course of our stroll about the garden I happened to mention the statue that stood in the alcove.

"I say, here's a thing," he began, his eyes lighting up for the only time in our brief acquaintance. "There's another statue of Christ, you know?"

"Really?" I replied. "I must have missed it."

"No, no, dear boy, not in the church. It's in the basement under the hall."

"Why on earth is it down there?"

"Excellent question. There's a story that goes with it, you see. A bishop in the eighteenth century went insane and tried to brick it up inside the walls of his palace. Said it kept whispering people's sins to him."

"Good grief."

"Indeed."

I thought about it.

"Surely a statue dating back to the eighteenth century should be on display somewhere rather than hidden away in the storeroom of a provincial church?"

"The same idea occurred to me," replied the Reverend Bartholomew, "until I went down and looked at it. It is not, in all truthfulness, a work of art."

Having taken his words on faith, I'd never been down to see the statue. Now he had been fully vindicated. Nonetheless, it was not the statue we worshipped, but God Himself. There was no reason why this likeness should not replace the other one temporarily while it was being repaired, even if it did unnerve me slightly to look at it. I'd never seen Our Lord portrayed with a furrowed brow before.

The route of our harvest procession by and large followed the boundaries of the parish until a point just over halfway around. Here it cut back inside in order to cross the brook that flowed through the village. The track to the bridge passed by the yard of the outermost farm of the area, owned by Tom and Julie Stead, and it was here that we usually stopped for some refreshments.

The Steads were not regular churchgoers, but Julie's mother, Maude, was. Maude lived in the farmhouse with them, unable to do any farm work but happy to cook and clean, potter about the kitchen garden, and spoil her grandchildren while their parents weren't looking. She sometimes brought seasonal flowers to the church with her—one of the surest signs of spring was the vase of daffodils that would appear in front of the altar. For several years now she had been too frail to process with us around the parish, but on each occasion she had greeted the statue with a garland of roses as it entered the farmyard. She had done as much this year, albeit a little taken aback by the frowning Christ, and I stood with her beside the pannier telling the story of the accident when I became aware of a commotion behind me. A mother was calling down the lane to her children.

"Ben! Tess! Stay away from the river! Get back here right now!"

Her words had little effect. There was the briefest of pauses and then a faint cry of "Help!"

This electrified our gathering. Abandoning the refreshments, everybody ran toward the cry. I had started farthest from the farm gate, and by the time I reached the lane I could already see Tom Stead climbing up the riverbank with a wet and shaken child under each arm.

Relieved, I turned back to let Maude know all was well, but my words caught in my throat. She lay crumpled next to the pannier, the only still thing on a breezy afternoon, and then I swear the statue's lips moved and I heard a harsh, whispered word: "Murder."

I was haunted over the next two days by the story the Reverend Thurrock had told me, yet I nearly convinced myself that I'd imagined it. I found it impossible to believe that Maude could ever have been guilty of such a terrible sin. Then the story broke. Shorn of the vulgar embellishments of the gutter press, the facts were essentially as follows. On opening Maude's will, Tom and Julie found another letter detailing how Julie's father had married Maude's best friend before realising he loved Maude instead. This being long before divorce was in any way socially acceptable, Maude would likely have lost her claim to inherit the farm. Maude and her husband-to-be thus conspired to kill his wife and make it look like a riding accident. The revelation of this sorry tale sent shockwaves through our little village. I did not think highly of whoever leaked the story to the press, but needless to say I had greater concerns on my mind.

If there had been no story in the newspapers, what would I have done? Could I have written off what I had seen and heard as a flight of fancy brought on by the adrenaline of my momentary exertion just seconds before? It was a moot point. The memory played in my head many times after I read the full story, and each repetition only served to reinforce my fears. In that open farmyard on that sunny day I saw the statue's lips move as it whispered to me the name of the sin that only Maude had known she was guilty of.

I was beginning to see why that bishop had gone mad.

The following afternoon found me in the church selecting hymns for the Sunday services. The statue stood in the alcove, and although I had no reason to, I could not help glancing at it now and then. I was unusually relieved when the doors opened and Terry entered.

"Afternoon, Vicar," he said. Then he noticed the new statue next to him. "Blimey, he's no looker."

I managed a smile. "I can only suppose that artists also work in mysterious ways."

"Ain't that the truth. God made man in His own image. It's a shame we couldn't return the favour."

I enjoyed spending time with Terry. That day he was there to put in sturdy picture hooks ready to hang some paintings that had recently been donated by the diocese. Unsurprisingly, he soon brought up the latest news.

"Strange goings-on up at the Stead's farm, then. I heard you were the one who found poor Maude?"

Again I caught myself glancing at the statue. "Yes. It was a terrible loss to our community."

Terry pondered.

"I suppose it was. Despite what them papers have to say. It seems a shame, though."

"What does?"

"Well, going through all that to marry the man you love and then him dying so young."

I hadn't heard this part of the tale. "Did he die young?"

"That he did. In his forties he was, not much older than you. He was the warden before the warden before me."

I stiffened. It was warm in the church, the late afternoon sun dappling stained glass saints across the altar, but I felt suddenly chill.

"What happened to him?"

"Reckon he fell down the stairs. Leastways we found him at the bottom with his head cracked open."

For a moment I relaxed, until Terry went on.

"Matter of fact, the only time I've been down in that basement was to help Billy Harrison carry him out."

I had to force myself not to look at the statue. "Which basement?"

"Under the hall. Reckon you've been down there yourself now." He laughed and nodded at the statue, then did a double take.

"What's wrong?" I asked.

"Nothing. Trick of the light. Could have sworn the ugly thing was looking at me."

I was a fervent believer in eating a good breakfast, and yet that morning I found myself contemplating rather than consuming my cereal. I was still sat at the table when Terry knocked at the door.

"Morning, Vicar," he said. "Feeling under the weather?"

"No, no. Things on my mind, Terry. Nothing more."

"Doesn't do to dwell, Vicar. Though I guess it's more in your line than mine. Are the paintings still in the spare room?"

"They are. I'll prop the front door open for you."

It was a glorious day, and the fresh air made me feel a little better. Terry left the vicarage carrying the first painting and I returned to the table. As I picked up my plate, I heard him yell.

Had it been anyone other than Terry who yelled, I might have run the short distance to the church and could perhaps have averted tragedy. As it was, my clouded mind and some implacable belief in Terry's ability to cope slowed me to a stride. Between the vicarage and the church doors I heard nothing more, and I was completely unprepared for the scene that confronted me.

The painting, splintered and torn, lay to one side of the aisle. To the other side lay Terry. His shirt was torn and his back scored, as though he had tried to run and been dragged back. The sun spilling through the doorway lit up his face, locked in a spasm of terror and lolling unnaturally in my direction. His neck was clearly broken.

I barely had time to take all this in before I heard a harsh whisper, loud in my ear: "Infidelity." The shock caused me to start sideways, trip across the hymnal stand, and knock myself out.

When I recovered, I telephoned the police. I told them everything I knew. It wasn't a lot, when I looked back over it. A Constable Lister took notes and then gave me the number of a local bereavement counsellor. It made no difference that I was not personally bereaved.

"People react to death in strange ways," he told me. "Anyone would be affected by finding two bodies in a week. The whispers are clear psychological signs, while the moving lips—well, in all honesty, that sounds like an optical illusion."

He promised to drop by the next day to see how I was.

That evening I sat despondently in my living room when I was roused by a knock at the door. To my surprise it was Margaret, Terry's widow. I invited her in and offered to make her a drink.

"No thank you, Reverend. I just need a moment of your time."

"What's troubling you?" I asked, with less than my usual tact.

She gathered herself and then spoke.

"An officer interviewed me earlier about Terry. I imagine they spoke to you, too."

I nodded.

"Near the end, he asked whether, whether—"

A solitary tear stumbled down her cheek.

"—whether I knew if Terry had been seeing anybody else. Another woman."

"Oh, Margaret." I felt sick. I hadn't meant my testimony to add to this poor woman's anguish.

"I told them no, of course, Reverend."

"Of course."

"I just need to know. Did I do the right thing?"

I met her gaze. "I'm sorry. I don't follow."

"I don't want anyone to think of Terry that way." She welled up. "Because there was another woman."

I couldn't speak.

"She lived in London. He saw her now and then when he was visiting friends. I found out not long ago and put a stop to it. I don't want people to know, Reverend. Should I have told the police?"

I was torn. I wanted to reassure her, yet I dearly wished she had backed up my own statement. I only had it in me to take the kinder course.

"Margaret, you did the right thing. I found Terry myself, and it could not have been anything but an accident. There was nobody nearby, and I really can't believe that anyone could commit murder without leaving any evidence whatsoever. It was an accident, Margaret. A terrible accident."

Lying to her made me feel utterly hollow, but I could see in her face that she believed my words every bit as much as I didn't. I assured her that I would tell nobody what she had divulged and she left with what comfort I could give her. Perhaps if I had told her of the statue she might have believed me, but without proof I would have been doing little more than taking advantage of her grief.

Insomnia was a curse of my youth that I had managed to conquer in recent years, but it struck me with a hellish force that night. What was I doing? Who was I up against? Was I, in fact, psychologically unbalanced? I did not think that to be the case. Had I seen movement in shadows or heard whispers in the night, then perhaps I could have believed my mind was tricking me. But I had always trusted in daylight, and I trusted in it still. The statue's actions were real. It seemed only to operate when alone with someone who had sinned gravely against the word of God. Yet what power truly lay within it? For if you could learn anything at all from the Gospels of Christ, it was that He Himself would never take the life of a sinner.

That was the thought I finally drifted off to sleep with.

A few short hours later it was Sunday. The little church was packed for the morning service, a congregation the size of which I expected only on Christmas day. I gave the first and only unprepared sermon of my life. Bolstered by the presence of so many people, I covered the full range of Jesus' teachings on forgiveness, from "Let he who is without sin cast the first stone" to "Do unto others as you would have others do unto you." After the service, I strode out of the church past the statue feeling as though I had won my first battle against that malevolent imposter-Christ.

Half an hour later, I was in the vicarage garden clearing out the shed. Terry had stored his tools there, and I wanted to be sure they were returned in good order. I had just picked up his hammer when I heard footsteps. My nerves got the better of me and I spun around, causing little Tess to jump back with a squeal.

"Good gracious," I said. "I'm sorry, my dear, you startled me. Has Sunday School finished?"

"Yeah," she said, "but Ben had football so Mummy has to pick him up. She said for me to wait here. What are you doing?"

"I'm just going through the tools in the shed. Some of them are quite old and not very useful any more."

"That hammer looks new and shiny," she said. "Oh! Would you like to see my new doll?"

"I'd like that very much. Where is it?"

Tess looked down and then behind her. "I think I might have left her inside. Back in a minute!"

She skipped away, and I turned back to the tool shed before the thought occurred: go with her.

"Tess!" I called, but she had just disappeared around the corner of the church. Surely a child wouldn't be in any danger? Then again, I had thought the same of Terry. I couldn't let myself make the same mistake twice.

Hammer in hand, I started to run. Skidding around the corner, I was mere yards from the doors when I heard her scream.

I wrenched the doors open and she tumbled out, landing heavily on the stone path. The back of her head was smashed in. The statue did not seem to have shifted, but one of its hands was stained red. The doll lay at its feet. I dreaded what was coming.

Its lips moved and it grated the word: "Idolatry."

I charged, shouldering it from the alcove onto the bright aisle of the church. It landed heavily but did not break, and I bore down upon it.

Nobody else believed. Nobody else understood. Nobody else had seen what I had seen. It had to be me. Only I could destroy this monster, this crude golem masquerading as my Saviour. In His name I would end this diabolical entity.

I brought the hammer down. The statue moved so fast I barely saw it. My wrist stung as it blocked the blow and I felt a strong, stony-cold grip at my throat. As my vision darkened, I heard that harsh whisper, close to my ear, grinding out the word: "Hubris." This impelled me to one last struggle. I twisted in its grasp and swung blindly. The hammer connected with stone, and the grip at my throat relaxed.

I fell to one side, gasping for air. It took a good minute for my vision to return to normal. I looked at the statue and found I had landed my blow on the side of its head. A large chunk had shattered off and lay in pieces on the floor around us. I felt so relieved that I could have danced and sung, had my throat allowed it.

Then I realised I was not alone. In the doorway stood Constable Lister, staring, shocked, at poor Tess and at the hammer still in my hand.

I don't blame the man, nor do I blame the court, the jurors, or the judge. I am not insane, though others believe me so, and I can well imagine how it must have looked from an outside perspective. I now go to serve my sentence, and I shall take the Lord with me, just as He was surely with me when I struck that blow and ended the foul creature I'd unwittingly set loose.

Hubris, it said. I'd say it couldn't recognise humility when it saw it.

The Heat Has Fangs
Trent Roman

B oy, you sure look hot, if you don't mind my saying so. If you're not in a hurry, you could always sit down for a spell right here. I've got shade and cool drinks and wouldn't mind the company at all.

There you go. Much better, isn't it? When it gets this hot, it's always a good idea to take a time-out and just cool off for a while. Heat can kill, you mark me.

I'm Memory Murray, by the way; pleased to meet you. They call me that because I never forget a face. I've been running this here newsstand since '63, and I remember everybody who has ever bought a newspaper or magazine from me. Also read my own papers on slow days like today, and I remember those, too. A fellow in a fancy suit once said my memory was eidetic, which is a fancy-suit way of saying photographic. He bought that day's *Chronicle,* the *New York Post,* and a *Penthouse.*

But listen to me ramble. When you get to be my age, you find that your lips just won't hold shut anymore. Then again, I've never been shy about flapping my gums. You ask anybody who remembers *me*, and they'll tell you that.

It sure is a scorcher. Hundred and ten, the weather said, and that's not counting the humidity. This is one heck of a heat wave, and it doesn't show sign of breaking anytime soon, either. But not the worse I've seen; no, sir. You should have seen things back in the summer of '79: asphalt was near well melting in the streets, honest to God.

Oh, sure, I know what you're thinking: here goes the old-timer, complaining about how easy people nowadays have it. Next thing, old Murray's going tell us about how he hiked ten miles to school in the dead of winter wearing only his granddad's linens. But believe you me, today might be blistering, but it doesn't hold a candle to those sweltering July weeks back in '79. That heat wave was a *killer*; it claimed thirty-six people before rains from up north broke the beast's back.

I remember most anything, but I remember that particularly well. One of the people we lost that year had been a friend of mine: Anders Svensen, the poor guy. He was such a card, that man; I remember once, me and old Anders had been out late drinking, and when we got back to the Barnyard, we got it into our heads that, just to be different, we'd switch apartments. Of course, Anders being Anders, that didn't mean just walking into each other's rooms, no: he was gung-ho on a total move, lugging about furniture in the small hours of the morning, and we passed out with cupboards and tables clogging up the corridor. Boy, did we ever get hell from the super and some of the other guys for that stunt.

That was March of '77 … two years before the heat got to him.

Poor Anders, he *hated* being hot. This, despite the fact that the man had roots down in Georgia, where he spent most of his childhood before his father moved them all to Chasm on some kind of laundry franchise operation. He said it was the Nordic blood in him. He was always the first to slip on T-shirts and shorts when the weather started turning warm. He had brown hair fading to a kind of ginger and perpetually pale skin that burned with naught but a stray beam of sunlight. It was a running joke at the Barnyard that the first day of summer was the day you spotted Anders Svensen walking around with his skin lobster-red and peeling like a dog sheds its fur.

I suppose it's only natural that Anders took the wave of '79 worse of anybody, then, although still a terrible shame. We all knew that it wasn't going to be a good summer, not after the bad winter. That was the year the Shah of Iran got himself booted out by the Muslim priests over there, although all that nasty business with the embassy and the hostages only happened later that year. Still, the situation over there was bad, and just like back in '73, war meant oil shortages and prices went soaring. Just like they are now, in fact; some things progress as the generations roll by, and others just stay stuck in the same ruts, I guess.

We were lucky that the winter was milder than usual, and the crisis in its infancy; otherwise, '79 would have seen a good number of people in the city freezing to death too, other than the usual hobos. Heating your apartment suddenly cost as much as eating for a week when February rolled around. The hardest was a cold snap at the beginning of March, weather way below zero; I remember several of us in the Barnyard decided to save cash by sleeping in the same apartment, with everybody pitching in to pay the super's heating bill.

But that was the worst part of what was really a mild winter, like I said, and we were back to bitching—pardon my French—about the price of gas for regular things like making your car go soon enough. We all hoped that the crisis would resolve itself soon; we all remembered the gas-pump line-ups and rationing coupons from '73. But we also felt, as the mild winter shifted into a warm and dry April and May, that if the temperature didn't give, we'd be sweating out of our skins by the time summer rolled around.

And right we were, though there wasn't anything we could do about it. I suppose the boys at the Barnyard could have gotten our petty cash together and sprung for an AC unit, huddled together in front of it as we had for the heater during the cold snap, but how would we have powered it? It was the middle of an energy crisis, and Chasm City was particularly hard-hit because the electrical grid hadn't been refurbished since the Fifties, and entire portions of the city were going dark. I remember Jimmy Carter, that peanut farmer, coming on the radio and telling us that we needed to work together to conserve energy. Ha! You think they switched off the fans in the White House when the air started to ripple?

What's that? The Barnyard? Oh, no, not a real barnyard. It was our nickname for the big old apartment complex where we all lived. It was on Fredericksburg, just past Columbus going east. Think it's still there, actually, although they've named it 'Aurora House,' added a whole bunch of stories, and I hear that it's considered part of the Projects now. Funny how the geography of cities can shift sometimes; you stay put, but after a few years you suddenly find yourself in a different neighbourhood.

Well, not me. I left the Barnyard in '81, after six years, for a nicer place here in the Core. We called it the Barnyard because it was a place for single men, mostly middle-aged farts like me and Anders, guys who were either lifelong bachelors or divorced. Sometimes we called it the Fraternity or the Bachelor Pad, but Barnyard's the one that stuck, I guess because a bunch of men on their own never maintain the cleanest apartments. The divorced guys were particularly bad; I guess they'd gotten too used to the missus taking care of picking up the joint.

When it started getting really hot, we really didn't spend much time indoors, though. The Barnyard used to have this awning, see, because it was built like one of those old-style hotels with a reception area and everything. Porches ain't exactly common this deep into the city, but we had one, and we spent most of our time sitting in its shadow during that summer, me and Anders and Don Vera and Shelby Masters, drinking lemonade or beer (depending on the hour), just shooting the shit and waiting for the sun to go down and hopefully a cool evening breeze to come by.

Anders really started interesting himself in the weather that year. Maybe he felt what was coming, who can say? But as May gave way to June, Anders started talking more and more about air currents and weather fronts, going on at length about the particularities of local climate until Don Vera told him to shove a weathervane up his ass if he was so concerned about which way the wind was blowing.

I remember this one time in June, before the heat wave really got going, me and Anders were sitting under the porch and he turns to me and says: "You know, Murray old buddy, I haven't been sleeping well at all. I can't; it's just so hot. I wake up in the middle of the night, near well drowning in my own sweat. I walk up to the window and stand there for hours sometimes, trying to catch what little wind there is. It's getting pretty bad. Yesterday night, I felt like taking a jump out the window to make some wind. Figured I'd flap my arms to slow myself down and cool myself off a bit. Funny the sort of things you think of when you're tired."

"Yeah, funny," I said, except I didn't think it was, not particularly. 'Cause Anders and I were neighbours, see, both on the third floor, facing the street. I'd stood at my window a couple of times, too, so I knew just how high a drop that was. Heck, just the drop to the awning alone would probably break your neck.

Ordinarily, I'd figure Anders was just kidding around. The man was a joker. But he didn't take the heat well, never did, and as he said this, his face was pale and beaded with sweat, and his eyes had this slightly buggy look to them, as though they had swollen just a little too much to still fit in their sockets. It wasn't a *healthy* look, is what I'm trying to say, and I got to thinking that if Anders felt like he looked, then maybe he really was considering punching his ticket.

It was a silly thing to think, maybe; after all, if he really couldn't stand the heat, then he could always try moving up north, haul his pasty ass to Canada or Alaska, live with the Inuit or something. But Anders was also a lonely kind of guy; parents dead, married for five years and divorced for fifteen, no girlfriend unless you counted his regular trick down on Pearl Boulevard. He never seemed depressed; he acted pretty jovial, and I'm sure that's how he felt most of the time he was around us, but how a man deals with others and how a man feels about himself are two very different things … and it's usually the latter that comes crawling out from beneath the stones in a man's soul during the late watches of the night.

I don't think Anders had been suicidal … oh, maybe he'd thought about it now and then, little mental games a person plays with himself, but not to the point that he'd carry it out. Hard to say; these days, it seems you can go crying to a circle of strangers every time you feel down, boozy or chubby. But men of our generation never spoke of such things; it was a sign of weakness, and you were expected to sort your shit out yourself. Maybe those feelings were part of the reason why the heat got to Anders. Why it closed in on him and ate him alive, when it left the rest of us alone, for the most part.

I remember sitting on the porch, July twelfth if I'm not mistaken, two days into the heat wave proper. Anders, who was looking more and more like Frosty the Snowman on a Cancun beach with every passing day, was sitting with me and Don Vera, whiling the evening away. Across the streets, those two Denney boys, Greg and Tim, had knocked the cap off the fire hydrant and were dancing around in the spray. A few days later, the fire department would shut down the water to that hydrant, and a couple of others around the city, claiming vandalism. Dangerous thing to do in the middle of a heat wave, but we learned that fall that the city's own water reserves had been dangerously low and that the fire folk had taken to pumping water by the truck-full straight from the Cherokee toward the end, despite how brackish and polluted the river water was.

But listen to me go on again; I swear I've more tangents than a geometry book. One of these days my tongue is going to come flapping right out of my mouth and just keep going down the block, honest to God.

Anyhow, at one point, Anders runs his hand through his hair—he wore it down to his neck, which I thought looked terrible but was fashionable at the time—spraying sweat like a wet dog, and with a terribly earnest expression, turns to us and says:

"I think the heat is after me, guys. I really do."

"After all of us," Don Vera says, and I nodded. Don actually seemed a bit pissed. By this time we were all getting sick and tired of Anders complaining about the heat. We were *all* hot.

"No, seriously, Don," he says. "I see it sometimes, hovering just down the road. It's all ripply and hazy, and you can see right through it."

"Mirage," I say. "Like in the deserts, right? You look at the horizon and you see that it shimmers because of the heat that's rising off the asphalt and such."

Anders nodded, but the look on his face said he was half somewhere else.

"It's not just that, though," he says after a time. "It *persists*. Most of the time, these heat mirages like you called it, you can tell they're just optical illusions because when you step toward them, they seem to recede, yeah? But yesterday, and today again, I saw one of those ripples, and I swear that when I stepped toward it, it didn't move. It just stayed there. I could have just walked up to the damn thing, I'm sure. Stuck my hand in it, even, watched it twist and fade if I'd wanted to. And you know what's worse? I'm sure that the damn thing *knew* I was there, too. The whole time I'm walking by, I get the impression that the heat is watching me, waiting for something. Like maybe it hoped that I would get close enough to it that it could swallow me whole."

Don looked at me then and gave me a sideways grin. Don Vera was a nice guy, most of the time, but he had a mean streak in him, and it usually came out whenever he was confronted with something he weren't familiar with or couldn't quite understand. This time, he twirls his index finger around this ear and makes a cuckoo sound, not bothering to hide one or the other from Anders.

Anders gets pissed off, of course, and not saying anything else, he gets up and goes back inside. Comes out a half-hour later—too hot inside, of course—but that had pretty much killed the conversation for the evening. He'd tried to confide something, but Don isn't the kind of guy you confide to. Makes him feel heavy, or worse, like he ought to reciprocate.

I tried to catch hold of Anders the next day, sort of to apologize for not saying anything when Don had thrown dirt in his face the day before. I crossed him on the staircase leading up to our floor after I'd closed up the stand for the day—not much business when it was that hot. He was stepping out somewhere and seemed to be in a rush. When I started talking about the evening before, he just shook his head and kept on going down. At the bottom of the staircase he looks back up, and with those slightly bulgy eyes he tells me:

"I was being serious, just so you know. The heat waits. I've seen it. The heat has eyes, the heat has fangs, and it waits."

Then he shook his head again, like a man who just walked into a whole nest of cobwebs, and he was off. I probably should have followed him—as a matter of course, one doesn't let people who rant about being stalked by weather simply walk off and drive—but I guess I was rattled by what he'd said … no, not *what* he'd said, but *how* he said it. So earnest, so solemn. Like he'd have no problems putting his hand on a Bible and repeating the whole damn spiel.

So I just stood there, middle of the staircase, thinking my good buddy had lost his marbles, until the sound of his car starting brought me round, and by then it was too late. Didn't see him again until the next evening, but I didn't say anything then. After all, I'd had an entire day to convince myself that I hadn't seen what I thought I'd seen. That it was dark in the stairwell, and his face shadowed. Having a picture-perfect recollection is no cure for selective memory; just like any picture, it's all in the interpretation, and if you want that interpretation to say, 'No, my friend isn't crazy, he was just kidding around,' then eventually that's what you'll remember.

In fact, I pretty much forgot about the whole thing—well, not forgot, but set it aside in the back of my mind, that cobwebby mental storage area where you keep the little trivialities that rarely come into play—until the evening of the eighteenth. Don Vera was downtown, seeing his lawyer about yet another snag in the divorce process, and Anders was out again, possibly to see his trick, so of the Barnyard Porch Regulars, it was just me and Shelby Masters. The Denney boys were sitting on the curb across the street, next to their now-defunct fire hydrant, glancing over our way every so often as though considering whether the relative coolness of our awning would be worth having to put up with the company of two men who were no doubt ancient in their eyes—they should see me now, right?

So there I was with Shelb, talking about everything and nothing, when the slight breeze that had been blowing in from down the street, out toward Old Town, ups and dies. That kind of puts a crimp in the conversation: bad weather was a good conversation opener, but it's boorish to keep harping on it, which is one of the reasons Anders was growing increasingly alienated. Neither of us wanted to mention the sudden stillness, but neither could we ignore it.

We both looked up the street, as though we could watch the wind and estimate its return … only there *was* something up the street. It was one of those ripples, the heat-mirages, hovering where Fredericksburg met Columbus, distorting the rest of the city behind it. It was a big one, stretching from one side of the street to the other, and more than that: it was tall. Usually these things hover on the horizon but stay low, because the heat coming off the ground will dissipate. This one just kept going up, though, all the way to the roofs and a little higher, such that the grey-blue sky itself looked wavy.

And it was *moving*. I know how that sounds, believe me, but honest to God, it was *moving*. You could literally track its progress down the street as it passed by buildings, leaving that hazy, broken, unreal kind of city behind it. It was like slow-moving tidal wave, given how tall it was. I looked at Shelby, wondering if he was seeing what I was seeing, if maybe I had just let the heat get to me, but his expression was tight and lipless, his eyes fixed on the nearing distortion.

Across the street, the Denney boys were looking at it too. Then they glanced at each other and by unspoken agreement got off their curb and strode up the walk to their narrow apartment complex. Shelb turned to me then and said:

"I think those boys have the right idea," and stood up. "Don't want to be outside when that thing hits."

I followed him, up to the doors giving onto the Barnyard's lobby, and then stopped. I guess I wanted to be sure, so I turned and looked back.

It was still moving, still pushing down the street. Watching it come closer, I had the queerest sense that my interest in it was being matched, and I was reminded of what Anders had said a few days before: the heat had eyes, and it waited. But it wasn't waiting now, was it? It was coming forward. It had acquired impetus. It didn't only track, it followed. And what for? Well, I think Anders had answered that one too: the heat had fangs.

Shelby called out to me from the lobby. I could barely hear him through the doors, but it was enough to get my butt moving again. I passed into the darkness of the lobby, heard the door swing shut behind me, and moved for the staircase on the other side. Shelby had already gone up after making sure I'd come inside, and I figured I'd join him. His apartment always was one of the cleanest.

Shelb had never married, never had a steady girl as far as we knew, and we suspected why, but that was something else we didn't talk about in those days.

The whole time I crossed the lobby, I didn't once look back. To be completely honest, I was scared. A little boy's imagination had stepped forward from the back of my mind, and it was whispering that if I turned around now, I would see the ripple pressed up against the glass doors ... see its hazy, blank-spot eyes staring into the lobby, watching and waiting....

Pass me another drink from the cooler, would you? Thanks. This is thirsty talk.

So, anyway, I went up to Shelb's apartment and we yakked the evening away. And by the next morning I had already convinced myself that it was just an unusual atmospheric phenomenon I'd seen, a combination of wind and smog, and that I had only read intent into it because Anders had given me the heebie-jeebies a couple of days before. It's not true that hindsight is always the clearest, no sir.

Anders passed away on the twenty-second of the month. I'd closed up shop early that day, so I'd gotten home at around the same time as Don and Shelby, who worked regular hours. After our bachelor meals—and yes, that's as appealing as it sounds—we moved to the porch again, settling into the nice wicker chairs we'd picked up one fall. After a while, I think it was around half past six, we saw Anders drive into the lot around back. When came back around the front—no back entrance, which was strictly speaking against fire codes, but nobody really cared—we saw that he was lugging a clear sack half as big as he was. The stuff inside was heavy, transparent, caught the light in prismatic rainbows, and was making his clothes wet where they rubbed together.

Ice. A huge heaping bag of ice.

"Christ, Anders, what'd you do?" Don called after him as he walked by us, his expression fixed and far-away. "Empty your bank account?"

Don was right: middle of a heat wave, energy crisis, ice wasn't cheap, and a bag that big could easily have cost several hundred dollars. That was no chump change at the Barnyard.

Anders didn't answer, though; he just kept on going as though he didn't see us. We all looked at each other, shared a laugh, figuring Anders was up to something again, and went back to our chatter. It was maybe a half-hour later that we heard the scream, faint but clearly frightened, coming from somewhere above our heads.

My first thought was that somebody—and I immediately flashed to Anders—had fallen out his window, but no: there was no bang on the awning, and the sound had an impression of distance about it. But still the image of Anders' face stuck in my mind, and I was sure something bad had happened.

"What the hell was that?" Don Vera asked, but I was already out of my chair and running for the lobby, quickly making my way to the staircase. I heard voices and footsteps echoing as I climbed and figured that Don and Shelby were following, but I didn't let up my pace, and when I reached the third floor, it was straight toward Anders' room I went.

His door was closed but not locked. Polite thing to do would have been to knock, but I just barged in ahead, knowing at some level that I wouldn't get an answer no matter how loud and how long I knocked. I rushed through the apartment, ignoring the stacked piles of clothes and men's magazines, looking for any sign of him. I remembered the bag of ice and looked into the kitchen but found nothing except slightly matured take-out food. I checked the bathroom next and stopped short.

Anders had filled the tub with water—he'd must have been stocking up, given that our meters were monitored—and poured his bag of ice in. He had then stripped and immersed himself in the ice water up to shoulder height. His head lolled to the side, his mouth hung dumbly open, and there was a fixed, vacant look to his eyes.

And next to the bathtub, a ripple, like on the horizons of deserts, hovering a scant few feet away from me. It was like a tiny tornado now, the back wall shimmering and fracturing through it. It was moving away from Anders when I had come in, and I got the distinct impression that it had turned to 'face' me, if that was possible. Something in the way it flickered there, some conjunction of heat and air, seemed to form blank spaces in the pattern, forming dead eyes and a hazy, malevolently satisfied rictus. I froze, convinced that it was going to come sweeping in for me next.

Then I felt pushed to the side as Don Vera barged in, heading straight for the bathtub and calling Anders' name. I tried to warn him off, but he didn't hear me and collided right with the ripple. He passed right through it, and suddenly it seemed to dissipate like morning mist in a strong wind, the last shimmers fading as though it had never been there at all.

Don, who was a large man, hauled Anders out of the tub in one go and laid him out of the floor, then stood above him, his expression confused. It was Shelby, joining us in the bathroom, who thought to lean down and try to perform resuscitation, but I knew it was futile even before he stepped away, shaking his head. Anders hadn't drowned, of this I was sure.

We called for an ambulance; they arrived without lights or sirens, since it was clear that Anders was already gone. One man, some kind of mobile coroner, gave Anders a look-over and then called for one of those black body bags. I remember thinking that it must be sweltering in there and that Anders would hate it; not particularly coherent, I know, but I suppose I was still in shock.

The coroner told us that Anders had a stroke, probably brought on from the sudden shift from the ambient heat to the cold in the tub. And it probably was a stroke, although I knew that wasn't the whole story (of course, I said no such thing at the time). The coroner asked if there was any next of kin to notify; we said there wasn't, as far as we knew.

And that was it. The coroner left with the body bag, there was a funeral, and the super cleaned out the apartment and put it back on the market. Three days after Anders had died, the heat wave finally went away: rains, coming down from the north, had broken the demon's back. There's never been one as bad since.

So you mind me when I tell you to get indoors and stay cool when it gets hot like this. Because sometimes the heat can wait for you, watch for you. It's killed before and can do so again. Remember: the heat has fangs.

In Lieu of Flowers
Chad McKee

A man might be expected to attend his own wife's funeral. I didn't. And I didn't send flowers, either.

This didn't seem to bother Ms. Helen Kellogg, our neighbor for the last twelve years. I hadn't seen her in six, due to my travels out of country. This she didn't mind either, as I was still a young man and she a widower of thirty years. Most of her time was spent in the Bingo halls or in her extensive garden or, on Sundays, the Baptist church. She had a strong and clear soprano voice that put her in the first seat of the church choir. She would sing for anyone, really; in the grocery store, at the bus stop, and even to her dog, Dunwoody Dan. Once upon a time my wife and I could hear her belting out hymns as she toiled for hours at a time in her kitchen.

In fact, the kitchen was where Ms. Kellogg spent most of her time. Food was her mistress. She didn't need a husband.

Her welcome was hesitant at the doorstep. I had slipped through the narrow grass alleyway between our houses, giving her a peep through the window to make sure she was home. She looked nervous. We never had much real contact before I left and had even less since I had come back. That went for the rest of the neighborhood, but Ms. Kellogg was our next-door neighbor and I knew her the best.

"Why, hello there! To what do I owe this pleasure?" she began, her artificially cheery smile weakened by puzzlement.

But once her eyes settled on the strawberry pie in my hands, an eager smile split her melon-like head. "What do you have there? Oh, it smells heavenly!"

I smiled. "It's Diane's signature pie. I made it for you."

I thrust the pastry into the woman's wrinkled old hands, which had been clutching her apron like a security blanket. She almost fumbled the exchange, which put a brief charge of anxiety into both of us. "Well, gosh," she said with surprise. "Why are you cooking for me? I'm sure *you* could use the food, not me." She made a good-natured allusion to her ample body, covered in a shapeless print dress.

"I want you to have it," I said sincerely. "I cooked it just for you, seeing how you ... found Diane. That must have been a shock. And I wanted to say thank you."

I didn't tell her that the ingredients were from her own garden, although I tapped absently at the pocketknife in my jeans. That bit of mischievousness had begun a dozen years ago, when Diane and I first moved to Pine Grove Estates and found that our garden was separated from Ms. Kellogg's by a picket fence. Its boards were spaced wide enough to stick one's hands through, grabbing a strawberry or a tomato. I nabbed the first booty but Diane soon started, herself, enjoying the little game of larceny—and the fresh produce. My wife had what I called a "brown thumb," because everything she tried to grow withered and died after she touched it. I wondered for a moment if Diane had kept up the minor thefts after I was gone, but I didn't consider the thought for long; she would never do it again.

"Please, have it," I insisted.

"Well," Ms. Kellogg began. I could see her mentally calculating the implications of accepting a pie from a man recently widowed. There was an etiquette to be followed in our little town. It wouldn't look so good among the neighbors, but what they didn't know wouldn't hurt them. "It smells wonderful. And if you made it just for *me*...."

"If you don't take it today, I'll just make more until you do," I warned lightly. Only thirty minutes to an hour apiece, I thought. That makes all the difference.

Dunwoody Dan made an appearance at the door and barked his approval. I gave him a scratch behind the ears and his tongue lolled out with pleasure. Animals had always liked me, at times had given me my only companionship. The years away from Pine Grove had taught me to appreciate attentions from any living creature. Once I was desperate enough to befriend a snake. I later had to eat it, though—or was forced to.

"Of course I'll take it. And thank you so much."

I backed out of the door, having been dismissed by her acceptance.

"I have something in the oven, too, if you'll excuse me." Then, as an afterthought. "And I'm so sorry about Diane. She was a lovely girl."

The door slammed shut with finality, although I could hear Dan give another bark, a farewell, perhaps. I did like that dog.

I enjoyed the weather as I drove into town. Spring was just approaching in our little village, which enjoyed all four seasons. The spring thaw was almost enough for me put off my meeting with David Granger of Granger and Granger funeral homes. But there was the issue of a headstone and funeral plot. The issue was that Diane had been given only the most rudimentary marker as the former and a randomly assigned plot for the latter. After the cheaply and hastily arranged funeral, Diane's body had been unceremoniously dumped into a small and desolate cemetery on the outskirts of town. It was little more than a potter's field. The problem was that she had no family other than me. And that hadn't counted for much, with me in Africa.

David Granger said as much when I visited him. "The body became state property when nobody *physically* came forward. We're all sorry about the timing of your return. Now, the condition of the body and all … the coroner wanted her in the ground," he said.

We sat in his office, a cramped and cluttered affair strategically placed between the preparation room, crematorium, and viewing parlor. The whole funeral complex was built onto the back of Granger's own home. Some might think it creepy, living with the dead. Then again, one becomes used to it, given time. I once knew a shaman from Congo who claimed he could speak to the dead. He dreamt of them, too, apparently.

"And she became just another corpse," I said.

"She had a proper grooming, internment, and funeral," Granger reiterated. "All very nice, very proper."

He was a gaunt-faced man, as all morticians seemed to be, and reedy thin with long, skeletal fingers tarred with a two-pack-a-day Raleigh habit. He wasn't scary or intimidating, though. He was sociable in a rough, crusty way. I knew him mostly by reputation. I'd met him at the burial of Diane's father and uncle, both of whom had died before I visited Africa. I had found him formal and professional at the viewings and funerals, but the business with Diane had shown his less generous side. He didn't hold the body, even when it was known that I was coming back. Even though I had beaten through jungle for nearly six years and had rarely slept in a bed and had eaten snakes and grubs for many of those days. Well, Granger hadn't known all of that. But now the body was in the ground and nobody had much to say except that it was a shame about the timing.

The shock was worse than when I'd first witnessed my first public execution.

"I want a real gravestone," I said. "In the church graveyard."

"There's no room. Hell, even the minister might not get one there."

"Then at Rosedale. Somewhere respectable."

Granger sighed with a hint of exasperation. "But she hadn't

bought a plot. If you want to get the body disinterred, that's state business. You can apply for that at the courthouse; I'm sure you can get the papers pushed through soon enough." He paused before bringing up the most delicate part. "But this issue with the infection … I'm not sure the health inspectors will allow a transfer."

I set my jaw at this, my teeth grinding a hateful melody. "Another reason why she's in that piece of nowhere beyond the highway."

Granger's shrug was partially sympathetic, mostly fatalistic. He eyed his cigarettes and I saw him snatch a glance at the bottle of Southern Comfort in an open desk drawer. It was barely hidden, Granger's drinking. It was deemed acceptable because most people considered mortician's work to be so ghoulish one needed to be a little drunk to do it.

"There wasn't much choice in the matter." A sense of firmness entered his voice. "But I'm not the one to talk to about it. I can make a headstone, but no doubt for the time being she'll have to rest in Holywell."

Granger gave a sharp nod at the end of statement, indicating it was his final word. I understood. I truly did. But I didn't like the arrogance in his voice, the set of his face that betrayed an overall indifference to my wife's fate. I used to see the same face on commanders organizing raids on mountain villages.

"Let's have a drink," I said.

"Excuse me?"

"A drink."

"Why?"

"To assure me that you did all you could and will do all you can to preserve Diane."

Granger seemed a little put out. "I don't follow you." Then: "But, if it makes you feel any better, we can have one."

He smiled as he brought out the liquor. "You have to have something to get you through the day. Do you mind if I smoke?"

"Go ahead."

He retrieved a pair of cloudy-looking glasses from the shelf behind him. I gave them a dubious look. "This one's a little dirty," Granger said. "I'll give it a quick rinse for you."

He ambled to the bathroom a short distance from his office, and I briefly heard water running from the tap.

Granger came back with the other glass, still damp from the tap, and handed it to me. He poured out a shot and a larger measure for himself, not bothering to inspect his own highball.

"Cheers," he said, and we emptied our respective glasses.

"Another?" he asked, lips smacking at the sweet whisky.

"Why not?"

We spoke casually for a few minutes. The good cheer of the liquor was short-lived, however. Soon enough an awkward silence settled in. Silence between two strangers. We sat in our respective chairs and stared for a time at the middle distance beyond our faces. Granger smoked. I took note of the objects in the office: a framed photograph of the governor; a faded and antiquated picture of Granger and his father deep-sea fishing, each with a fish in hand; a cheaply mounted degree for mortuary science; a battered file cabinet; an outmoded desktop. The chairs were straight-backed and upholstered with cheap leather that looked expensive but felt rough and cloying. Over the years I've learnt to be comfortable in silence. It is the best way to survive when rival guerrilla factions are passing in the night. No, it didn't bother me to sit motionless. But it clearly did Granger.

"One more?" he asked hopefully. His hand was poised on the bottle neck.

"No, thanks," I said. "I have another appointment."

"Oh. Well, thanks for stopping by," he said, standing up. "Got a new visitor to welcome anyway." He hooked a thumb to the preparation room. He stamped out his Raleigh. "I'll get that headstone arranged, don't you worry."

"Yes, I'd appreciate that," I said, rising.

"First thing on my list," he said.

I bet.

County Hospital was the Johns Hopkins of our little town. There were two other establishments dedicated to the advancement of medicine, but they were a poor second and third. The best were at County, or so they claimed. I'd never had the pleasure. It wasn't until I awoke in the Red Cross hospital, sheathed in bandages, sundry tubes intersecting my body like spaghetti junctions on the highways, that I can remember an overnight hospital stay. Even then, I can't honestly say how well they treated me, being unconscious for most that time. Perhaps it was a blessing, as the tent was piled with dead or injured and the smell was worse than a morgue.

I might have been responsible for putting some of the men there. At least one, but I can't be sure. I was at my breaking point then, and the trappings of my physical life were as chaotic as my dreams.

I didn't go to County. I went to Paul Master's house, instead. Right to the source, you might say. He lived in a mock-Victorian home on the edge of the city, not unlike my wife's grave. However, instead of a token burial in a forgotten pasture off a country lane, Master's house rested on a escarpment, before the landscape dipped into a bowl-like valley. It was a privileged position, a wealthy enclave of the town's finest. From Master's house one could see the full breadth of the city and its outlying counties.

Masters had written me a note when I returned to town, expressing regret about Diane and suggesting that I should visit him if I ever needed to discuss what had happened. I felt that that moment had come, though Masters was clearly baffled as I stood on his doorstep. Perhaps he had not expected me, after all.

"I'm so sorry about your wife," he began, as everyone I met began. "She was a very brave woman. A fighter."

He sat me in his living room, which was decorated with elegant period antiques in keeping with the Victorian fashion of the house. He had good taste, and the leather couch I sat on was certainly more comfortable than the chair in Granger's office. Then again, I would expect nothing less from a surgeon.

He sat across from me, one leg crossed over the knee, relaxed in a light blue polo and slacks. He might have been en route to his sailboat, if our town had a marina.

I learned soon enough that Masters had little to say. A repeat of the hospital inquest, long on generalities and short on details.

"She cut her radial artery," he said. "Tending her garden, apparently. She needed immediate assistance—"

"But the call came at least thirty minutes late."

"Yes," Masters said. "It's hard to put an exact time on things, but it was a tragedy that someone didn't get to her faster, otherwise we probably wouldn't have needed that surgery...."

"So the cut didn't kill her?" I asked.

"No." For an instant Masters stared at the ground. Possibly in shame, more likely wondering how to phrase his next statement. In the end, he simply said: "Not directly. It was the infection. Respiratory failure, ultimately."

"Was she aware of things? At the end, I mean?"

"Certainly not," he said quickly. "She was heavily sedated."

I said quietly. "Then she didn't know I was returning. After six years."

"I couldn't tell you precisely," Masters said carefully. "She was in need of rest. I can tell you that she was in no pain when she passed. In fact, the infection itself is not known to be terribly painful. More of an itch, really."

"More of an itch," I repeated. *Liar.*

"Yes."

"And how far had the infection spread?"

"Half of her body."

"I suppose the only question is: how did she get it?"

"We would all like to know that."

An uncomfortable moment followed as we measured each other. I held my gaze as Masters crossed and uncrossed his legs, then watched as the color in his face changed, darkening. Only a guilty man blushes in silence. I have an interrogator's eye.

The moment passed when the phone rang. Masters appeared relieved as he went for the cordless. Before he answered, I asked if I could use the restroom. He indicated upstairs.

When I returned, Masters was just ringing off.

"My apologies," he said. "Work."

"There's always something to be done."

He nodded with agreement.

"I won't take any more of your time," I said. "It just seems so sudden. And not getting to see her when I was so close...."

"A tragedy," Masters agreed, with a reassuring nod. "Again, I'm so sorry."

"So am I."

He hesitated briefly before asking me a question, probably the only thing about my visit that really interested him. "Where were you at before you returned? Nobody really seems to know."

"I was in Africa," I said. "I was there to collect plants for a pharmaceutical company. As you know, many plants contain anticancer agents, that sort of thing. But I had to stay longer than I wanted—I was coerced, so to speak, into working for the local government."

"How interesting."

"It was life-changing."

I felt better already. Social interaction was the best medicine for pain and loneliness. But I had not quite fulfilled my apology to my wife.

It took half an hour of driving before I was able to be with her again. I swung through the rusty little gate under an arch that said

Holywell in ancient, blackened iron. Holywell had once been the only cemetery in town until the small Methodist church had been burned to the ground and later rebuilt closer to the town center. Now the grass was overgrown from disuse or lack of care. Only the unwanted were exiled to this furthest reach of the township. That was why I wanted her to be moved back with the rest of the world; the only one she'd ever really known. She hadn't traveled far. Only me.

The soil she rested under was still disturbed, churned, and mixed. At least the quiet and privacy had allowed us to be together alone.

Allowed me to have my own private viewing.

The dread I'd felt on that first visit was gone. I could concentrate on little else then. The shock of discovering you had missed your wife's last breath by a mere handful of days after six years in exile weighed on a man. That was what had ultimately led to the frantic digging, the defiling of the grave. To view that last bit of flesh before it returned forever to the earth. To see her face one more time.

I knew how fast a body decomposed; I knew that formaldehyde and other fixatives were only the most temporary of preservatives. But what greeted me was beyond decomposition. I was surprised that they had not simply cremated her. That would have destroyed the evidence.

Perhaps Masters had been truthful when he'd said half of her body had been affected by the infection. But after the passage of a few days, the bacteria had feasted. Even before I'd opened the coffin lid, I could smell her. I knew then that Granger was a liar. There had been an internment, but no grooming, no embalming. She was wrapped in a semi-clear body bag, parceled for disposal. When I sliced it open, I could only tell it was my wife by her wedding ring. Her face had been a ghastly blue-black, her eyes filmed over an odd gray. The skin had become taut in rigor, pulling the flesh away from her mouth, exposing the teeth in a death's head grin. But her body was the shocking bit, the image that couldn't be pushed away, covered up, or otherwise erased: she was crawling with bacterial lesions. Her skin was gone altogether in most places, allowing the infection to consume her viscera. Her flesh appeared to actually undulate; the bacteria were so concentrated that they were pulling away chunks of tissue like ants carrying leaves back to their nest. Masters wouldn't want a body like this to be in his hospital. That would be bad for business.

I thought again of the Congolese shaman briefly in our camp. He had dreamt of his wife dying. However, his dream had not foretold his own death at the hand of a poisoned dart. I've never forgotten the look on his face.

My dreams had started soon after his death and haven't stopped since. I could see Diane in those dreams, tending her garden. She wore a sundress and a pleasant smile as she gazed at me through the window. But with each passing night her smile had faded as her color had darkened and the tendrils of vines had grown around her still body. Before a fortnight had passed, she had become more earth than human. When I related the dream in confidence to another man in camp, he said the Congolese had cast a *boloki*, a festering spell. Perhaps I was bewitched still.

I examined her headstone again. It denoted only her name and life dates in small, block script. For now, that was enough. Perhaps later I would buy her a sepulcher. An extravagant tomb would allow her to lord over this forgotten plot. She could be the Lady of Holywell, the baroness to the begotten dead. I thought back to my time in East Africa and my former employers: they favored mass graves. This was the next worst thing.

My contemplation of her headstone reminded me of Granger. He would probably be waiting for me. For anyone, by now.

I returned to the funeral home. The door was open, as expected. The Granger family kept an "open house," as it were. I encountered no one in the parlor, with its newest models of coffins, floral arrangements, and other death paraphernalia, and I barely glanced into Granger's office. I continued to the preparation room, whose door was closed but unlocked. A strong chemical smell rushed out when I pushed it open. The chemical overlaid the cloying, putrid smell of fleshy decomposition.

The enclosure was an odd mixture of morgue and dressing room. On one side of the room were shelves lined with fixatives and solvents. The other side was occupied with a broad mahogany table, not unlike the kind one might have in one's dining room, but scuffed and dry. It was piled with make-up kits, wigs, and cotton balls. Hooks and thread of various colors lay nearby, along with scissors and a few varieties of knives. One appeared to be for filleting. With a few lures, one might have thought Granger had left his tackle box on his wife's make-up vanity.

The bleeding table sat in the center of the room. A big industrial embalming machine stood at its side, cold and imposing, like a steel centurion. An elderly lady rested on the table, awaiting its services. I didn't recognize her, only that she had ripened since being removed from the refrigerator. I ignored her and instead moved around the table, my eyes tracking the black-and-white squares of the linoleum.

Granger lay under the cosmetic table, his eyes closed. I knelt down and checked his pulse. A faint heartbeat, shallow breathing. His skin was turning as yellow as the embalming fluid he'd wanted to fill the old women with. Granger's lips were dry and purple. He was suffocating.

It would not do to die like this, under a table of wigs and plastic eyes, beneath the room's only window. No, that would not do at all. I closed the window tightly and took hold of Granger's legs, dragging him toward the door. A small moan escaped him, but it was a soft, ineffectual sound. It barely carried beyond his lips before being absorbed by the air conditioner. I dropped his legs then, near the chemical shelves. Formaldehyde, methanol, acids. Each were in gallon-sized, smoked-glass bottles. I noted how close they were to the edge of the shelf. Grabbing a paper towel, I moved each a little closer. Granger roused, his eyes fluttering open. A little glassy but soon focusing, concentrating. He could understand what I was doing, possibly. No, definitely.

I was a little surprised that the man was alive. The dose of calcium oxalate I had slipped into his whiskey glass should have been enough to kill. Nevertheless, he was mostly paralyzed, which was sometimes preferred. Once in Africa I had been commanded to prepare such a compound—that which would take a few hours to kill a man. In Africa one might use delphinium. But enough ground rhubarb leaves were just as good.

I'm not a torturer. At times I have made poisons at the hands of men who do torture. I don't enjoy seeing a man suffer, even if he has made me suffer. But when the men of the so-called civilized society will not even allow you a final look at your wife … the bewitched hold no quarter. Perhaps the shaman *had* cast a spell that day.

I let the formaldehyde fall to the floor. The bottle crashed violently next to Granger's body, its spray marking the man's lab coat and the cupboards nearby. The pungent, biting odor of the chemical immediately flooded the tiny room. Granger's eyes, the only part of his body still responding to his brain, tracked me as I left the room. I wanted to close the door quickly, not wanting to dissipate the asphyxiating properties of the chemical. Perhaps it was a stab of guilt. Or a nasty impulse to assert my vengeance. But I felt that the man deserved an answer to his death.

"I saw what you and Masters did to Diane," I said. "Properly groomed and interred, right?"

If Granger felt remorse, he did not show it. He was not allowed to. The vapor off the shattered bottle induced convulsions. The only thing that escaped Granger's mouth was a line of frothy saliva.

My adrenalin dropped into the red by the time I was a block beyond Granger and his mortuary. I had to force one foot in front of the other to return home. Nonetheless, I stopped by Helen Kellogg's house. I rang the doorbell without answer. I walked around to the back yard, letting myself through a gate that was never locked. Good morals were the cornerstone of our little town, of course. No one stole in this village. A quiet enshrouded the house, which normally would be either filled with the television or her soprano voice.

I tapped on the back sliding glass door that led to her kitchen. I could see something obscured by the kitchen table, something large. I took my handkerchief and slid the door open. It took only a step inside to see that Helen Kellogg was facedown next to her beloved oven. The appliance was still warm. So was the pie, which she had reheated for consumption. A plate with a fork rested on her plate. Perhaps three bites had been eaten. I could imagine her savoring each morsel, not hurrying.

She was very meticulous, Ms. Kellogg. Nothing was rushed.

Then, the stomach pains had begun. She would wonder if she had eaten something bad from a previous meal, perhaps, and use the toilet. But the pains would not go away because poison does not simply pass through one's bowels in a moment's time. Sweating and heart palpitations would occur as the toxins raised her blood pressure. Fear of a heart attack would raise it further, causing her to hyperventilate, at which point she would certainly rush to the phone and call 911. Imagine the surprise when she did not receive a dial tone, the wires having been cut by my pocketknife only moments before giving her the pie. Her muscles, after only ten minutes, would begin to go rigid with numbness. A slowing of breath, then the arrest of the heart. Mrs. Kellogg was not a young woman. And she foolishly had ingested a few leaves of oleander from her own garden.

I figured the whole drama may have lasted thirty minutes. Possibly longer. Just like Dianne when she had been dying on our back lawn. *Sun-bathing*, Mrs. Kellogg had said. That's what she thought Diane was doing that day. Perhaps that was so. I can't tell you why, but I didn't believe her.

Perhaps because we stole from her garden. She was a petty woman, like most everyone else in our little village. If I had been a pariah since returning, then I imagined Diane must have been, as well.

There was a sound to my left. A soft padding accompanied by a whimper. I froze for an instant before I realized it was just Dunwoody Dan. The dog glanced at me and then at the body of his master. He seemed to be in a state of indecision.

"It's okay, Dan," I said. I noticed his supper dish was empty. "You're hungry, aren't you?"

I picked him up in my arms. He was shaking slightly, unsettled.

"Let's go to my place," I said. "I'm sure I can find something for you."

Dan and I went, through the grassy alleyway and past Helen Kellogg's garden of oleander and rhubarb, and into my own empty house. I don't deal with loneliness well. Particularly when you return from six hard years battling for your life. It makes you realize who appreciates life and who doesn't.

I took a couple of bowls out of the cupboard, one for water, the other for some leftover chicken. Dan looked suspiciously at the food but was soon eating after a tentative inspection. Probably he was used to dry dog food; never had the pleasure of real meat.

I went to the sun room connected to our porch. There was a box there, transparent so the sun could shine through. Although rather large—Helen could easily fit one of her home-baked breads inside—only a small object occupied its interior. I put on my gloves, respecting it. Something that Dr. Masters had not. I then used a pair of gloves to lift it from the box, the same type I had used in Master's home.

I was pleased with the preparation I had left in his en-suite. A simple compound, really; most anyone could make it. The color was clear, so Masters wouldn't notice it drying on his razor. The consistency was smooth like oil but finer, like a film, so he would never detect it on his toothbrush. Its scent was muted with the lavender I had taken from Mrs. Kellogg's garden. So it was unlikely that Masters would smell it in his facial cream. I was perhaps most proud of this, as the culture's odor had become particularly unpleasant after incubating in the sun.

It didn't look like much. When I'd cut it off, you could still tell what its origin was. Now, after sitting in the box for a week with a bit of wet cloth and the aid of some flies, the thumb had become completely grown over with the bacteria that ultimately led to Diane's death. *Macerating fasciitis*, the hospital had said. Flesh-eating bacteria. The hygiene of the town had dropped to a sorry state when such an infection had become common in its best hospital. A shiny polish could hide only so many things.

Nonetheless, my wife's flesh had fulfilled its usefulness; she had reached beyond the grave, with my help. Now I would no longer have to look at it and be reminded how I cut it off when I visited Diane in her grave.

I felt the beginnings of satisfaction. I may have not arranged her burial or been at her funeral, but I had given her something more than just flowers. I had given her revenge.

And what memorial was better than that?

Down Where the Blue Bonnets Grow
Daniel R. Robichaud

D on said, "It's true, and you can see the spot." He was the youngest of us, not yet fourteen, and notorious for improving on the truth. His story smelled like a pickup truck hauling horse shit. Stuff like this just did not happen in southern Texas. Or anywhere else.

He had run the mile and a half to Maurice's grandma's porch, arriving at two o'clock and sweating up a storm. The June afternoon sun had turned his face, arms, and neck an angry red. He sucked down lemonade and scratched his burns and winced while he told us about seeing the girl lie down and vanish.

"So, show us," Rade said. He was half-black, half-Mexican, and knew all the best jokes. The dirtier the better, so far as we cared. He had a natural talent for everything nasty: he told us what smegma was—dick cheese—and he showed us our first pussy. Four years before, he had found a thrown-out porno mag in his complex's Dumpster. *Tang Poon*, it had been called, and it had been all about the Asians. Most of the photos had been ripped up. Stained. One of the few good ones showed a girl spread wide as could be. He scissored out the pussy and carried it around in his pocket. Showed us, when we asked, and we asked a lot. After a few months, that picture became so folded and faded it looked like a rancid burrito.

"How'd you find out about this?" I asked.

Don hesitated, and Rade said, "Daryl asked you a question, boy."

"She come and told me. Her brother had shown her—"

"Who she?" Maurice asked. Even when he was not laughing, he had a natural smarm to him. An eternal smile. I'd seen him cry once, after Jaffrey Laffy had punched him a couple times, and through it Maurice had still worn that smile. He was stuck with it.

"Thersa Doublet." An eleven-year-old Don talked about from time to time. The gal had a crush on him.

"And how did you know her?" Rade this time.

"She and her twin brother Tommy are in my complex." That would be on the other side of Babcock Road, what my Daddy called *the poorer stretch*. "I was on the hill, hoping for a squirrel to pop, when she came from the far field, crying. I asked her the matter, and she said it was Tommy. He laid down out where the blue bonnets grew—"

"This is San Antonio," I interrupted. "Blue bonnets grow everywhere." It was the Texas flower for a reason.

Don nodded. "I said that, too. So, she showed me."

"Just like that?" Rade said and snapped his fingers. "She laid down like her brother, and—?"

"Just like that," Don agreed a little too fast. He even snapped.

We three looked at each other, equally unsure of Don's story. Finally, Rade said, "So, show us already."

"Fine, fine. But I ain't laying in it."

"No one's saying you have to," I said. The others nodded in agreement.

This should have been my first clue something was up.

Don led the way out of Maurice's grandma's complex, down Bandera Road, through his folk's complex, and out into the overgrown fields behind. We ran up and over the seven-foot-tall dirt hill where Don sat and shot rats and rabbits and squirrels. Beyond this waited overgrown fields and the rusting sign for the coming development.

The "Coming Soon! A Grrrreat New Place to Live! Coventry

Fields Apartments" announcement had been standing on the earth for as long as any of us could remember. The ownership had changed hands several times. Money problems. The graffiti had grown graffiti.

The low hills were full of long grasses and weeds and blossoming wild flowers, most of these blue bonnets. The dry blades crackled when we pushed through them. The place was abuzz with bees, and it reeked of sweet, growing things.

Two hundred yards in, Don said, "Right here."

Bare earth under the baking sun. Blue bonnets grew around the edges, but no weeds, no grasses, no nothing grew in the spot itself, which was strange because the earth was a fertile black-brown. Similar to the stuff my mom bought by the bagful from Lowes, stuff called "growing medium" because that sounded better than "good dirt." It even smelled like garden soil after a rain.

"See how it looks like a figure?" Don continued. "Arms poked out to the sides, legs spread." We all agreed it did look like a person maybe six feet from toe to crown.

One Christmas, my family visited kin in New Hampshire. I got to see the things a person could do in the snow. My little cousin Jennifer taught my sister to lie down and sweep her arms and legs to make what she called "snow angels." This bare spot looked like someone had lain down to make a dirt angel and stopped early.

I trudged around the spot. Found a hat on the far side, up near where the head would be. White hat decorated with pink ribbons. The kind of cutesy stuff my mom made my kid sister wear.

I picked it up, and Don pointed at it like his finger was on fire. "That's hers! Thersa's! Must've fallen off her head when she lay down. She wore a white dress and matching hat."

I remembered the girl. Little blonde Thersa Doublet. I had seen her the previous week, squatting in the parking lot near Don's folks' place, chucking rocks to try to hide the fact she was mooning over him. Hell, far as I knew she thought he set the stars in the sky.

Don pretended it was no big whoop, but he sure liked to talk about her socks—powder blue or starched white or whatever color. He was fixated on her ankles. Rade had called him a foot sniffer and after that Don had stopped talking ankles and socks so much. But I figured he still thought about them.

I got to wondering. "She lost her hat, huh?"

"Duh." Don eyed me like I might have grown a second head when he wasn't looking.

"Girly shit," Rade said. He dug among the weeks and came up with a rifle. "Now this's what I'm talking about."

"Hey," Don said. "That's mine!"

"Salvage, man," Rade said. Rade's Uncle Tim was Coast Guard, so Rade knew all about international salvage laws. He told us if you found something, it's as good as yours.

"Give it to me. It's got my name on the stock!"

Rade tossed it to Maurice, and Don raced after it. Maurice tossed it to me, and Don almost ran for me but stopped when he realized he would have to cross the bare spot. "Come on, Daryl," he said. "Give it back."

"Not just yet," I said.

"But it's mine." Don dragged the "i" to obnoxious lengths. He sounded like a ten-year-old. Hell, maybe a five-year-old.

"Don't be a pussy," Rade said. "Let's try this out." He palmed the air over the bare spot.

"Try it," Don said with a loud gulp, "out?"

"Yeah." Maurice chucked a rock into the dark earth's middle. We waited, but nothing happened. No longer a pickup truck of manure, Don's story had become a loaded tractor trailer. A sixteen-wheeler.

I had to admit, though, something about this place made my skin crawl. It had an atmosphere.

The bare patch was too neat: too clean and too well-designed. It felt as natural as a perfectly straight line: No such thing occurred without a hand behind it. If I had come here alone, maybe I don't know how long I would've remained. Gave me the creeps. Though the rooftops of Don's complex peeked over the rough, they seemed too far off to be helpful. Even with the fellas there with me, I was weirded out.

Instinct made me train the rifle on the bare patch. If the earth itself sat up, I could take a head shot. Of course it didn't. The earth just lay there, as earth is wont...

"I think it has to be alive," Don said to Maurice. "To disappear, I mean."

I suggested, "Why don't you lie down there?"

"Don't be an asshole," Don said, suddenly nervous.

Rade's grin got nasty when he said, "Why don't you?"

"Because I don't want to disappear. I seen it happen. Makes you think I want it to happen to me?"

The holes in his story clicked for me, then. "She led you here? Thersa Doublet, did?"

Don said, "That's what I said."

"Because she saw her brother lie down?" I asked.

Don said, "Yeah."

"And she saw him disappear?" Maurice asked. I knew what had clicked for me had also clicked for him.

Don said, "Yeah."

"Now why would she come back here?" I asked.

Don said nothing. Just shrugged.

"And why," Rade said, "would she just lie down?" I knew the story's fishy quality had clicked for him, too.

"Because," Don said. "Because she wanted to show me."

"And she lost her hat, lying down?"

"Yeah," Don said.

I was still three paces away from the naked earth. "Then don't you think it should've been stuck in the blue bonnets inside the patch? Not way the hell back here?"

"The wind," Don said, "must've kicked it up."

Rade said, "It fell off before she got to the earth?"

I asked, "If we look around, are we going to find any more of her clothes? Socks, maybe?"

"What the hell you saying?" Don demanded. Didn't take a shrink to see terror underneath the outrage.

"She wouldn't be any more eager to lie down where her brother disappeared than you were," I said. Now, I realized I had pointed the rifle at him. He realized this, too, and he said nothing.

"You knocked her hat off, didn't you?" Maurice asked. "What'd you do, hit her upside the head?"

When Don remained mute, Rade asked, "Why, man? Did you want to sniff her feet?"

"You fuck her?" I asked.

"I didn't do *that*," Don said. "She's a kid, man."

"But you knocked her hat off," Maurice said.

Don's head jerked down and up.

"Hit her on the head," I said. "Why?"

"To shut her up," Rade suggested. "Was she screaming unholy hell, Don?"

"Thing I don't understand is, where'd she go?" Maurice asked. He looked at the bare patch. "Holy shit, did you *bury* her?"

"I didn't bury nobody. She lay down and the blue bonnets blew across her, and then she was gone. Just like—" His mouth snapped shut.

"Just like what?" Maurice asked.

Not what, I realized. *Who*. "Just like Tommy?" I asked. "You saw him go, didn't you? You and Thersa saw it together. And then she started carrying on, or maybe you got to thinking you could touch her ankles or something. Just the two of you, out here. Alone."

Tears rolled down Don's cheeks. He glanced toward the rooftops, then back at us. He knew he would never make the run, never get to safety before we caught up to him. Hell, even if a miracle occurred and he did escape, what then? Hide from us forever? From Thersa's parents? The cops?

As far as I knew, there was no crime for making a girl disappear with a magic trick. Then again, no magic trick I knew made someone disappear for real. Wasn't magic to kill someone, though.

Her blood might be on the gun stock. Her hat was here. If our parents let us, we could testify to his involvement in her disappearance somehow. He might get tried as an adult. Crime of passion or something.

Don had to be thinking along similar lines.

"Tommy said he wanted to show us something," Don said. Then he backed up. "Thersa and Tommy were on the hill with me, fetching the kills after I popped them. There was a rabbit I'd winged good. It was wounded but not dead. I was going to smash its head, but Tommy said he had something to show us, and he brought us out here and tossed the rabbit in. The blue bonnets covered it over and then it was gone."

"And then what happened?" Maurice asked. "Why'd he lie down if he knew—"

"It was an accident," Don said.

"Accident, my ass," Rade said.

"It *was*," Don replied, shaking like a leaf. "Some guts or something slicked his soles, and he tried to turn around to say 'ta-da,' like a stage magician, but he slipped, and he fell over backward, and I tried to grab for him, but ... I didn't."

Didn't reach him, I wondered, or didn't try?

"And then he was gone." End of story.

I asked, "And Thersa?"

"What *about* her?"

"What happened to her?" Maurice asked.

Rade added, "Spill it, Donny."

"She screamed. Why didn't I do something? Why didn't I save him? She swore she'd tell on me..."

"And you hit her," I said. "And then, what, you shoved her in there?"

Don's head shook. "I made her lie down. She cried a lot because she's a kid, but she did what I said."

"Why would she?" Maurice asked. "Were you pointing the gun at her?"

"If he was holding onto his rifle, then why'd we find it in the weeds here?" Rade asked. "I think you must've put it down for some reason, Donny. You sure you didn't toss her around? Touch her a little?"

We took Don's silence for assent. A wind came through, shaking the blue bonnets and the dry grasses as though the world itself was verifying his guilt.

"Cold-hearted motherfucker," Rade said. I detected admiration mixed with the revulsion.

"Why the hell bring us out here?" Maurice asked.

"Excitement is my guess," I said. "I think he really wanted us to know about this place. About what he did."

"It's," Don said. "It's cool. If you think about it, I mean."

"It's disgusting," I said. "Shit, man. Thersa Doublet's in the same class as my *sister*."

"But the Doublet twins were skanks!" Don said, as though this excused him. "White trash don't matter! They want to be fucked with. They pose for *Tang Poon*!"

"That'd be Asian trash," Rade corrected.

Don said, "I'd never do that to your sister, Daryl!"

"Damn straight you wouldn't," I said. "But I still don't buy it. People don't just vanish."

"They do here." Don's hot head now prevailed over his cold feet. Rage brought apple red to his cheeks. "You have to believe me!"

"Show us," I said.

This stopped his anger dead.

"Daryl," Rade said, "what are you—?"

"I think the twins're both dead and buried somewhere. I think Don is full of shit. But if it's for real, then I think he should prove it." To Don, I added, "Prove it. Or so help me God, I'll shoot you. A .22 might not break skin, but it'll ruin your eyeball." For emphasis, I aimed to the left of his nose.

Maurice said, "Daryl—"

"Prove it, motherfucker!"

"You wouldn't," Don said. "You won't shoot me."

"Won't I?" I squeezed the trigger, the rifle bucked, and his cheek developed a red crease. I chambered a fresh round in less than two seconds.

"Jesus Christ." Maurice sounded ready to barf.

"Residents will know the sound of Donny's gun," I said. "Folks round here are probably used to him popping the varmints."

Don's frown told me I was right.

"So lie down, Don."

"What are you going to do, when I'm right?"

"But you ain't right," I said. "You ain't right at all, are you?"

Don looked at the bare earth. Sweat slicked his face. I read the quandary running through him: Was this worth losing an eye? "Okay, okay, I lied about them disappearing," Don said. "They're back in the complex, playing. I can take you to where."

"No," I said. "I think you're trying to cover something. I think something disappeared around here, and I think it was a part of you that pulled the vanishing act. I think you're afraid to lie down here. Lie down with your guilt. Your sins. So, that sounds like the best punishment possible. Lie down, Don. If you do, I won't shoot you."

He decided to run.

Rade, Maurice, and I caught him before long. He wept like a baby as we dragged him back. He pleaded for us to let him go, to let him turn himself in. When we tossed him onto the bare earth, he went mute. His mouth remained open and his eyes wide, but his terror remained soundless.

Then I discovered just how wrong I had been.

Despite the lack of a strong breeze, the blue bonnets bent over him. His hand shot up through them and then disappeared among them again as though wrenched back. Seconds later, the flowers stood up once more, revealing the barren black-brown earth. Don was gone.

Rade threw up. Maurice whimpered, "What happened?" I stood resolute, knowing Don had got what he deserved.

We all knew the desire, God help us, to see it happen again. That was the real reason Don had taken us there. Once you see something like that, there's a part of you that won't rest until you see it again. And again. I've been out three times since, and I'm itching to return.

Want to come with me? Out where the blue bonnets grow? You won't believe your eyes...

The Infatuate
Adam Walter

*Why do you want to persecute yourself with the question whence all
this may be coming and whither it is bound?*
—Rilke

H e has never known another way. As usual, it will begin with a
look and finish with a song. Someplace in between comes
contact, and then he knows the limit of days left to him. After that
the two attendants, the two giants, will be sent to find him and bring
things to an end. His single, absurd hope is to delay. Still, he will
give it his all. And though it can only serve to worsen matters, he
knows that this time he will, himself, be required again to provide
the song.

It was a rainy morning in the beginning of September when Lia saw
the man appear at her bus stop for the first time, transferring off a
255, a bus that ran south along the near side of the lake until it
reached this downtown stop on Third Avenue. Like everyone else,
he melted into the quiet, drowsy mob of commuters to wait for his
connecting bus. But Lia noticed him immediately. He was four or
five inches taller than she was and had the most striking silver hair
beneath his old-fashioned felt hat—a fedora, she thought.
Otherwise, there was nothing unusual about his appearance: black
overcoat, dark brown suit, black umbrella. She was embarrassed to
stare, but she looked at him again and again in the ten minutes
before their buses arrived. It was as if, no matter how many times
she looked, whenever her eyes left him she couldn't really be sure

she remembered his face. He looked at her also—twice, longer and more boldly than she. Despite the silver hair, she couldn't decide his age. He might have been in his early forties, her senior by more than a decade. Maybe, and yet (ignoring the hair color, which may or may not have been natural) it was conceivable that he was her same age, even a year or two younger. Something about that face—the thin nose, lively eyes, and small, nascent grin—refused to be charted by time.

Eventually the wave of buses arrived. The crowd came to life, separating into distinct streams beneath the rain. And Lia's first, unremarkable encounter with him abruptly ended without promise or presentiment.

The next morning when the 255 arrived, Lia's eyes lingered on it until the silver-haired man stepped out and opened his umbrella. The two of them watched each other much as before, and she found herself slipping into a series of adolescent, almost involuntary fantasies, as sometimes happened in the presence of a man who attracted her. In short, cartoon-like dreams—concocted in a single moment and forgotten in two—she imagined how they might meet by chance at a party, a bar, or a second-hand bookstore and suddenly recognize each other from the bus stop. In these fantasies she tried to fit him, like a puzzle piece, into her life. He might be a divorced man, well-to-do but lonely, a man ready to offer a young woman a comfortable and colorful new world. Or maybe he was a destitute artist with only the one good suit that he wore into town each day, and he would draw her into a taxing but rich, authentic love. For Lia these were simple daydreams, dalliances in her mind's eye, flirtations with the idea of the man, and nothing more.

Generally she paid as little attention as possible to her fellow commuters: the inscrutable foreigners, the middle-aged office workers, the occasional homeless man, the sometimes sociopathic teens. Lia, who was a great reader but saved all her books for home, was profoundly disappointed whenever she let herself notice what people around her were reading. It was rare that any but the worst authors were represented on public transit. Books read on a bus, it seemed, could only be used as bland alternatives to the other conventional insulating options: a newspaper, a magazine, or a pair of headphones. Lia herself was one of those commuters who always find a window seat and spend the entire ride staring out at traffic and the weather. Once she had commented on James Joyce to a girl seemingly engrossed with a copy of *Dubliners*. The girl had responded by looking up from the book and saying, "God, it's the worst, but I have to read this for a class."

So it was unusual for her ever to find something on the morning commute that could pull her out of her own thoughts. But this man—he seemed to possess something elusive and exceptional, something hidden.

The second time Lia saw him, she took the trouble to notice both his buses: first there was the 255 and then the 486, which ran up the northeast side of Tower Hill. She herself headed in the opposite direction, down to the financial district, getting off in front of the bank where she worked. The 486 and her own bus usually arrived at the bus stop about the same time, a few minutes before 7:30.

It was the third time she saw him, a Wednesday morning, when he finally approached her. The rain was coming down steadily as he left the 255. He had some trouble opening his umbrella, but eventually it went up, and he took his place in the crowd, coming much closer to her than on the mornings before. He removed his hat briefly to shake the water from it. For the first time, Lia saw his full head of silver hair. Suddenly she resolved to give up watching him, resolved to not allow herself even one more glance at him that morning.

A small commotion broke out near her, under the crowded bus stop shelter, when a disabled woman began maneuvering her wheelchair back and forth. The crowd shifted and Lia, along with a handful of others, was jostled out from under the shelter and into the rain. When Lia regained her footing, the space where she had been standing was taken. She usually arrived at the shelter early enough to find a place there but always kept a compact umbrella in her bag for the times she needed it. She was groping for it when she saw the silver-haired man walking directly toward her. She stopped rummaging through her bag and was startled into complete immobility, knowing that he came to offer her the cover of his own umbrella. He reached her and, saying nothing at all, simply stepped beside her and tilted the umbrella to cover them both.

What he did next, she could hardly believe. Without warning, staring kindly down into her confused eyes, he took her right hand in his left.

They continued to stand like this, and neither said anything. Did he think he knew her? Was that what this was about—had he mistaken her for a woman he'd once known? Or had they, in fact, met before? Had *she* forgotten *him*? No, it wasn't possible. It just wasn't.

His hand was large and warm, his hold on her delicate yet anything but tentative. She knew she should say something, make it clear they did not know one another. But she had been jolted beyond a capacity for speech.

The buses arrived, and he walked Lia to hers, holding the umbrella high above until she reached the door. He gave her a steady look, then one of his slight smiles, and he let go of her. He jogged off across the wet pavement to the 486, where he lowered the umbrella, collapsed it, and disappeared into the bus.

She thought about him the rest of that day.

It was a long time before she could grasp what his small but bold act, his bold familiarity, had provoked in her. When he had first taken her hand, she had felt an impulse toward fear and then anger. Somehow the impulse had almost immediately been driven out, to be replaced by curiosity and a sense of daring acceptance.

And for much of the day, those were the feelings that governed her thoughts of him. Now and then she would again feel a twinge of fear. Anyone, she knew, would tell her there was something wrong, whether socially or psychologically, with such a man; anyone would tell her he could only turn out to be crazy, dangerous or—maybe just as disappointing—a common opportunist. Those worries, though, were brief, fleeting, much like the girlish daydreams she'd had when she first saw him. What dominated her thoughts now was the quiet thrill of something new and strange, something filled with mystery and possibility.

And soon that morning proved to be no fluke, no isolated incident that could be ignored or rationalized. In the days that followed, he continued to come to her. Thursday there was no rain. When he arrived, he came and took her hand, and until their buses pulled up they stood as before. On Friday the rain returned. They held hands, and again neither spoke. It was as though this silent clasping of hands came as a natural and inevitable extension, though somehow miraculous, too, of the glances they had shared early in the week.

Each morning an eerie tension hung in the air as Lia stood in the bus stop crowd and held onto this man. Though the two of them knew nothing of each other, they shared the most improbable secret, and no one looking at them—now, in this place—could ever hope to guess it. Again and again she thought: Who, seeing them like this, would believe they were strangers?

Though her curiosity about him grew daily, Lia remained unable to begin a conversation. For his part, he seemed fully content, behind his kind smile, with their silence. A couple of times she found herself wondering, absurdly, if he weren't simply mute. It was absurd, yes, but also just the sort of thought that, all things considered, she could not avoid. And then she remembered seeing him, days before, saying goodbye to another man as the two of them had stepped down from the 255 and went in different directions.

That was what she believed she had seen, and yet she could not be certain she was recalling such a minor, ordinary incident with absolute clarity.

She was left that weekend to wonder if he would be at the bus stop without her on Saturday morning and Sunday. And would he be there again on Monday, when she returned? Perhaps by then he would have vanished from her life.

But all the next week he was there to hold her hand and stand with her in the rain. From that first day, the Wednesday when he came to her with his umbrella, this continued a full two weeks.

Because it was the most tangible thing they shared, she became attuned to the rain as she never had been before, and to the dark, overcast skies that added an aching somberness to the quiet between her and the man. Their hands were often wet, and it seemed that no matter where they stood, eventually the water always puddled around their feet as they gazed at the miserable, endless ranks of cars, trucks, and buses passing them by. In the sidewalk, every twenty feet or so, stood an emaciated tree with slick, limp leaves. Not for the first time, Lia felt that this was no place for the organic, this desolate landscape of wet asphalt and concrete from which even the sun hid itself.

At work Lia had been, for almost a year, taking her lunches with a coworker, a woman named Meris who was a few years older. Once, Lia decided to tell Meris about her silver-haired man. At lunch that day—the second Wednesday—Meris had been talking about her in-laws. Her husband's parents were a pair of intense social activists, and on the previous night they had taken Meris and her husband to a new play with political overtones. Meris went on about the evening and the play for nearly twenty minutes, though Lia had said hardly a word. And finally, Lia gave it up. She could not imagine any outcome in which Meris might take this confidence of hers seriously. Besides, there was so little to say about the thing, and how could she speak to anyone about him before the two of them had even talked?

When the second Friday came, Lia was more anxious than ever. She felt sick at the thought of the coming weekend, at the uncertainty of it, and she was disgusted with herself, knowing she still would not break their silence.

The next Monday he did not arrive with the 255 but appeared, as if from nowhere, five minutes late. They touched and she felt a flush of relief. Then, almost immediately it seemed, their buses pulled up.

"It's too much," she said, her heart pounding. "I can't keep it this way any longer. I'm Lia. Please, won't you tell me your name?"

His gentle and ever-present smile grew. "It's Isaac," he said.

"Tell me more," she said. "Tell me about yourself." She was prepared to stand there in the rain and talk for an hour, if only he would.

But all he said, taking her to her bus, was, "Tomorrow, I promise."

When he got off the 255 on Tuesday morning, his hat was missing, leaving his silver hair in full view, and he moved more slowly than usual as he raised his umbrella and walked toward her. The rain was light that morning, a misty drizzle. Behind him two men, both half a head taller than Isaac and wearing blue suits, seemed to be following. One had dark hair; the other was bald. Before the three of them reached Lia, the bald man patted Isaac on the shoulder and then led his companion away and up the street.

Holding Isaac's hand, Lia now noticed the state of his clothes. Wet marks dirtied his knees. His coat was missing a button, and one pocket had been torn along the seam.

"Are you all right?" she said. "What's going on?"

His face was untroubled, and not even a hint of concern entered his voice. "What do you want most to know?" he asked detachedly, as if it were a riddle.

"I want to know who you are."

"That's going to be difficult. There is almost nothing I can tell you that would make sense."

"Then tell me something that doesn't make sense. *Who are you?*"

"I'm someone who wants to give you a gift, Lia."

Immediately a primal apprehension filled her. But this fear was a frail thing, and a moment later it began to collapse. "A gift? What kind of gift?"

"I'm giving it to you right now." He lifted her hand and curled it toward him as if asking for something; her trust, perhaps. "It's the sort of thing, though, that you can't say much about without changing the nature of it."

He went silent. Finally he drew in a breath, took a moment to consider her face, and began speaking again.

"Then there was the time you and I took that trip out east," he said, his voice lilting ever so slightly. "The earth was so dry and hot, and the sky was like an endlessly blooming flower, offering up one impossible beauty after another. It wasn't long before you were looking exhausted, worn out by it all. I wanted to stop for a while, spend a few days in one of those little half-deserted towns along the way. But you insisted we stop for only one night; you were hungry for that trip like I hadn't expected. Soon we were on our way again, and we crossed the river, its pure, shimmering water rippling under us like the wall of a dream world. And then we reached the city.

"There we walked for miles among the poor and the lost. First you gave away that big jacket I'd been so foolish to bring along. And before we knew it, we'd emptied our baggage, giving it all away. And so, unburdened, we moved with the lightness and ease of natives through that place."

He stopped a moment, lowered his eyes, turned further inward. Lia did not know how to respond to all of this. If it weren't for the earnest, personal tone in his voice, she would think he were reciting a story from memory; a sort of parable or a hypnotist's monologue.

He looked at her again and continued.

"We had money enough for just a few meals when we bought sandwiches one afternoon to eat on the steps of a massive, ancient cathedral. When we'd finished, we went inside. Somehow we ended up talking to that young, soft-spoken priest who offered us the job of picking a few baskets of apples from the grove behind the cathedral. The grove was part of a narrow, isolated retreat for the clergy, walled on the sides and running along one end of a large cemetery. The retreat ran much deeper than we could see at the time. The apple trees were nearest to the cathedral, and a thick clump of evergreens was all we saw beyond.

"I still remember the scent the apples gave off that hot afternoon as we climbed up and down the wooden ladders. When we finished, sweating and tired, the door to the cathedral was locked, and no one answered our call. We walked into the evergreens to find shade. When we saw no wall before us, we kept walking. We went farther than we thought the retreat could possibly extend, but the parallel walls to the left and right remained constant. Finally we came to a small opening in the trees. There, sitting on the bright grass, was a wizened old priest, bald, milky-eyed, his skin reddened by the sun. Two large blue jays stood unmoving not far from him, as though listening. Perhaps a full minute after we appeared, they stirred themselves, rustling their wings, and then flew away, up into the trees.

"I suppose the priest spoke to us for more than an hour, but if you asked me today, I couldn't tell you a single thing he said. I do remember that at one point you and I both had tears on our faces. Then, just as I realized the day had begun to cool, the priest invited us to sleep awhile on the grass. He kissed us each on the forehead and left us. And we slept.

"When I woke everything was wet, and the rain seemed to have been falling a long time. You were gone, so I looked for you in the trees. After a time I found a way out of the place—a small, stone archway. As I left, some deep part of me knew we'd lost each other.

"Before long the streets held standing water, and I was glad you were not there. The grassy fields outside the city were thrashed back and forth continually by a wind that might have had devils in it. I was glad, too, that you were not there. And when I saw the river twisting and jumping between its banks, I felt that you were someplace distant and safe. They said the rains there that year were like nothing that had been seen in living memory."

For a time he simply held her hand. Then he said, "So often, I thought I would never see you again. But here we are. How much better all things work for those who simply trust."

The two men in blue suits appeared again on the sidewalk a few yards from Lia and Isaac, but Isaac seemed not to notice. The men looked taller and more menacing than before, as though, like military men, they had consciously adopted an imposing attitude, a commanding posture.

Isaac studied her eyes a moment, searching for something he seemed desperate to find. Then he sighed, and his face relaxed.

"Don't worry, Lia," he said. "I know it wasn't you who took the trip with me that time. No, but she was so like you. She might have been a sister. Or, someday, a daughter." He leaned toward the side of her head and whispered. "But this—this gift, now—is for you. Only for you."

"Those men," she said, instinctively tightening her grip on his hand, "what are they—?"

"Don't worry," he said quietly, his gentle tone turning almost lighthearted. "You think that I need protection from them, or maybe that they *are* my protection? But would you believe that, today, I'm the dangerous one? You can trust that; they do."

He leaned in again, this time kissing her forehead just as the bus drew up. He smiled at her and then walked to the men expecting him. Together, all three joined the line waiting to board the bus.

Without warning, everything went soft and dreamlike around

Lia, and she experienced a prolonged sensation akin to déjà vu. The light became hazy, the street noise receded, and all movement in front of her turned slow and deliberate. Both her body and mind seemed to freeze momentarily, assaulted by a numb exhaustion.

She saw Isaac board the bus, stepping up from between his two companions on the street. When he was inside, the other men followed. They swung into step behind like a pair of doors shutting, one after the other. Watching the two large men squeeze their way into the bus, suddenly hunched and drawing their limbs in close to fit through the door, Lia again had the notion that they were taller now than they had been only minutes ago.

Then the bus was gone.

It was some moments later, when her own bus and the 486 arrived, that Lia realized Isaac had not taken his usual bus.

So it was that, after just two weeks, the strange wind that had blown Isaac to her returned and carried him away. She never once saw him after that. In the days following, she found that she cried easily, and she realized it would be a very long time before she stopped looking for Isaac whenever she was on the street or encountered a crowd. And eventually, not quite a month after he disappeared, Lia began walking four blocks out of her way each morning to catch her bus at its next stop. She did this rather than stand in the old place alone.

Autumn passed into winter. Snow fell on the city: on roads, roofs, and trees. It melted, and then the cold turned pitiless, cruel. And snow came again.

One morning after a full day of heavy snowfall, a snow plow operator came upon a terrible sight. He found the small form of a woman frozen, curled as in sleep, on a bus stop bench. She wore dark pajamas and a thin, green-striped robe. When the TV news interviewed him, the plow operator said she had seemed merely asleep—peaceful and dreaming. "She was young, so young and pretty," he said, more than once. Her frozen hair was the image he couldn't shake.

When regulars at the bus stop were interviewed by the police, it was mainly the women who remembered Lia and could describe her. It had been some months, though, they said, since they'd seen her last. The two men who remembered Lia both mentioned the boyfriend whom she had been with during two of her last weeks at the bus stop. The men mentioned also, each in his own way, how the joy had vanished from her face when the boyfriend no longer appeared.

Each time that he finds her again, she wears a new disguise. And yet it is *she* who always fails to recognize *him* for who he is. Still, he holds to the promise, to faith. One day everything will flow together. One day everything will be right, and finally, hand-in-hand, they will make their escape. One day he will pull her through the keyhole with him.

So he hopes and he perseveres. He will pursue her to the end. Amid all the variations, all the uncertainties, a few things will never change, and these constants are what bind him.

Next time, too, it will begin with a look and finish with a song. He has never known another way.

Fiddleback
Lorna D. Keach

"Six, in three pairs of two," he muttered. He rode the elevator up to the third floor of the hospital, holding a Mason jar filled with daffodils.

Betty would be pissed at him for pulling them up from the yard, but he knew she didn't care much for store flowers. He wanted to bring her something that reminded her of home. Something that felt like home in this place with sterile white sheets and the plastic tubes and needles—but it wouldn't matter. Betty was pissed at everything now. The doctors kept telling her that her kidneys could fail (and her red blood cells could explode, but even Walt thought the doctors were making that up), but all she wanted was a cigarette and a whiskey. Sixty-two years old, and it was a miracle she'd lasted this long with all her smoking and drinking, the doctors said.

Walt unfortunately agreed. He should've been a widower years ago.

Once the elevator came to a lilting halt, Walt stepped out and closed his nose to the smell of the hospital. Too damned clean. He was used to the smells of damp earth, cow patties and fertilizer, cut grass, horse sweat. Dust, in old abandoned houses. Rotten wood had a smell, even when it was just dry and splintered. Betty must've been going crazy from the smell. Of course, she was also going crazy from the IV stuck in her hand and the fact that she had to pee in a bowl and call for a nurse every time it needed to be emptied. Betty had gone crazy from this place. As Walt trudged down the hall to room 310, he figured he just might, too.

He heard her yelling at one of the nurses when he neared the door.

"I'm done with the goddamned patch and your goddamned gum. I'm gonna go outside, you hear me?"

The nurse was a young man in purple scrubs who just smiled at her. When he patted her hand, Betty yanked it back, ready to slap him with it.

"Now, Betty," Walt said, after deciding it was too late to turn back. "Are you being sweet today?"

"The hell I am. I'm fuck-all tired of this place." She watched the nurse scoot out while he still had the chance. Then her watery eyes fell on Walt. "And just where have you been? It's almost four." Her voice cracked a little when she said it.

"I brought you something."

He set the jar on the rolling bed table; the one Betty could pull over her knees to eat on. She took one look at them and a fat tear ran down her left cheek.

"You bastard," she whispered.

"I only took three."

"Flowers ain't meant to be in a jar. They're meant to be in the ground." She turned away from him and looked at the window. "You coulda brought me a potted plant or something."

"I'm sorry." Walt said. Seemed he'd been saying that a whole lot lately.

"You coulda stayed last night."

It took him some time to answer. "…The animals needed tending."

Betty got quiet. There was very little she could say to that, even though Walt knew he could've stayed last night and then gone in the morning to feed the horses and let the cows out to pasture. But he couldn't stand it here, with its clean smell and all its terrifying needles. He'd watched his father sink into a hospital bed not unlike the one Betty lay in; all his daddy's organs had melted inside his body, shrinking him, like he'd been sucked dry. As a kid, Walt had been convinced the doctors were vampires drinking his daddy's blood. They were predators; they'd run his daddy down until he couldn't run any more.

But Betty hadn't shrunk yet. She was still a thick, solid woman—a *capable* woman, no matter what that paper gown said. (And a sweet woman, really, when she'd had her sleep and her smokes and whiskey.) She'd done her hair and put on a bit of powder that afternoon, Walt saw. She'd outlast him for sure, he thought. No matter what her habits were, Betty would long outlast him.

He closed his eyes and tried to think of something else.

"I dreamt of things crawling in my veins." Betty muttered, now not facing him because she didn't like it when he saw her cry. "Of the hour or two sleep I got, I had bugs in my veins."

Walt just nodded, still standing by the bed. He couldn't make himself sit down.

"It's really hard, being alone in this place."

I'll stay tonight. Walt knew it was what she wanted to hear, even though she was too proud to ask it outright. He felt the words in his throat ... but the box-machine on her IV stand beeped and he saw it drip another drop of saline into the long, clear tube running to her hand. His throat seized up. Suddenly it was too tight to get anything out.

Betty waited, then wiped her face off with the towel they had wrapped around her ice pack. She put the sweating plastic bag back under her arm. Walt caught a glimpse of the red, softball-sized knob there, just above her armpit. The knob wasn't hard; when she poked it, it jiggled like it was full of jelly. It was why he'd driven her to the emergency room in the first place. Fever and chills were one thing, but "I think something's wrong with this bite, Walt," she'd said. At the tip of knob was a tiny black spot; something the doctors said might get bigger.

The flesh might die, might eat a necrotic hole right through her. Fiddleback poison did that; it ate holes into people.

But there was nothing they could do about that. Right now, it was just saline and antibiotics, to work on the infection, and they'd find out later how much flesh rotted off Betty's arm.

"Cellulitis can affect the hemoglobin in older patients," the doctor had said. He'd described a patient he'd had a few years back, over seventy, whose red blood cells had swelled up and burst. The infection made his blood explode. It still sounded like bullshit to Walt. But even though that kind of reaction was rare, "there's a good chance the infection could become systemic." It could go to her organs; make them melt.

"Jeopardy's on." Betty pointed at the TV on the wall.

Walt nodded. He understood she wanted him to sit and watch it with her, and he supposed that wasn't as bad as sleeping there overnight. Walt wanted nothing more than to turn on his heels and bolt and not stop until he got to the truck, but he'd already done too many unforgivable things. No one would ever forgive him again after this was over, he was sure of it....

Just as he was about to walk around the bed to the chair on Betty's right, he caught movement from underneath a daffodil petal. Betty had her eyes on Alec. Walt froze and watched as a small brown spot crawled down the petal to the jar, tripping over the leaves. It dropped to the table. Betty didn't see, but Walt did. The thing seemed to look at Walt for a second—*six, in three pairs of two*. Walt could see its eyes.

And, suddenly, he thought of the old farmhouse on the edge of their property. Built in 1856, it was too far gone to be restored. "The place needs to be torn down," Betty had said. "Put to rest." The roof had long ago buckled under the weight of rain and wind. All the wood had rotted. And, after Betty hinting for years, too proud to ask him to do anything but always needing his help for something—she needed him, and Walt suspected she hated herself for that—Walt had finally borrowed a bulldozer from their neighbor up the creek and gone to take care of it. The smart plan was to just run the house over, bury it. But Walt had wanted a look around first—the house his grandfather built, the one that had fallen into disrepair when no one could repair his daddy. He'd taken his sledge with him, just in case he found anything interesting in the staircase banister or in the floorboards. People from that era hid their treasures in secret places in the house.

Walt found himself hoping he'd find something of his daddy's. It was slow going to get to the entryway; the bay window had collapsed and the front door lay crookedly across the frame. When he got there, he put his facemask and goggles on, like their neighbor up the creek had suggested. "You don't just tear a place down with your bare hands." He'd worn gloves. And he'd smashed open the banister even though it broke his heart, busted it wide open....

They'd poured out. glowing like dust in the sunlight leaking in through boarded windows—thousands of them, all startled and skittering back to the walls and up through the fireplace. Walt had hollered something, something about Jesus, and jumped back. They ran over his boots. One latched onto his sledge; he'd had to shake it to get it off. Most of them tiny and brown, little specks of babies; some of them the size of a dime or a nickel. A few were far too big—quarter of an inch in body length, that was as big as they were supposed to get—but Walt saw a few that were bigger than quarters, bigger than half dollars. Change was all he could compare them to, for sizing. They were round, almost flat. But they ran, and Walt saw the fiddles on their backs, their even brown markings that made them brown recluses. They weren't supposed to be aggressive.

For the most part, they weren't; in half a breath they'd all run back to the secret places left in the house. Except one.

One paused on the tip of the shattered banister, facing him. It was so big, Walt ran out of coins to compare it to. A giant spider, like the granddaddy of all brown recluse spiders, staring at him with cold intelligence in its eyes—its six eyes in three pairs of two. Walt's heart had nearly stopped. He'd never been afraid of fiddlebacks, as prolific as they were in this country, but this thing wasn't any common spider. The size of his fist, it was an avatar— the necrotizing accumulation of all brown recluses.

And it *knew* Walt.

The giant fiddleback had looked at him, and one skinny leg lifted up like a bony finger. An accusation. Or a promise, maybe. Walt had tread somewhere he wasn't meant to be.

And Walt knew it wanted reciprocity for the destruction of its people's home. It wanted sacrifice.

The spider on Betty's table didn't lift any legs. It just waited like it was expecting Walt to crush it. Walt looked at Betty with the knob under her arm, wearing that paper gown that made anyone seem invalid. She'd survive one bite, but surely not two. But, if the spiders were in the daffodils, they must have taken the house—the farmhouse was under a foot of earth, now. Where else could they go? Where could he go? For the rest of his life, he'd be shaking out his clothes and checking the bed before he lay down, but what good would that do if there was a score to be settled?

Walt thought about crushing the spider with the jar.

Betty called out "Venice!" and Alec awarded someone two hundred dollars.

Walt closed his eyes. She had such a hard time loving him, he knew, when all she wanted was to be alone. Or maybe that was what he wanted. The IV machine beeped again and sent another drop down the long, clear tube crawling up Betty's vein.

And Walt said, loud enough so the spider could hear him, "I'm gonna go grab some coffee. You want any?"

Betty nodded, silently. She didn't look at him.

Walt walked out of the hospital room.

He didn't go back.

The doctors called him at 8 a.m., saying Betty had passed away suddenly from massive organ failure. They hadn't gotten to her in time. It seemed the infection had flared up in the night, spreading violently to her liver and her kidneys. She'd gone in her sleep.

A second necrotic bulge had appeared on the palm of her left hand, like she'd been trying to swat something away.

Walt hung up the phone afterward, knowing that the doctors wanted him back at that terrible place so he could make arrangements. Instead, he sat for a long time on the porch, staring at the daffodils clustered around the steps. He breathed in still morning air with the smells of cut grass and cow patties, and he saw the lawn move.

Thousands of small brown spots on a mass exodus. The grass twitched and waved as though a breeze were passing through it and, bringing up the rear, he saw the granddaddy fiddleback run over the ground like a retreating general. Walt watched and held his breath until it and the last spider was gone, vanished into the fallow fields.

With his sacrifice, his penance was paid.

And then he wept.

Daddy Long Legs
Harper Hull

The soothing female voice of the bright GPS unit on the dashboard kept on counting down to the next move.

In one mile turn right.

Marvin knew exactly where he was going and how to get there, but the almost-human voice purring to his right made him feel like there was someone in the car with him. He'd even named her—Veronica. After his sister. He'd activate her even on a trip to the store three blocks away from his home, just to have her around.

The gloom was thickening quickly, prompting Marvin to flick the headlights on. It had been years since he'd been home last, years since he'd seen his dad, yet the looming, reaching trees that lined the narrow road still felt familiar. There was something inherently wrong with the nature in South Carolina, as if everything living were out to get you. Including plants. Especially plants. Marvin knew the idea was ridiculous, but it was one he'd kept with him after leaving his home state for Pennsylvania all those years ago with his mom.

In one half mile turn right.

Marvin kept glancing up at the blackening trees as if he expected to see a body swinging from a sturdy bough. The road was quiet, the sky was cloud-covered, hiding the stars, and he felt claustrophobic all of a sudden, boxed in and trapped in the last place he wanted to be. He shivered despite the close warmth and wondered what he'd say to his dad. Dear old Dad, good ol' boy

Marshall Derry, on his last legs for the final time and with only one person left to turn to. Number one faithful son, on his way back to the original family house like a prodigal dog.

In two days it walks again.

"What did you say, Veronica?"

Marvin shot a look at the GPS, which looked normal and in working order. The little cartoon representation of his vehicle was straight along the green line. He shivered again.

He knew exactly what *it* was and where *it* walked. He could never forget the long-legged tree thing. *Daddy Long Legs,* he'd named him. Once he'd seen him; once in his life he'd been terrified beyond his wits and bad things had happened. *Great,* he thought, *and now I'm imagining things too. My own Veronica turned on me! Welcome home, Marv—dredge up every ghost you got, this is the place for 'em!*

He really, really didn't want to go home to that house and that room and that garden. As he took a right, cooingly encouraged by the electronic Veronica, he couldn't stop himself from reliving the time the man atop the trees had appeared in his life, as he relived it every bright, sunny morning of his life. He believed if he ever saw it again he would drop dead right there.

He'd been seven years old when it had happened. Back then he'd shared a room with his little sister; they had been lucky enough to get bunk beds and he had, as elder brother, claimed the top. King of the room. His mattress was higher than the windowsill, and he used to wake up every morning to a slat of light slinking through the gap at the edge of the curtain and draping itself across his face. It was a good way to wake up, that scarf of warmth.

That particular morning, it hadn't been the sun that had awakened him but the noise from the back garden. It had sounded like a godawful ruckus out there, and Marvin had pulled himself up onto his elbows, leaned to the side, and shifted the curtain a few inches. The garden had been filled with squirrels; the angry little ragtag balls of brown fuzz were everywhere, with more joining them as they descended from the line of tall trees that fenced in the back yard. Squirrels had filled the grassy spaces between the tool shed and the covered, above-ground pool, all the way toward the house itself. The noise was deafening, even through closed windows. All the creatures had been chattering and screeching at high volume, up on their back legs and practically waving their tiny fists toward the trees.

That was what had struck Marvin the hardest: the fact that every single squirrel had been facing the exact same direction; tiny black-eyed, bushy-tailed receivers all picking up the same signal. Marvin had started scouring the sky, looking for an owl or something else predatory and dangerous, when the garden had suddenly gone silent as a tomb.

Marvin spotted him in the upper right quadrant of his vision, all limbs and hat, before he quickly shifted his focus to take a full-on view of the thing and had gasped so hard he'd almost choked.

It couldn't be real!

You have reached your final destination.
   As Marvin pulled up the familiar driveway, he shivered, shaking the old images out of his head. His sister had died that day, all those years ago. He blamed the man in the trees; always had. He glanced at the clock on the console and breathed deeply. Not even 9 p.m. yet. He had a good ten hours of cool, dark safety before the sun rose and woke him in a feverish sweat. He could see his dad silhouetted in the living room window, looking out at him, now raising an arm and waving weakly.

Marvin scooted round to the trunk, grabbed his suitcase, and headed for the front door of the house, mentally preparing himself, shaking old conversations out of their dusty coverings in his head. He didn't even know if he should address him as Pa or Marshall anymore. Maybe Sir or Mr. Derry.

Maybe just Dad.

Sitting at the dining room table with a beer and a roast beef sandwich in front of him, Marvin lied to his father.

"You look good, Dad, considering."

"I look like crap and feel worse. Miss my 'baccy like a sumbitch."

Marvin smiled weakly. It was true; his dad looked terrible. He'd aged twenty years in half a decade. A triple-bypass could do that to a man who already had problems with his lungs, liver, and back. The old man looked a faded, shrunken, badly photocopied version of himself, all loose skin and tiny, pointy bones. A threadbare sheet thrown over broken chair parts. When he spoke, Marvin almost expected rusty pocket-watches, small black moths, and tarnished coins to fall from his mouth.

"Well, I'm going to look after you and the house for a while, so think about resting up. Think of what you want to eat, too. I'll get groceries tomorrow. No bacon, though."

His dad made a huffing sound and shook his head sadly, imagining the horrors of a healthy diet.

"No tobacco, no meat, no Scotch. They may as well just leave me in the woods so I can truly live like an animal."

Marvin laughed and pointed toward their beef sandwiches.

"No meat? What's that on your plate, Dad? Don't play the martyr; you could be a lot worse off."

"A one-off to *celebrate* you being here," said his dad sarcastically. "I suppose you'll be sleeping in your old room?"

Marvin tensed and looked down at the table.

"I was thinking I could stay on the couch in the living room."

"I pass out there myself many a night; you take your old bedroom."

Marvin nodded as he screwed up the fear in his chest as tightly as he could, visualizing it as a piece of lined canary-yellow note-paper covered in scrawled, black sketches of long-legged beasties that warped and disappeared with each mental scrunch.

"Son, I'm glad you're here." His dad's eyes looked a little moist. "It's been lonely. I know it wasn't your fault, now, too."

Marvin's old bedroom still had the bunks assembled up against the far wall. After Veronica's accident, he had begged his parents to let him keep them. He remembered lying there at night for that short, oh-so-short period of time before they'd left and imagining that Veronica was alive and well and sleeping safely, a tiny, soft, curly bundle of warm girl below him and out of sight. That was when the darkness first became a comfort to him, a safe, all-encompassing mass that hid the frightful things that appeared in the sunlight. He could have reached a hand down and felt her warm, soft fingers grasp it. Now it just made him sad to see the tiny mattresses in the white-painted wooden frame. He threw himself down onto the adult-sized single bed that was against the near wall just inside the doorway and made a mental note to disassemble and remove the bunks the next day. Maybe donate them to a local church or charity; surely kids still enjoyed them. Who didn't want to be king of the room?

He managed to kick his shoes off and pull his belt away from his pants before he started to drift off. He hadn't realized how tired the drive had made him. Within a few minutes his eyes were moving frantically beneath their lids and he was snoring, low and heavy. The safety of night didn't come this time, and the familiar dreams began to flicker and roll in Marvin's imagination.

He was back in the garden, a kid again, some hours after the tree walker had been by. His parents had gone to the hardware store to pick up supplies and a lot of trash bags; the squirrels had reacted insanely when the tree walker had come: part woodland creature massacre, part suicide pact, and dozens of bodies littered the garden.

Marvin had been given the task of removing the cover from the pool and fishing out the floaters; some of the animals had managed to wriggle their way beneath the tight cover in their frenzy and had doubtless drowned in the deep, dirty water filled with rotten leaves and dead bugs.

Marvin had untied the plastic cords that held the thick cover over the lid of the pool and cinched it away enough to pop his head in and peek inside. Little bodies dotted the surface, most of them face-down. Marvin shivered and reached for the net at his side that usually only removed leaves. He glanced at his little sister, blowing bubbles up on the safety of the deck.

"Veronica! Come here!"

She obediently trotted over to him, carefully stepping around the dead squirrels with a look of disgust on her face and holding her heavy knitted cardigan together tight across her tummy.

"Come look! Drowned squirrels in the pool! Their eyes are all bulgy!" Marvin added a theatrical touch.

"Eww, no! Get them out, Marvin!"

"Just look first; come on."

Marvin reached down and took his sister's little hand, led her up the small steps that led to the pool rim, and held the cover up so she could peer into the shimmery, dim interior. She gave an exaggerated shiver of disgust. Marvin grinned, reached up, and, grabbing her little waist, performed a mock push-then-pull, shouting out "Saved-your-life!" really fast.

His hands slipped off her on the pulling part of the joke. She tumbled headfirst into the pool with a high-pitched sound, her body and legs making a rough, rasping sound as they rubbed against the inside of the tarpaulin cover. which fell heavily back into place, closing the small gap.

Veronica's death had been blamed on Marvin by everyone except his mother. She had held him close, both of them sobbing, as the white-faced, lantern-jawed men quietly and grimly removed the little girl's body from the now uncovered pool, solemnly wrapping her in a red blanket and ceremoniously carrying her to the front porch to await the sheriff and his county coroner.

As the neighborhood men remained on the porch, all smoking cigarettes and pipes, standing around the coddled body of Veronica and looking away into the distance in complete silence, Marvin's father had returned to the back garden. He'd attacked the pool with a fury he had never shown before, smashing the frame to pieces with a sledgehammer and standing steady, gasping, as the green water had spilled forth and washed across him, up to his knees, before settling across the lawn in a massive, filthy puddle. The dead squirrels lay sopping yet rigid; the man kicked them out of his way as he moved toward the house; toward Marvin.

If it hadn't been for his mother, Marvin would have been beaten to death that day by his own father, he was sure of it. He understood, too; it *was* his fault, but it was also the fault of the tree man. He had been the portent of death that day, but no-one had believed Marvin when he'd told them what he had seen. Well, his mother, anyway; she said it was his imagination reacting to the trauma. He didn't dare speak to his dad about it.

Within eight days the situation in the family home was deemed unlivable. Marvin's mother left his father and took her son with her to Pennsylvania, where they stayed with Marvin's aunt until finding a new place of their own, where they intended to live a long, happy life. As happy as they could get, at least. That was the goal.

The sun rose, crisp and white, and Marvin woke to the normal sounds of a southern garden. He sighed in relief and stretched his arms, his shoulders sore from a bad night's restless sleep. Just to be sure, he looked out of the window and scanned the tall trees that bordered the land; nothing but branches, leaves, unidentified nests and the odd squirrel circling a trunk like a wind-up toy. No Daddy Long Legs, today.

No death.

A long shower and a change of clothes later, Marvin found his father sitting in the living room watching some old movie on the television.

"More coffee, Dad?"

"Go on; fill 'er up."

"I ... I meant to ask you last night but I was too tired ... what did you mean, you know it wasn't my fault now?"

"I seen him. Old Tall Hat."

Marvin sat down hard in the easy chair across from his dad, shocked at the revelation.

"You saw him? Dad? The ... the tree walker?"

"Yup, the man you told your mother about the day your sister ... that fella. Saw him clear as day, striding across those top branches with those spindly legs like he was on the sidewalk. It was the morning that Ella—that your momma—my Ella, the morning she died. Not the first time I've seen him, either."

Marvin stood up and took his dad's mug from his clasped hands.

"Mom told you about that? Wait, I'll go get that coffee. Then we can talk some more."

Marvin's mother had been killed in a car wreck when he was still in high school. She'd driven headlong into a bus on the highway on a beautiful July morning after swerving into the oncoming traffic trying to overtake a truck. No-one knew where she'd been going or why she'd been in such a hurry to get there.

Except Marshall.

Marvin listened to his father as he recalled the events of that morning, rage, pity and hopelessness all tumbling in his chest like socks in a spin cycle.

"I called her up in Pennsylvania right after I'd seen that sumbitch. Told her you were right all along, said I wanted you back with me, wanted her back with me. A real family. She wouldn't have any of it, called me crazy and a deluded old bastard. She never forgave me for the way I came at you that day, you know. I don't think she would have if she'd lived a thousand years. Anyway, I got mad, told her I was calling from the town you lived in and was about to pull you out of school and bring you home to South Carolina with me. Then I hung up. I was in a bad way after she let loose on me the way she did."

Marvin hung his head in his hands and cried. He cried as his dad came over and awkwardly patted him on the back. He cried as his dad leaned down and held him. Then they cried together until the sun was high in the sky and the coffee was cold beside them on wicker-topped tables.

When their faces were red and there were no tears left to spill, Marshall told Marvin more.

"My poppa—your grandaddy—was a bad, bad man. You don't know what he looks like, do you, boy? Never been a photograph of him kept, not in this house, not even by my daddy. All burned and sent to Hell, just like him, and rightly so."

Marvin glanced around the room and realized there were no photographs at all on display anymore. Too many bad memories for the old man, he reckoned.

"His name was Ernest, mean old Ern, and he's the reason we both seen that thing in the trees. It has a name, but I daren't say it, never will, and I won't tell it to you, so you never have to even think about saying it. My nanny—a good woman she was, always gave me the creamiest milk when we paid a visit—she didn't deserve being with Ern. For some reason the bastard got it into his head that she was cheatin' on him with a fella who lived down the road a ways; undertaker, he was. Hell, maybe she did have an affair. Maybe this fella treated her nice. I actually like to think so, considerin' what happened."

Marshall lifted a papery hand to the chest pocket on his

overalls, patted the place where he used to keep his tobacco pouch, and sighed.

"Ern was known for his liberal fists and feet; looking back, I remember Nanny often had a bruised face or a bad arm. At the time I didn't think nothing of it, being just a young 'un. Got in fights with men, too; big man, spent a lot of weekends in the town jail. Well, one day Ern completely snapped, and he took Nanny out into the woods and tied her to a tree. Beat the tar out of her. Then he went and found the poor bastard he suspected of having the affair with her and knocked him clean out with his rifle butt and dragged him to the same spot in the woods. In front of Nanny he tortured the poor bastard half to death, then strung him up in the trees. Left him there flayed and broken for the animals to have their way with. Shot Nanny in the face and turned himself in, sayin' he'd take what was comin'. The police found poor Nanny's body still tied to that trunk, and Mister Won't-say-his-name was high up in the boughs, strung by his ankles and wrists, joints popped and bones broken. Barely looked like a man no more."

"What happened to Ernest?"

"They were going to string him up, but he managed to do the job himself before they had a chance. Choked to death on his own tongue in his cell. The mean old fucker had chewed it off and swallowed it."

Marvin put his coffee mug down, turned it in a circle, and picked it up again, his mind racing.

"So the tree man is…?"

"Yup, it's him. No point running, I found that out,. He'll get you one way or another. Doubt he'll stop 'til there's none of us left. If you ever have kids of your own, think on that, boy."

The story told, they made a vow to never talk of the long-legged man in the tall hat ever again.

That afternoon, under the high sun, Marvin made a bonfire in the back garden, in the indent where the pool used to be. He brought the bunk-bed out in pieces that he placed one-by-one into the flames. As the paint cracked and shriveled, sending black smoke curling into the clear sky, the trees at the back of the garden swayed ever so gently in the breeze. A large raven flew across the lawn, cawing, and Marvin retreated indoors to medicate and feed his father as if it had been an alarm reminding him of his new duties under death's shadow.

The fire quickly sparked out, leaving one slat of wood from the bed intact and slightly scorched.

"You're all I have left, son."

"I know, Dad."

"What about you; you got a nice young woman back home?"

"No. This is my home again now, anyway."

"I'll understand if you want to get on with your life up there."

"I was only there to be away from you. I don't need to be away from you anymore."

"I'm sorry it took this long. I miss your momma."

"Me, too."

Marvin slept soundly that night. With the bunk-bed gone, the room felt different, more comfortable. No nightmares came to him. No dreams either; just dense, deep, black-blue sleep.

Morning crashed into the bedroom with a symphony of awful noise, bird cries, and squirrel screams, startling Marvin out of his bed and pulling the bleary-eyed man straight to the window. After a moment to gain his composure after being awakened so abruptly, he felt a cold, hard stone lodge in his throat.

The familiarity was crushing and terrible.

Pulling the curtains wide open in one swift move, Marvin pressed his palms against the glass panes and shot his eyes to the trees outside.

"Oh fuck...."

He was coming. Just like the first time, all those years ago, he moved into sight from the right, his ridiculously long legs appearing before any other part of him. Three times as long as his torso and as skinny as drainpipes, they picked their way across boughs and branches with the utmost care, like a water beetle skimming across a pond. They bent and switched at impossible angles, those limbs, and Marvin shuddered as he recalled the horrible story.

With the sun behind him, when he came into full view, every inch of him was shadow. Black from toe to head to the tall stove-pipe hat that perched atop it. He looked to be wearing a frock coat, only now Marvin knew that his back had been flayed to the spine and it was flesh flaps that hung down like discarded, off-the-shoulder suspenders.

He moved like an insect, quickly taking center stage in Marvin's field of vision, where, amazingly, he stopped a moment and seemed to turn his head toward the house. Marvin froze, feeling sad, furious, and terrified all at once.

The man in the trees reached one of his long, zig-zag spaghetti arms upward and tipped his hat before continuing his acrobatic, impossible walk.

Marvin roared and sprinted from the bedroom in just his pajama pants. He took the stairs three at a time and bombed through the kitchen toward the back door, not seeing his father until he had barreled through him and sent him sprawling hard onto the dirty, parchment-colored tile floor. In a blood-filtered rage, Marvin burst out into daylight, not hearing the gasps coming from his father, and reaching down on his way across the garden to grab a singed piece of burned wood. He headed for the tree line, shouting obscenities and spitting through his speech. He twirled, looked, moved, looked again.

The tree walker was nowhere to be seen.

"Come on, you bastard! Come on! Get down here! No more! I'll fucking kill you!"

The garden became quiet; no bird cries or squirrel chatter now, just Marvin's ranting at leaves and wood. Sobbing with anger and failure, he flung the piece of wood toward the treetops and stomped his way back to the house.

Marshall's body was taken away and examined by the county coroner. Cause of death was determined to be heart failure. The old man had died quickly on the dirty floor, listening to his only son rage at ghosts outside.

That night Marvin set himself up in his old bedroom with the curtains open and his dead father's shotgun leaning against the wall. He prayed that Daddy Long Legs would come back, literally prayed on his knees, his elbows resting on the bed, his muddled words sent upward toward God in the belief they would be deciphered, translated, and understood by a higher power.

He just needed to see the man in the trees one more time and this would all be over. The shotgun was loaded with one shell, and Marvin had spent the previous hour making sure he could hold the weapon between his legs, beneath his chin, and still reach the trigger.

All he needed now was that one final appearance—one more glimpse of that crooked shadow blocking out the wide, white morning sun.

Miss Riley's Lot
Gregory Miller

How 'bout when my big brother Chris took me up on Still Creek Hill during huntin' season and let me watch while he and his buds shot a woman? I guess it's true enough, since I saw it all happen, more or less, and the parts I didn't, my kin and friends did.

I was fifteen, and it was the day after Thanksgivin', and the year was nineteen-forty-seven, and Chris, he was nineteen that year, a real bruiser who liked to drink and get in brawls around town, but he got along with me better'n most. When he got kilt a few years later down on Route Eighty-one, drunk as a skunk, I couldn't believe it. He was the kind of fella that could stop a truck, or so I thought.

Well, he and Jim and Dale, that's his friends, they took me up in the woods above town, the part where all us kids got up to no good, and farther in, deep in, until Still Creek Hill reared up and we was breathin' hard in the cold, and then Chris ran up ahead to the clearin'. He had us wait, then came back and said, all breathless, "She's there, OK."

And I asked, "Who's that?"

And he said, "You'll see" and nudged his pals.

We went on up the hill together until it broke clear from the woods. There was wheat all up on the top, and we had a pretty good view of the lay of things. North, McKellen Street roped away toward Plumville down below and miles off, and farmland spread off into the distance. East was Still Creek, from where we came, all hidden by trees but still peekin' out here an' there, but west and south was all woods as far as the eye could see. And down the south side of the hill, out of sight of the road, was an old woman sittin' on an old stump. She was all wrapped up in a shabby black knit shawl and had on black stockings and a black, stained bonnet and a natty old black dress and a tattered, dirty pair of black old wooden clogs like some foreigners or old-times wear. It was like she was in mournin' or something, dressed up in so much black. White hair streamed out from 'neath her shawl in long, thin strands. Her face, oh, it was like lookin' at one of them maps with mountains on it, the kind that stick up a little. She was all wrinkled, and her eyes, I remember when we got close thinkin' how they musta once been green but now was all faded, kinda olive-colored, and red, too.

"Well, Chris, that's Miss Riley!" I sorta shouted.

All the other fellas laughed long and loud at that, but I can't say as I knew why, 'cept we wasn't sup'osed to say a word to her 'cause she was 'touched,' like they say, and she had always kinda skeered me. She liked to clump around town now and again, but 'specially out in the woods and through the fields, and she muttered and laughed and smiled like there was somethin' real sad and unspeakable behind those four black teeth of hers.

"You ain't frightened, now, are you, Jeff?" Chris asked, nudging Dale.

"No, no, I ain't a bit."

"That's a good fry. Now you follow close and watch real good."

So they moseyed on down to Miss Riley, me followin' behind, and Miss Riley came a'clumpin' up the hill aways to meet 'em, and Jim, he said, "How's it goin, Miss Riley?" And Miss Riley, she stopped and smiled that smile, then laughed, and it sounded like a sqallin' baby seeing somethin' all shiny for the first time in its l'il life. And she said, "I'll show you a thing or two!" then turns and walks on down the hill again to her dead ol' stump and takes a seat.

"Here now, whose turn is it?" Jim asked.

"I thought we said it was mine," Chris said.

"No, I don't remember that," Dale said.

"Three's better'n one!" Miss Riley piped up, and I thought to myself, 'What's she runnin' her gums about?' And then I found out.

"You say so," Chris said, and set his point three caliber against her chest, just as Jim and Dale did the same. And then I'll be damned if they didn't lift up the safeties, pull the triggers, and the world went up in smoke and flame.

What I felt, it's kinda hard to put into words. All time, it seemed to hang on edge, and I let out a whoop! and a cry and fell on my knees as Miss Riley, she got blowed backward, knocked straight outta her shoes, and a fine red mist sprayed the ground, my brother, his buds, and my face.

Then Miss Riley, she lay all still, her chest pretty well gone to glory and her bones and innards all on display, and I closed my eyes and pinched my arm and tried to wake myself up, but a'course I couldn't 'cause I was waked already.

That then is what happened to begin with, and it's bad enough, I guess you'd agree. But with my eyes still clamped shut so tight I saw stars, I next heard a rustlin' and a whisperin' and a grunt from one of the boys, and then high above it all, shrill and clear as winter water, Miss Riley's laughter.

I opened my eyes real slow, 'cause I didn't want to see no more, but there's no way I could keep 'em shut after hearing *that*. And what did I see once they was wide again but Miss Riley standin' there in the knee-high wind-blown wheat, puttin' her shoes back on, balancin' from one leg to another. Her hair, it was all wild 'cause her bonnet was knocked clean off by the blast, and her face was covered in blood, but she was alive, though I could still see her innards wavin' as she moved.

There's no point lyin; I passed out cold on the ground at that, and when I came to Chris was lookin' down at me and shakin' his head.

"Sorry 'bout that, fry. We didn't figure you'd take it so rough, though it *is* a bit of a trial when you don't see it coming. But that's always been the best way to let a newbie know what's goin' on with Miss Riley, since no one'd believe otherwise unless they saw for themselves what happens, and without time to back off or put a stop to it first."

I wiped my mouth and sat up. Jim and Dale were outta sight, but Miss Riley was sittin' on her stump again and starin' at me with those faded olive eyes of hers, smilin' that hoary, black-toothed grin.

"You're dead," I said, and pointed at her. "You gotta be."

"Ha!" she spat.

"You saw her chest," Chris said. "Look again."

I peeked over at her again, and that big ol' hole was still there in her gullet, but it didn't look too bad from what it was before. There was less blood, and she'd kinda stuffed her hanging bits back inside herself or somethin', and I could see bits of pink skin around the edges. Scar tissue, I guess it was.

"She'll get better," Chris said. "She always do."

"Come on by and do the same any time! Donations accepted." Miss Riley cackled at me, but I couldn't look at her again, and I didn't feel too steady on my legs. Otherwise maybe I woulda said somethin' back, though I don't have any notion what.

Chris put a hand on my shoulder. "Come on, let's get back to the house and go for a drive. You'll get your answers. It's time."

We got back to the house and didn't even go inside at all but went straight for the old Model A Chris'd bought from Doc Weaver for twenty clams. And when we was inside and rollin' down the road toward nowheres, Chris started talkin', and I sat there all quiet and still except for when he asked a simple question or two.

"Here's the thing about Miss Riley," Chris said, staring ahead.

"How old would you say she is?"

"Eighty-five," I said, cause that was the oldest I could imagine.

Chris shook his head. "That end of town she lives in? Back when Grampa's pa was a boy there was a big flood, and a heap of people died, you know that, don't you? You better, the way Gramma keeps on about it. OK, so most everythin' from there was either warshed away or left to rot, so nobody'd have to think about all the people that got kilt, and so they wouldn't disrespect nobody's memory by buildin' it all up again. Except Miss Riley stayed, because she was there then, and already old, and she lived through it even though she was swept away a mile or so. She came back when no one else did."

"That flood was a hundred and twenty years ago!"

Chris nodded, keepin' his eyes on the road. "I ain't saying anyone understands it, but I don't doubt but she *is* the oldest woman in the world. And I guess you're wonderin' how she does it? Well, she doesn't do much of nothin', as I can tell. She just can't damn well lay herself down and die.

"Before Grampa passed on when you was little, he took me out for my first hunt and showed me what I showed you today. Miss Riley, she goads hunters into doin' it, and finally long ago one of 'em did it for the first time, and ever since it's been kinda traditional-like for some of them to take a shot at her every year at the start of the season. Good luck, they say.

"But Miss Riley, I know why she keeps at 'em. She keeps at 'em 'cause she keeps hopin' one of 'em will do her in right and kill her. It don't happen, though. Sometimes it takes longer and sometimes it takes shorter, but she always gets better. Even so, she won't never give up.

"Hell, I've shot the ol' hag five times in so many years. Once in the neck! Blew her head almost plum off her body. Almost thought she was done for a minute, and boy, was I scared. I didn't want to be taken in for murder, 'specially in such a queer way. But a

minute later her pale old hand started twitchin', and the next she
took a big, deep breath of air and let it puff out white from her
lungs, though a good bit went through the hole in her gullet, too.
And ten minutes later she was staggerin' off, real slow but real sure,
and even though she had a bit of a wheeze for the next year or so,
she was pretty well right as rain for buck season."

We was both quiet for a bit, and I watched the blue November
sky meet the road as Chris kept drivin'.

"How come she don't die?" I finally asked.

Chris sighed like, and he shook his head and wrinkled his
nose. "There was talk of great tragedy and all the kind of things
you'd think'd go along with such a queer situation, goin' all the way
back to the War of Eighteen-Twelve. Somethin' 'bout her son gettin'
kilt and her swearin' to stay until he got back, and him not gettin'
back, so her stayin'. Could be pucky talk. It don't matter, I guess.
But now she's ready to go, and she's been ready for a long bit now."

"You think that's true?"

"Mebbe. But one thing I know is that when folks don't get the
ins and outs about any given thing, they make up somethin' so they
think they do. And that's what happened, I guess. But you know
what I think? I think there *ain't* always no reason for everythin'. I
think she don't die 'cause she don't die. That's her lot, jus' like it's
some's lot to die young. She's durn tired, has been since anyone
alive's known her, but that's her lot."

That stuck with me like glue, and I come to think maybe Chris
was right 'bout a story makin' people feel better. I like to think the
tales were true, meself. They give what happened to her some
reason, bad or crazy besides. Better than none, for sure. But I'll
never know one way or t'other, and so be it.

Chris snuck a glance at me.

"So you're probably wonderin' why the hell you ever need to
know 'bout all this business. Well, you've heard stories told, and at
your age you'd be hearin' more shortly as all that gossip talk begins

to take hold in you. But the more talk there is, the more likely the chance some outsider'd hear and start studyin' up on things, and pretty soon there'd be cameras and those goddamn reporters and town would be in a tizzy and nothin'd ever be settled again. And that'd be a damn shame, 'cause privacy's a right few don't deserve. So most of you boys need to be told and have it all out in the open and understand how things is, and that way you won't need to talk 'bout it ever again unless you're careful who with and when. And that way you know what's what. You see how things stand?"

I guess I was starin' out ahead at me and didn't say nothin' fast enough, cause Chris reached over and punched my arm real hard.

"You see how things stand?" he repeated.

"Yeah, I guess I see how things stand."

He nodded.

"Now, that's what I wanna hear. Now she's harmless, I'll say. She's odd, but she won't hurt you. So if you wanna take a shot—"

"No!"

"That's your good choice, either way. But if you wanna keep away from her, there's a couple things you should know. First, next time you go swimmin' down at Spring Creek's deep hole on a hot summer day, better be careful not to go too far under water. I've heard it told she sets herself at the bottom of the pool with a rock tied to her ankle. It's her way of keepin' cool, since drownin's death, and she can't die. So if you feel someone grab you, that's what it is. And if you don't want to get grabbed, use the hole downstream by the hill.

"Second, if you ever walk in the woods and see her hangin' from the old oak tree over on the edge of Mr. Scot's, don't get scared. She do that sometimes, too. You just ain't ever seen it yet, but you will if you keep on huntin'.

"And third? Once in a while, usually at night, she'll climb up the tower of Still Creek Public Library and take a leap. It's the highest buildin' in town. She don't do that often any more, not since

Sheriff Rogers had the borough add on that grate. And she usually only does it when she's been hittin' the bottle, and no one in town's allowed to sell her any hard stuff anymore, neither. But you might see that, too, so it's best to keep one eye out and the other open." He paused and laughed. "That way she won't land on you."

We drove back home just in time for Ma's supper, and it was good but I didn't have much stomach for it. Boy, what I wouldn't do for just a taste of that pot roast now. Nothin' like it anymore. But I wasn't hungry and hardly ate a thing. And Chris and I, we never spoke of Miss Riley again.

What happened then? You might well ask. Did I let her be, or did I see her again? Well, time fades old frights. I had a good group of friends back then, Philip and John and Drake (the first two's dead now; the other livin' with a wife and kids in Chicago), and as we growed up we hunted together despite what all our dads or mas or brothers or cousins told us 'bout crazy ol' Miss Riley. Now we was good boys for the most part, even if we got in our share of trouble…. Still, good or no, we was also of the age that liked to walk the line with things, and death was the biggest line of all. So we hunted. And so one early Saturday we was back in the woods huntin' and came up Still Creek Hill, and Miss Riley was there all right, sittin' on her stump, and she came up on us like she came up on my brother, and said, "You wanna go? I'll show you a thing or two!"

And so we talked a fair bit about it, then Drake went up and shot her right in the gullet.

The old woman staggered back a step, and her face screwed up in pain, and she let out a whollop of a holler, almost as loud as Drake's, but she didn't drop, and when she looked down and saw her stomach, she started laughin', then walked off like nothing much was the matter. Just as before.

"Now you'se a man!" she crowed, hobbling away. "Now you'se a man."

I gotta admit I shot her, too, when I saw her next, and the scary thing is, it felt *good* in a way I don't understand. But I can't say as I felt like a man. In fact, I kinda scared myself, doin' that thing.

And so we'd see her around and got used to the idea that she couldn't die, and life went on. She was crazy and not worth talkin' to, otherwise I guess I'da tried to get a better relationship goin' with her. Knowin' someone like that? Couldn't help but be interestin', but she never had nothing to say. And she was a bit of a creep, stalkin' around in woods and hidin' in lakes and hangin' from trees and laughin' and smilin' with those rotten teeth. And that's all there'd be to the story, 'cept for one more thing that happened a few years later, and it ain't often discussed now, though there was plenty in town that saw it and don't forget. And since no one's likely to believe you, even if you believe *me*, I guess I'll spill.

There was a house up on Barnaby Street, about three blocks from my little place. It was abandoned after some fella got killed down in the mines during the nineteen-thirty-one cave-in. A whole blasted mountain fell on him. His family couldn't keep the place without no money, so it went back up on the market and ended up belongin' to the state after a time. The coal was beginnin' to give out a space, and people was startin' to take up farmin' again, but no one new was comin' in, and the folks in Still Creek already had homes.

Well, fifteen years is a long time for a house to go without bein' a home, and it started fallin' down in places, but us boys used it for all kindsa things. We used to go there nights when we was bored and knock back a few, and do all the other sorts of stuff most young folks get in trouble for, nothin' major. But we went even though we knowed it wasn't a safe place. There was wires and electrical fixins and rotten wood all about.

Shortly after I turned seventeen, me and my friends was up there one afternoon with some young ladies, and we was havin' our own party in a way, and someone dropped a match in the wrong place. A bunch of old heavy yellow curtains caught fire, and before we knowed it we was runnin' for our lives out into the open air. It was December, so I remember the cold of the air and the heat of the fire hittin' each other, and then I heard the screams, but they warn't like those of us who was runnin'. They was of pain, and they was from inside that house.

I was in quite a state, and my lungs was all filled with smoke, but I looked around and took in who was missin', and it was Drake. He was still inside. But I took a look at the house, and I couldn't do a thing. There wasn't no way I could get back in the house. The whole doorframe was blazin'. All I could do was cover my ears and cry and watch and, you know, wait for what I felt sure would happen.

And then Miss Riley showed up.

She came stridin' up the walk in her old black clogs, and she handed one of the cryin' girls her tatty ol' shawl, and there was a look in her faded eyes I never saw in nobody's before or since.

"Here's sumpin' I haven't tried!" she said, and she didn't stop walkin', just strode on in through the flamin' door.

There was a long moment when nothin' happened, except Drake's screams stopped, and we all feared the worst. But then out comes Miss Riley, and the fringe of her dress was burnin', and her face was all smudged and black, but she had Drake slung over her back like a cord of wood, his legs held tight in her wiry old arms.

She dropped him down on the sidewalk, and I caught his head in my hands, and he was breathin'. His face was black, but it was only soot, and I guessed right it was the smoke that had gotten him mostly and that he'd fainted dead away. And sure enough he got better with only a few bitty burns and some singed lungs, and he's the one of my three old buds with the family now, the one still alive and happy.

But Miss Riley, she had plans. She took a deep breath, and my lan' she looked so sad. And she looked us up and down, and then suddenly her eyes blazed bright, and they didn't look so old, and with a wide smile and a screech she ran back toward the front door. A big lick of fire reached out to meet her, and a second later her white hair was nothin' but burnin' light, and the light wreathed around her head, and she was gone.

We could hear her laughin' for a long time, and her shadow flitted by the windows, and we could see her burnin' in the flames, and then the whole house, it come down and she warn't laughin' anymore.

I figgered Miss Riley would come out chucklin' again soon enough. She'd taken worse in her day, I thought. But when the ambulance came, I was taken away to the hospital in Kittaning and didn't see no more of it. But I heard the fire department got there right fast, and it took ages to put out all the smolder, and the next mornin' they dug under all the mess and rubble, and there she was, but there warn't much left, and she wasn't movin' a whit. And I heard it said a great winter wind came up ahead of a storm not far behind, and it scattered her ashes all over town and beyond.

Well, it looked like the tired ol' lady'd found her rest at last, and I must say I felt mighty good about it, even if town was a little less … well … interestin' without her in it. And Drake? He went on talkin' to everyone who asked 'bout how she saved his life, which a course she did. But out in Chicago no one believed him anymore, and that makes sense to me.

So then life kept goin'. I got older and graduated high school by the skin of my teeth and got a job down at the lumber yard since the last of the mines was gettin' ready to close.

That said, I guess I was twenty when I first heard it.

Sure, it kept away for a good few years, but then there it was, and there was no hidin' from it. Not in town and not in the woods, neither. And I guess that's what drove me halfway across the state, and how come I don't visit the old family home no more.

It was laughter, and it came from nowhere but the wind.

Sometimes it'd come on fast and leave quick; sometimes it seemed to circle 'bout the house or down the street and back and stay awhile. And sometimes it was cryin' I heard, high and hard one time, soft and tired-like another. 'Course, it coulda been just the wind, and not sumpin' else carried on it, say, like ashes. The wind can be funny sometimes, soundin' like a person. But how many times you ever recognize the voice? How many times it sound like it's singin' through the dust of four black teeth?

So that's old Miss Riley's lot. I guess it don't fit in really as a ghost story, seeing as how all this was all 'bout a livin' person, more or less. But then I guess some kinds of livin' can be just as scary as dyin'. Truth be told, I ain't half as scared of droppin' dead now as I once was. No, not half as scared.

Closing the Deal
Lee Clark Zumpe

S tan cracked the front door and glared at the little man standing on his porch. He tipped his head to the right and watched as the scrawny salesman read the NO SOLICITING sign through squinting eyes behind bottle-thick glasses. The evening thunderstorm had tapered off into a soft drizzle, but the salesman had clearly been caught in the summer downpour. The long sleeves of his button-down shirt stuck to his bony arms, and his shoes made squishing sounds as he shifted his weight from one foot to the other.

"Beggin' your pardon, sir." Awkwardly, the salesman forced himself to make eye contact with Stan. Rivulets of water cascaded down from his matted hair over the acne-pocked landscape of his face. Even as he spoke, a bead of water rested on the rim of his upper lip, dangling and quivering with each breath. "I'm not here to sell you anything you don't want."

"That's what they all say," Stan grunted. Stan stood in the doorway like some ancient Roman statue guarding a shrine. Skirting the uppermost borders of middle age, his hair had thinned and grayed over the last decade, and his once-youthful expression had finally begun to deflate. Still, he exercised daily—he kept lean and fit. He remained the envy of the remnants of his teenage clique; a constant reminder that they, too, could have kept themselves from swelling into soft, lumpy, bitter loafers. Stan eyed the salesman, his face unconsciously curling itself into a disclosure of his disgust. "Take it next door, buddy—there's a woman there who'll drop a twenty for just about anything."

"You don't understand, sir," the salesman stammered, summoning up the most imposing voice he could. He leaned in toward the doorway gracelessly, trying to position himself to keep Stan from slamming the door in his face before he could cast his bait. "Despite my appearance, I don't just go door to door. No, I'm better organized than that. In today's world, you have to be very familiar with your potential markets—you have to know your clients intimately. You have to react to their needs promptly."

"I don't follow...."

"Point is, sir: If I show up at your door—you must have summoned me." The salesman coiled his lips up into an unsettling grin. "If you'll permit me a few moments of your time, I'd be happy to explain."

Stan shook his head.

"I've got too much to do to waste the time ... like I said, the woman next door."

"I'm not interested in the woman next door." The salesman backed away from the door, swaying back in his shoes so that he could see the next house down the street. "She has nothing to offer me at this time, and I can offer her nothing—therefore, we have no business to conduct. I understand she drove her husband off a few years ago—cheated on him with some drunk she picked up down at the Rusty Nail Tavern, didn't she?" He shrugged. "To each her own, I suppose."

"How'd you know...."

"She doesn't like you very much, I gather. You're the one who tipped her husband off, aren't you?"

Stan nodded, smirked mechanically. The thought of it filled him with a sick sense of satisfaction. He had hated having to break the news to the man who lived there, but....

"How do you know all this?"

"Like I said, you have to know your clients intimately..."

Ten minutes later, Stan and the salesman sat at his dining room table. The salesman had declined the offer of a cold soda, but he did gladly accept a towel from the linen closet to mop up his soggy clothes.

Gluttony
Saturday, 1:10 a.m.

Midnight washed away half the patrons at Just One More, a seedy little bar on the outskirts of town near the rows of dilapidated warehouses and processing plants that had been abandoned when all the corporations had moved to Mexico in search of cheap labor. Stan arrived as the lightweights were pulling out of the parking lot, swerving down the two-lane highway toward nearby trailer parks and cheap motels. His timing was intentional—being nocturnal animals, crack pushers rarely closed deals in crowded pubs no matter how sordid and sleazy their reputation.

Stan sat at the bar nursing a warm beer, perched on a barstool desperately trying not to touch anything. The place was crawling with cockroaches. The bartender intermittently smashed a line of ants besieging a bowl of peanuts on the bar. Afterward, he would wipe their tiny corpses across his apron.

After only a few minutes, two scrawny men in white T-shirts disappeared into the bathroom.

Stan stood and followed them.

Through a slit in the door, Stan watched as one coughed up a wad of bills. In exchange, the other handed him a plastic sandwich bag that he quickly stashed in his jeans pocket.

Back out in the bar, Stan did not bother to put his glasses on as the men returned to their respective tables. Instead, he held them up to his face, peering through the lenses cautiously. The tint of their bluish skin shocked him, but it was the roiling of their flesh—seemingly displaced by a multitude of vermin just beneath the surface—that made him cringe and shudder.

"Hey," Stan said, slapping a 10-dollar bill on the counter. He casually glanced toward the jittery addict across the room. "You know that guy?"

"Think his name's Trevor," the barkeep said.

Back in the comfort and security of his car, Stan added Trevor's name to the list.

"Nice place," the salesman said absently. He looked around the room, at its Spartan décor, at the eggshell-white walls that spread out in every direction. Stan's house had an overwhelming and overpowering element of neutrality about it. He had never been one for accoutrements and ornamentation. "Life has enough distractions of its own. No need to pin on any more to your environment, right, Stan?"

"I guess."

"Well, look around you. I can see by the way you keep your house so neat, so organized, that you do not believe in that modern notion of amassing material possessions."

Stan eased himself into a self-assured smile, not having given much thought to it. He squirreled away as much money as he could from each paycheck, paying the mortgage and picking up enough supplies to last him until the next payday. He had plain furniture, white blinds and dull drapery over his windows, and a drab gray carpet blanketing the floor of the house.

"Keep it plain and simple. No attachments, right, Stan?"

"It doesn't seem necessary."

"Precisely—and that's a very ancient concept, one that not many people understand these days. Aside from food and shelter, everything you really need is housed inside your skin."

"I suppose so. I've always thought the best investment you can make is keeping yourself in good shape."

"That's true, Stan—that is absolutely true." The salesman leaned forward, resting both arms on the dining room table, slanting forward in his chair as if he were about to whisper something to Stan that he did not want anyone else to hear. "And the shape you're in—physically—is a reflection of the state you're in morally."

"Well, I don't...."

"No—think about it, Stan." The salesman bounded up from his chair and began circling the table. "If a man can't be trusted to maintain his only important possession, how can he be expected to maintain his integrity, his decency? If a woman lets herself go—doesn't take care of herself, doesn't keep in good condition—how can she be expected to preserve her virtue?"

"What do they say, your body is your temple?"

"Exactly. You don't have to go far to see it. Look around you. Immoral behavior, perversities, wickedness and corruption—they all show right through the skin, Stan. Sin is a form of decay, and though the decay may begin deep inside, at the core, eventually it makes its way to the surface." The salesman stopped in front of the window, peeled back the curtain a few inches. "Look out there. Look at your neighbors. You *can* judge a book by its cover: You know who the sinners are!"

Sloth
Friday, 5:30 p.m.

"It's not my responsibility, ma'am." The expressionless pharmacist stood on the opposite side of the counter, one hand in his pocket and the other fidgeting with a pencil. "You'll have to call your doctor's office and have them prescribe something else. Your insurance doesn't cover this brand."

"I already spoke with the lady receptionist," the elderly

woman said, leaning against the counter for support. A line had formed behind her. Stan stood at the back, waiting to pick up his monthly allotment of beta-blockers to control his high blood pressure. "She said that everything would be taken care of."

"Well," the pharmacist said, frowning, "she apparently doesn't understand the paperwork. Your husband's plan doesn't include brand-name medication of this nature."

"Of this price, you mean?" The old lady's unexpected barb visibly rattled the pharmacist. "If you would just call the doctor, I am sure that they could straighten all this out."

"It's not our policy, ma'am," he said, dismissing her. "I have other customers."

"What about this prescription? My husband needs it...."

"I've told you what to do, ma'am."

"But it's after hours—I don't know if I'll be able to get anyone at the office...."

"Next, please."

Stan slipped the glasses the salesman had given him out of his pocket. Through their telling lenses, he saw the slate gray hue of the pharmacist's flesh, the featureless expression which lacked both eyes and ears. There he stood, a monument to indifference, a cold, marble sculpture completely devoid of compassion and empathy.

When Stan reached the counter, he read the pharmacist's nametag and made a mental note of it for future use.

"So," Stan said, "You're selling religion...."

"Oh, no, Stan: Religion isn't something you can acquire through some form of business transaction." The salesman shook his head, frowning at the very thought of it. "You either have religion or you don't. You can't pick it off a clearance shelf at the outlet mall any more than I can peddle it door to door."

"What then? Exercise equipment? I'm sorry to disappoint you, but I don't need...."

"Wrong again, Stan, but I'll give you points for trying." The salesman sat down again, retrieving a notepad from his breast pocket. Simultaneously, he produced a small carrying case that he placed at the precise center of the table, opening it with a moderate tap and revealing a pair of tortoise-shell horn-rimmed glasses with unusually thick, smoky lenses. "I do hope you'll forgive the outdated style. What they lack in aesthetics they make up for in utility."

"Glasses? You want to sell me a pair of reading glasses?"

"Absolutely not," The salesman kept one finger hovering above the glasses, the digit swaying gracefully from side to side to affect an almost hypnotic phenomenon. He scribbled a few lines on his notepad, glancing at Stan occasionally as if recording certain physical traits and general impressions he deemed worthy of cataloging. "No, sir. In fact, these are our gift to you." He paused, dropping his pen. "Doesn't seem like much of a gift at face value, does it, Stan?"

"Not really."

"You'd be surprised at just how valuable those glasses can be. And by value, I mean fiscal value," the salesman said, a decidedly sly smile spreading over his face. "You see, my organization seeks out individuals with acute observational skills—expert insight and acuity regarding the human condition. We consider your gift of perception a valuable resource, and we would like to take advantage of it. What's more," the salesman said, narrowing his eyes to accentuate his offer, "we intend to compensate you for your contributions."

"I already have a job," Stan said. "I enjoy what I do."

"That may well be, Stan." The salesman nestled his chin into the palm of his right hand. His index finger tapped the pallid flesh of his cheek as he considered his next line of reasoning. "It's really a pity, you know. A man like you, thrifty, prudent, spending years saving money. Yet, here you are. You've come to a realization in the last few months, haven't you, Stan? You can't afford this place anymore, can you?"

"I've never missed a mortgage payment," Stan said coldly, all trace of affability abruptly obliterated. The salesman suddenly reminded him of those covetous bankers questioning his ability to match the annual rate increases. "I'll decide when it's time to put this place up for sale."

"I think you already have, Stan," the salesman said, allowing his gaze to wander around the room, mocking the interest of prospective buyers. "Maybe you haven't been completely truthful with yourself about the decision, but I think that you've already made it. Rising property taxes, increasing insurance rates—it's a disgrace that an honest, sensible, practical man like you can't even manage to preserve the American dream."

"Times are tough," Stan said, echoing the resilience of generations of Americans who'd faced similar hardships. "Things will get better."

Greed
Saturday, 8:17 a.m.

"I'm sorry, Stan." Lou Masters had worked with Stan for years, refinancing his mortgage and monitoring his IRAs. "Looks like this market has just priced you out. As your financial advisor, I think that it would be prudent of you to start shopping around for more affordable housing."

"This is my house we're talking about, Lou—I practically built it." Stan sat across from Lou in a booth at a local eatery, waiting for a stack of pancakes and a pile of bacon. Two coffee cups discharged strands of ethereal steam that quickly dissipated in the dry, cool air. "There must be something that you can do—shift money around, extend the mortgage. What have I been paying for all these years?"

"You watch the news: The bubble's burst, Stan. Hit this

market particularly hard." Lou sipped coffee without shifting his eyes. "Home values are falling, taxes continue to rise, and insurance rates are skyrocketing." Lou maintained a casual but professional relationship with each of his clients, remaining strictly detached in situations that pitted the bottom line of his institution against the wishes of its patrons. "It's business," Lou said, siding with the bank. The institution boasted a genial and accommodating attitude in its omnipresent advertising campaign, but when it came to actually helping people—particularly in times of economic hardship—it was merciless. "And you don't want to risk a foreclosure. Get out from under it now, while you still can."

"That wasn't really what I wanted to hear from you this morning, Lou." Stan did not bother with the glasses—he needed no validation. He pulled out the form he had been carrying around for the last 16 hours and jotted down Lou's name. He looked up in time to see the inquisitive look on his financial advisor's face. "It's nothing," Stan said. "It's just business."

"Such composure and optimism—it's truly admirable to see such traits in an age of rampant cynicism and negativity. Let me reward you, Stan. Let me make a proposition I believe you'll find quite agreeable."

The salesman paused, waiting for any sign of lingering opposition. Stan leaned back in the dining room chair, folded his arms, and pursed his lips. The reality of his financial situation had, in fact, kept him up nights as his mind raced over fiscal scenarios. No matter how he juggled his budget, though, he had concluded that eventually he would have to put the house up for sale—move out of the county entirely and find some place where the cost of living would not bleed a man dry of both his savings and his hope.

"I'll take your silence as an acknowledgement of interest, then," the salesman finally said, sliding some paperwork across the clean, polished walnut of the dining room table. "It's all quite simple, actually," he continued, reading from a prepared statement that had evidently been composed by wary attorneys. "We seek a specific class of transgressors and malefactors for a combination of institutional castigation and cultivation. Due to certain contractual obligations, my organization is unable to directly accumulate these subjects and therefore enlists the willing assistance of an intermediary scout, hereafter referred to as the liaison. The liaison shall accrue the names of seven subjects deemed of interest to the organization, one in each of the following categories: *luxuria, gula, avaritia, acedia, ira, invidia* and *superbia*. In return for providing these leads, the liaison will be remunerated. The amount of recompense will be no less than $1 million, payable in gold bullion, to be disbursed when the liaison has fulfilled his obligations to the organization. The contract between you and the organization will be considered null and void if the liaison fails to fulfill his obligations, provides unsatisfactory information, or withholds an identity due to a conflict of interest."

Wrath
Saturday, 11:47 a.m.

It had been easy so far. His nominees had exposed themselves without much effort, without any hesitation. Stan had basically placed himself in civic situations—some routine, some disreputable—and all the reprobates had emerged.

Just like upending a rotten log in the forest to uncover a host of vermin, society's underbelly swarmed with perverts and self-servers and junkies and bullies and cheats. Stan had always known this, had always been keenly aware of the unbridled carnality and corruption plaguing the world. It had always sickened him and kept him from forming lasting relationships. His understanding of human nature had brought about his early conversion to the religion of misanthropy.

Next on the list, wrath, immediately called to mind its most fanatical progeny, murder. At its core, though, Stan recognized something more fundamental, more universal, particularly in today's rushed environment. Wrath, Stan realized, often grew from impatience with the due process of law, be it the law of the land or the laws of the universe. That impatience bred impulsiveness, intolerance, and vigilantism.

Sitting in a traffic jam on the interstate system that dissected his town and drove adjacent property values deep into the ground, Stan found himself surrounded by routinely calm individuals overcome with rashness, aggravation, and antagonism. Delayed drivers pounded dashboards with their fists, uttered profanities, and made irreverent gestures. Some stewed quietly, their exasperation building beneath the flesh as they stockpiled their compounding road rage in shadowy corners that would eventually erupt in a fit of anger channeled at some unsuspecting spouse or child.

Watching them through the glasses, watching them writhe and squirm in flames fanned by their own fury, Stan felt no remorse for them at all.

Stan picked the most vocal of the bunch, recorded the make and model of his car, and noted the license plate number.

"If you want to pay me a million bucks for a list of names," Stan said, tempering his enthusiasm, "I'm in—assuming this isn't some kind of scam. The only problem is I didn't quite catch all those fancy categories you rattled off."

"First, Stan, it's no scam. I'm not phishing for personal account information, a Social Security number, or your mother's maiden name—we need none of that to proceed. There's no investment required, no buy-in to some employment scheme or pyramid deal. You just use your powers of observation to find seven candidates within the specified amount of time." The salesman signed and dated the contract from which he had just read the primary requirements of the agreement. "As far as the categories, the sheet of paper in front of you lists them in more modern terminology. Even if you're not a particularly religious man, I think you'll recognize them as the Seven Deadly Sins."

"Oh," Stan stammered, glancing at the form on the table. Like a worksheet, it listed each sin followed by a blank space that he would have to complete with the name of the sinner. In order, the sins included lust, gluttony, greed, sloth, wrath, envy and pride. "Yes," he said, scanning the document, "I get it now."

"Our prospective liaisons often ask the same questions, so I can probably clear up any uncertainties you have with a few additional bits of information. You needn't fill them out in order; a full name is preferred, but, if unavailable, a partial name or even the precise time and place where you witnessed the individual will suffice; your name will not be published and will not be made known to those you select; and your acceptance of the payment on completion of your obligations will not constitute an act of greed on your part, since you were approached by our organization—however, I strongly recommend that you don't inquire about further employment." The salesman sat back in his chair, having completed his well-practiced spiel. He pushed the contract across the table toward Stan. "A few more tips: People always think *fat* for gluttony, but alcohol and drug addiction are just as much forms of gluttony as excessive consumption. People always think *lazy* for sloth; apathy is a far more destructive derivation of sloth than lethargy."

Envy
Saturday, 2:45 p.m.

Stan stared at the blank spaces on the form. He could not remember exactly what time the salesman had come calling the previous afternoon—had it been 3 p.m.? 4 p.m.? Everything else had fallen into place so easily, so perfectly, so decisively, that he wondered why something as simple as envy could cause him so much angst.

Dante described it as the "love of one's own good perverted to a desire to deprive other men of theirs," according to Stan's spur-of-the-moment Web search—the results validated his understanding of the concept without offering much inspiration. For the first time, Stan felt pressed for time and on the verge of defeat. The other sins evoked certain stereotypes that presented ample aspirants among the iniquitous, nefarious folk that populated his town. Envy, though, seemed much more abstract and ultimately less evil than its more destructive cousins.

Envy, nurtured to fruition, might make a jealous man commit an act of vandalism against a neighbor with superior material possessions; might make a covetous loner stalk the object of his desire; might sour friendships, disintegrate marriages and impair familial relationships.

Stan glanced at a portrait of his family, taken when he was still just a teenager. His younger brother, Stephen, had not spoken to him in years. He had always complained their parents favored Stan, provided Stan with more affection and rewarded Stan's achievements with enhanced praise, exceptional attention, and excessive significance.

Stephen had been consumed by envy and had spent his lifetime using it as an excuse to veil his own mediocrity.

Stan looked at the photograph sitting on the nearby credenza, this time through the glasses. The vision he saw repulsed him: Even at that young age, the spite and resentment had begun to disfigure Stephen, transforming him into a shadow-like effigy of his older brother.

Reluctantly, Stan scribbled his name on the form.

"What about these?" Stan tapped the glasses sitting in the center of the table.

"I almost forgot," the salesman said, slapping his forehead

with the palm of his hand. "These glasses will help you by validating your selections. Don't use them unless you're relatively certain, because the effect is quite unsettling."

Lust
Friday, 4:56 p.m.

The salesman had concluded their dealings with a firm handshake and a promise to return in 24 hours. Stan watched as he walked down the sidewalk, rounded the corner, and disappeared.

Next door, his neighbor hovered over a flowerbed. Petunias poked out from a covering of cypress mulch, swaying eagerly as she watered them with the garden hose.

He felt the glasses in his hand, felt them burning his flesh as if urging him to use them. The compulsion stirred him, even though he needed no confirmation of her sin. The whole street knew how she had cheated on her husband. It gossiped still about the strangers she brought back to her place in the dead of night.

Looking at the ground, he hooked the frames over his ears. The bridge sat snugly on his nose.

When he looked up into her yard, what he saw made him gag a little. Covered head to toe in the filth of her numerous lovers, she stood naked to the world, a mass of swollen breasts and cracked lips and writhing black tentacles sprouting from a copious number of extraneous orifices.

Stan staggered back inside, pulled the glasses off his face, and let them fall to the carpeted floor.

After regaining his composure, he scrawled her name on the form the salesman had provided.

"Well," Stan said, looking over the contract. He scratched his upper lip as he rationalized his decision. He only had to collect the names of those who had committed sins, after all. Pointing out the immorality of others seemed a passive activity at best, particularly compared to the zeal with which organized religions upheld their own ideals through ostracism, persecution, and the occasional witch hunt. "Where do I sign?"

"At the very bottom," the salesman said, smiling. "But first, the only stipulation we have not discussed is the time frame. Each liaison generally requires a different amount of time to fulfill the obligations. How long do you believe it will take you to come up with seven names?"

"I don't know; shouldn't take too long," Stan said, boasting. Considering the number of sins reported daily on the local news and in the newspapers and considering the fact that he could pin a sin on two or three of his own neighbors, his confidence redoubled. "What's the normal time?"

"It averages anywhere from a week to a few months," the salesman said. "Had one fellow recently who managed to get all of his names within 48 hours."

"I could do it in less, I bet," Stan said, his competitiveness getting the best of him. "Let's say 24 hours."

"Very well," the salesman said, watching as Stan signed the contract. "I'll see you in 24 hours, Stan."

Pride
Saturday, 3:35 p.m.

Stan shambled out of the bathroom, the preternatural glasses abandoned on the terrazzo floor near the edge of the bathtub, at least one lens shattered. The salesman's insistent knocking had finally stirred him from his humiliation, reaching some part of him that still believed a reprieve might be possible.

"Time's up, Stan," the salesman said, barging inside the moment the door opened. His presumption and audacity would have solicited a stern reprimand from Stan on any other day, but today he found himself incapable of putting up a struggle. "Let's see how well you've done. Where is your list?"

"There," Stan said, pointing to the coffee table in the living room. The pen with which he had added his brother's name to the list sat dormant alongside the piece of paper. "I'm not finished," he said, the words spilling awkwardly over his lips. "I've only been able to get six names...."

"Oh, come now, Stan," the salesman said, "I'm sure you've got the seventh name ... I'll be happy to give you a moment to add it to the list."

"No ... I ... there's nothing more," Stan said, sounding nervous. "Only six, that's all."

"Strange," the salesman said, reviewing the names on the list. "The only one missing is pride. Are you sure you haven't managed to find anyone that might fit that category?"

"I couldn't," Stan stammered.

"Well, this is unfortunate," the salesman said. "Not only have you failed to meet your obligations by not finding seven candidates, you have also withheld a name due to a conflict of interest."

"What are you talking about?"

"Stan, your glasses transmitted every sin you beheld, every soul you scrutinized." The salesman eased himself onto the sofa, his fingers toying with the drapery covering the front window. "I watched as you judged them all, watched as you ferreted them out like the parasites they are. You lived up to your potential ... until you stumbled over your own pride. I know what you saw in the mirror."

"What will happen to me now?" Stan had never realized just how discriminatory he had become. What had been academic dignity in school had become arrogance in adulthood. What had been attention to personal fitness in his youth had become narcissism in middle age. What had been a predisposition for virtue and decency as an adult had become unwarranted righteousness and elitism in his later years. "Will you add my name to the list?"

"Of course not, Stan—I can't do that." The salesman picked up the form and scanned it, line for line. He appeared impressed with the candidates Stan had selected. "Shame, really—some very good contenders here. We've had our eye on some of them for some time. Some, on the other hand, are new to us." He wadded up the paper, set it back on the coffee table, and scowled as it erupted in a small ball of flame. "Look, I'm not the devil, Stan. It's not my job to track these people down and haul them off to hell—not yet, anyway. So relax."

"That's it?"

"That's it. I'm sorry about the money; I know you could have used it." The salesman stood and showed himself to the door. "Good luck," he said as he left. He paused in the doorway and looked over his shoulder. "And, Stan: You might want to try to keep yourself off anyone else's list in the future."

Customs
Mark Rigney

Here's what Michalis said to me before I left Athens: "It's not Bulgarian; it's not Greek; it's definitely not English. In Macedonia, you won't understand a word they're saying. In fact, you won't understand, period."

He'd laughed, as if not being understood could in some way be a good thing, and then he pressed a fifty denar coin into my hand, a brass-colored disk a little larger than a quarter and featuring, on the back, a prowling, life-like lynx.

"For luck," he said. "An uncle brought it back last year. I can't spend it, so—it's yours. But personally, I don't think you should go."

"Why?" My Greek is middling at best, while Michalis' English is fantastic. Does this help me in truly understanding him? Not a bit.

"Jon," Michalis says patiently, "you have no idea why you want to go in the first place, and that can be trouble. Truly."

The train from Athens to Thessaloniki was amazing, fast and comfortable and clipping along through scenery that made my head spin. Cliffs and gorges and tunnels; death-defying feats of engineering.

Thessaloniki made my head spin the other direction. My own fault, yes? For staying too close to the rail station in a hotel both noisy and squalid. Worse, this morning's train is a not-so-nice train, an old junker ash-tray of a train. Literally. Ashes everywhere. The whole place, six coaches long, smells of slow, cancerous death.

The journey north is slow now; clanking. The scenery flattens and we crawl past it. Grass grows between the sleepers. I keep looking out the windows for mountains, but in vain. I try jiggling with the switches that supposedly work the air conditioning. That, too, is fruitless, and it makes the Polish woman who shares my compartment giggle privately when she thinks I am not looking.

Then the train grinds to a stop. We are at the border, the homey little station on the Greek side. The Greek conductors come by and check our passports. "Pass-a-porta," they say to me, as if bastardized Italian or French is the best way to handle the difficulty of English. I hand over my passport. One page receives a definitive stamp and the passport gets slapped back into my hand.

Ten minutes later, after the Greek conductors have stamped every pass-a-porta and disembarked, the engine snorts ahead, the coaches clank and bang, and my Polish friend lights up a Greek cigarette.

"Next one takes long," she says. She knows I don't speak Polish, and she doesn't speak Greek. English, her version, will have to do.

"How long?" I ask.

She shrugs and folds herself tighter into her corner seat by the window. The smoke drifts out of her nostrils and curls its way outside as if pulling her soul out with it. I resign myself to a long day's train ride.

It's less than a mile between the Greek side of the border and the Macedonian side, but the scenery could not be more different. Here the station is dilapidated, the plaster peeling, the reddish wood roof in obvious need of repair. The old wall clock lacks an hour hand. When the customs police come out, looking disheveled and possibly drunk, they straighten their uniforms as if they'd only just hauled them on, perhaps after sex or a brawl. They do not bother with entering the train; they merely walk up to the windows, one at a time, and bark out orders of which I understand, as Michalis promised, not a word.

The gist, however, is clear. I hand my passport through the window. So does the Polish woman. The customs officers take the collected passports and disappear back into their station building office. The wait begins, and this time it is more than a little unnerving because we have been separated from our passports, the little booklets that legitimize us, make us official and human and real.

The Polish woman is twenty-two. When she first got on, I thought she was thirty. Hard living, Poland. Michalis told me there's a filter between Poland and the sun that screens out all the joy. Contractors have been hired to scrub and remove this filter, but so far they have been completely unable to find it.

We wait for an hour. We spend the time reading glossy magazines; diverting but empty-headed drivel. No wonder we don't talk; our brains are filled with gloss. Passengers sometimes walk past us down the corridor. They are easy to see because the compartment doors have glass windows, and there are windows to either side of the door as well, alongside the passenger seats. When the people in the corridor go by, they sneak glances inside the compartments; we are like fish in a bowl. A dirty, filthy, ash-strewn bowl.

We wait another hour. The Polish woman is smoking again. I open the window wide and lean out, hoping to breathe fresh Macedonian air, but it is not Macedonian air at all, it is Greek air; the wind is from the south, strong and steady, and I can almost smell the salt of the Aegean Sea. The dry grasses rustle with it. The bright red-and-yellow sunburst of a Macedonian flag billows and shakes as the Greek wind passes through. The Polish woman's smoke gets ripped away, hauled off deeper into the heart of the undiscovered country ahead.

Another hour goes by, and one of the Macedonian border

police has sat down on the edge of the platform, cradling his machine gun and dangling his legs and, like the Polish girl, smoking. There are three empty, rusty tracks between him and our train. I have never seen a working station with rails so rusty.

I turn to the Polish girl, who has given up on her book.

"What's your name?"

"Maryla. Common name."

"Common name, beautiful girl." I let one hand lightly brush her ankle.

Her expression is frank, amused, her chuckle accepting. "No, stop. Look, the window curtains draw. Then."

I had not realized the curtains could go across not only the corridor windows but the corridor door as well. Privacy! That chore done, I tug off the Polish girl's skirt and momentarily forget her name. She is blonde with a wide, flat nose, and pale, slightly pitted skin. Maryla. Delectable. She whispers things in my ear that I did not imagine any woman would ever suggest.

Three hours later, half dressed and annoyed with the world, each other, and ourselves, we have run out of snacks, run out of water, and no longer have any feeling for each other's bodies beyond revulsion. Our compartment is sweaty and hot, stuffy beyond toleration. Maryla sits in a slouching sprawl across her side of the compartment's seats, and the sight of her sex is so sickening that I have to turn away.

She laughs.

"You look bad, too." She points, derisive. "What's your word? 'Limp.' Look at you. Limp like you will curl and die."

"I'm going to see what's going on," I say, and I haul on my jeans.

Maryla lights another cigarette and stares out the window. One finger absently toys with her left nipple.

I exit the compartment just in time to witness a fight breaking out between two men farther down the car. They are fighting over a water bottle: twelve ounces, flimsy. I don't know what language they're speaking, and I'm not sure it matters because the fight is in deadly earnest. Pretty soon the smaller man has the other by the hair and he slams his opponent's head into the sidewall once, twice, three times. Blood, oozy and red, seeps down the wall to the corridor floor, and the winner stands up and spits on the back of the loser's head. He then uncaps the water bottle and takes a long, slow drink.

I duck back into my compartment and lock the door and pull the curtains firmly across the windows. Maryla looks up, so incurious that it's only habit that makes her ask "What?"

"Are you sure you don't have any water left?"

"Sure, yah. But she does."

Maryla points out the exterior window over to the station platform. On the single rickety bench sits an old babushka-type woman, short and thickset, head in a shawl, fat black shoes clasping fat stockinged feet. She is eating a meaty sandwich, or something like one, and she has a grimy bottle of water at her side. My mouth waters just watching. If only the train would move, we'd have a breeze, but as it is, we're an open-air oven. That's just what a train is with the power off: A slow-roast of all aboard.

"I'm going to get that bottle," I say. "This is ridiculous."

"Wait," says Maryla. "Watch."

Down the train, another man has just stepped off our train, and as he does so, the customs officer rises, raises his weapon, raises his voice. Again, the shouting is in two languages and I recognize neither one, but the meaning is clear: The man without the gun wants to go the platform, presumably for water, and the man with the gun wants the other man to get back on the train. Now.

More yelling, then a burst of automatic weapon fire. The man from the train staggers back with jerky steps, then weaves forward and collapses face-up across the tracks, blood spurting from a ragged hole just over his heart.

I gasp, I turn away without so much as an oath. What can be said when something like that happens? And when I look out the window again, I see the babushka still eating, smacking her lips and sucking down water while the fountain of blood from the dead man's chest spurts lower and lower with each struggling thrust of his dying, punctured heart.

"Maryla, we have to get out of here."

She shakes her head. "We have wait. Is only customs."

"Only customs! We've been here six hours already, maybe more! A man just got shot!"

Maryla's face is resigned, detached. "We wait long enough, maybe I have your baby."

Outside in the corridor, there's a war going on. Tightly contained, yes, but a war nonetheless: The war for what we have left. I hear shouts, screams. Thuds. Running feet. Then the train itself jerks, heaves, and bucks. We're moving.

"Maryla!" I cry, probably unnecessarily, but I can't help it, I'm elated. "We're moving!"

"Not far."

"What do you mean?"

"They put us on siding."

"How do you know?"

She gives me that weight-of-the-world Maryla shrug again. "Where do we go with no passport?"

Turns out, she's right. A switchyard engine the color of spent coal backs us onto a siding. I dare a peek into the corridor so I can look out through the windows on the opposite side. I don't know why I didn't realize it before, but for such a small station, the adjacent rail yard is huge. Freight trucks and coaches as far as the eye can see, all huddling in the blowing wind, all dry, so dry that I desperately need a drink.

"Maryla. I'm going for water."

"Okay," she nods, and she pulls on her skirt. "But so jammed up like this, with one place only to go? You have, um, gun?"

"Are you kidding? No."

"I have butter knife. Knife and spoon."

I take the spoon. It's beyond absurd, but I feel armed holding it; I feel dangerous. I will get water with this spoon. With this spoon, I can get anything.

"For war, we paint," says Maryla, and she bends, smudges a finger into the ashes at her feet, the gray-white ash covering the floor. When she stands, she presses her newly black-tipped finger onto my face. She draws a circle around my right eye. I let her do it.

"Now you paint me," she says. "Paint me all over before we go on war."

I reach down to the floor, first with one finger, then with all five fingers, all ten. I scoop up the ashes and press them into the pores of my skin and then I rub the soot into Maryla's skin, and she undresses all over again, and I undress, too, and we fuck there on the black-ash floor, and then we rise, breathing hard and striped black like demented carnal skunks, and she takes her butter knife and I take my spoon and we spill out into the hall, feral and stalking, and we go in search of the war.

Most of the fighting has left our carriage and moved farther back, toward the last coach. We charge over the already fallen and fling ourselves headlong into the melee, me first, Maryla right behind, and the woman I tackle lands hard, too hard for her to react as Maryla jams the butter knife into her chest, but the knife breaks without doing any real harm, and I don't have time to look back, I'm grappling with a teenager wearing a Greek football jersey and I know that if I can just pin him against the wall for half a second, I can use my spoon to gouge him in the eye, I can scoop out his eye like an a oyster, an egg yolk, I can blind this boy and eat his moist wet eyes for my supper.

But I can't get a good grip. The boy is too slippery and fit and young and he squirms away, and my spoon clatters to the floor, and ahead of me a man looms with a real knife, the point sharp as a wildcat's tooth, and he lunges for me. I dodge by falling through the doorway of the nearest compartment so that the man misses me and falls on Maryla instead, and the knife drives home first in her belly, then in her neck, and she looks so—alert. Alert and surprised. Then I tackle this man, this killer of my Polish girlfriend, and I hit him until he isn't moving any more and then I throw the knife out the window because I don't want to see Maryla's face when I use that knife to kill someone else, to steal their water or yogurt or whatever it is they have, and I stagger back toward my coach, my compartment, and I realize that Maryla has written LOVE on one of my thighs with cigarette ash, and KOCHAC, love in Polish, on my other thigh, and I have never been so thirsty in my life.

I reach my compartment. I don't bother going in.

Instead, I loll against the window, desperate for water and hating that steady Greek wind and how it dries my throat, dries my tongue, leaves me licking my chapped lips as if the licking can possibly do anything but hurt me more. Outside, I see movement in among the endless waiting train cars, the sea of freight and passenger coaches—the many other waiting travelers, most hanging out the windows just like me, eyes sunken, tongues engorged, all keeping an eye on the steady march of a single lynx that's padding through the rail yard, carrying in its jaws a dead or dying mouse.

The lynx spots me, meets my gaze. Its eyes burn with yellow green fever-fire, steady and perfect and deadly and cold, and as I watch, the lynx gets a gulping better grip on the mouse in its jaws and starts to hurry away.

I watch it go from the prison of the siding, the prison of the customs yard, the prison of the train I thought I was supposed to be on, and I realize I would give anything, anything at all, to change places with that lucky, beaten mouse.

A Day at the Beach
Lawrence Conquest

"Just look at our daughter," Sally's mother cried in delight. "Isn't she the most *gorgeous* thing?"

Sally's father lowered his copy of *The Times* and essayed a playful wolf-whistle. "You're right! Hey—looking good, Sal!"

Sally Wallace wilted under the combined force of her parents' gaze. Their eyes seemed somehow magnified, as though pressed against glass. Sally felt uncomfortably like one of the pickled exhibits in her school's biology class. She hugged her arms about her and tried to hide her body from view. Sally didn't care what her parents said: she was ugly and she knew it.

"Don't squirm so, dear," Mrs. Wallace admonished. "There's no need to be embarrassed, really. It's a lovely outfit."

Maybe it was, if you had the figure for it, Sally thought. But why did *she* have to wear it? Sally had felt self-conscious enough in her old one-piece swimming costume, so what had possessed her mother to buy her a bikini?

"But Mum—people will be able to see my belly!" Sally cried. She cradled her hands about her midriff, mindful of its swollen size.

"Oh darling, that's just puppy fat," her mother replied. "You'll grow out of it soon enough. You'll see."

Sally wasn't so sure. Michael and his friends were always teasing her about her weight. They'd already managed to spread a rumour around school that she was pregnant. 'When's it due, Sal?' her brother would ask in mock earnestness, as if twelve-year-olds giving birth were a regular occurrence.

"Why don't you take it down to the beach, Sal?" her father asked. "Go on—give it a trial run. I doubt anyone will see you, especially once you're in the water. Besides which, Michael's down there already. You like playing with your brother, don't you?"

Sally scowled. Sometimes she wondered what planet her parents came from.

The midday sun glared upon the Hasting's seafront, fixing the scene with an unblinking stare. Sparks of sunlight glittered across the crests of waves, the brightness failing to penetrate the depths below. Here, summer was only surface-deep, a biting wind leeching away the heat from the day. Bright red buoys swayed gently in the water like inebriated clowns, gaudy and fat.

Sally strolled along the promenade, eyeing the human tide that ebbed and flowed across the beach. Would-be bathers trod gingerly over the pebbles that littered the sand, fully aware that their jutting edges could slice through flesh as easily as glass. Their opposite number dragged themselves from the sea like amphibians learning to walk, their bodies hunched against the weight of gravity.

Running parallel to these ever-flowing lines was a group of three teenage boys. Sally eyed her brother and his friends with distaste. At home in neither water nor land, the group had staked claim to the boundary that marked the shore's ever-changing edge. With trousers rolled, the boys stalked through the frothing surf like belligerent wading birds, kicking plumes of water and sand at any who dared crossed their path.

Sally wrapped her towel closer about her and descended the promenade. She steeled herself for the abuse to come, determined not to let their barbed words hurt. Inevitably, as soon as the boys noticed her, the cat-calls began.

"Morning, Fatty!" called Michael cheerfully. "What are you doing here?"

"Nothing much," Sally pouted in reply. "Just came for a walk, that's all. What are you lot up to?"

"We're heading up to 'Neezer's place in a bit." Michael cocked his head at Martin Little, a rotund fourteen-year-old who had come by his extravagant nickname after being picked to play Ebenezer Scrooge one year in the school play. "He's got a stash of lager. We're going to get right royally pissed tonight, ain't we, lads? You coming, Sal?"

Sally didn't bother to reply. The last time she'd accepted an invitation to visit 'Neezer's the boys had locked her in his shed and thrown spiders at her through the windows. She doubted any of the gang had access to alcohol, either. Despite being two years above her, none of them looked old enough to drink. The acne-scarred faces and patchy attempts at facial hair were a bit of a giveaway.

"What you hiding under there, anyway?" asked Donald Frick, a pasty-faced Scot with red hair and matching freckles. Not waiting for an answer, he grabbed ahold of one corner of Sally's towel and ripped it away. Sally did her best to hide herself with her hands, but the laughter from the boys was immediate.

"Look at you!" laughed Michael. "What the hell are you wearing a bikini for, Sis? You haven't even got any tits yet!"

"Yeah! Tiny tits, tiny tits!" chanted Donald in sing-song voice.

"Give it back!" cried Sally, reaching for the towel, but Donald immediately tossed it over her head to her brother.

"And what's with that belly?" Michael continued. "You look like a fucking whale!" 'Neezer laughed uproariously at this witticism, seemingly unaware of the rolls of fat that quivered about his own chin.

Sally knew better than to attempt to regain the towel. The boys would only turn it into a cruel game. 'Piggy in the middle,' with her as the pig. She ran away down the beach, tears stinging her eyes.

In her wake she could hear the sound of hysterical shrieking. Deprived of her company, the boys had turned upon each other.

Laughing and snarling, they whipped at each other's flesh with the stolen towel, deriving callous amusement from causing each other pain.

Sally trudged along the beach, away from the gang and toward the Old Town. The area was practically devoid of tourists, the original heart of Hastings now a ramshackle collection of residential homes and dilapidated antique shops.

Numerous upturned rowing boats clung to the beach like limpets. A ripe smell hung in the air as a few hardy fishermen tried their best to keep the old ways alive. They hauled their catch slowly up the beach, each bulging net teeming with dying life. The eyes of the condemned seemed to fix upon Sally as she passed, their mouths puckered into silent screams as they failed to gulp oxygen from air.

Past the fishermen, a parade of tall black huts ranged across the beach. The net shops were half-buried by drifts of shingle, their timber exteriors worn smooth with age. Closer to the shore, several large rock formations thrust themselves from the pebbles and sand, their surfaces pitted and stained a deep, dark red.

Bored and tired, Sally made her way toward the nearest of these outcroppings. Climbing the crest, she noticed that the departing tide had left a portion of itself behind. The hollow interior had been transformed into a stony womb, an oasis teeming with life. Nymphs and larvae swam in endless circles, while tiny crabs and flatworms stirred the sediment below. Rows of barnacles clung to the rock pool's sides, their off-white shells nestled in a verdant carpet of algae and moss.

Sally leaned further over the pool, entranced by the display. As she did, she began to make out the image of another form of life staring back at her: a young girl, ugly and fat, her cheeks wet with tears. Sally considered her reflection a while, searching for a single positive aspect to her features.

Finding none, she bowed her head, and a single tear dropped to the water below. The motion disturbed the liquid mirror, the ripples turning her reflection out of true. Suddenly, the girl who stared back at her seemed bloated and piscine, less a vision of a living girl than that of a drowned corpse turned pale from lack of sun. Sea creatures appeared to have nibbled at the dead girl's flesh, leaving curious indentations in her pasty skin. Waterlogged hair framed her head in a gently waving halo, insect life darting about its tangled strands. And below it all—inevitable, inescapable—lay a bloated reflection of her hated belly; a loathsome mass, swollen and huge.

And then the impossible happened. Her reflection appeared to loom before her, its dimensions increasing as if rising from below. Then the image broke the surface: first the forehead, then the nose, then the chin. Water cascaded until it came to rest shoulder-high above the waterline.

Sally rubbed her eyes, but the vision remained: a distorted bust of herself seemingly resting upon the surface of the pool.

Examining the features carefully, Sally could see that it was both a reflection of her and yet something entirely other. The creature bore the surface characteristics of humanity, and yet its features had been skewed out of true. Its eyes were gelatinous and set far more to the sides of the head than any normal human's would be. The nose was little more than a narrow stump, flattened out across a too-broad face. Puckered lips framed a circular mouth, an impossible number of saw-like teeth visible within. The creature's hair was really no hair at all, but some kind of segregated fin that extruded from atop its head. And every inch of its skin was threaded with scales, the wet material sparkling in the sun. And yet, somehow, the resemblance remained.

The creature opened its mouth, and a gargling nonsensical sound emerged from within. It raised one spindly arm from the water, the appendage studded with rubbery nubs. It curled the limb toward itself, uttered another unknowable word, then gestured toward the sea. Finally the creature threw both of its front limbs aloft and uttered an ululation to the sky that sounded both mournful and surprisingly musical. Seemingly exhausted, it sank back into the pool, curling itself around its own bloated stomach.

Sally knew that on some level she should be afraid of the creature's otherness, but its obvious distress struck a chord inside. She knew what it was to be ugly and alone. She gazed out to the sea, some fifty meters distant. Presumably the creature had been swept ashore during high tide and had become caught in the rock pool. But would the tide simply return and wash it away, or did it need her help?

Sally knew that the tide came and went twice a day. It was still early afternoon, and she would not be missed for a few hours yet.

She decided to wait.

Sally only realised she had been sleeping when the seagulls' cries awoke her. The birds were chasing each other through the sky above her, shrieking and cawing as they swooped and dived. Looking around, Sally realised the colour had faded from the day. How long had she slept? Was the creature still there?

She clambered back up the rock formation's incline and gazed hard at the pool within. Had she not already known of the creature, she doubted she would have spotted it at all. The strange girl appeared to be sleeping, a gentle flaring of her gills the only sign of life.

Sally wondered how long the creature had remained hidden in the pool, cut off from its own kind. She looked to the sea and was surprised to see circles of light moving across the water. In stately procession the ghostly circles flowed, ever onward, two by two. Sally imagined some eerie parade beneath the sea, unknowable alien creatures turning their lights upon the roiling surface above, and then cursed her stupidity. It was nothing more than the reflection of cars turning above the promenade; flickering illusions cast by their headlights as they swept across the water.

Sally shook her head and tried to focus on the here and now. The tide was closer than before but still a good fifteen meters distant. Perhaps it would come closer yet, but Sally couldn't afford to wait any longer. Her parents would be worried. If she were going to help at all, it had to be now.

Sally reached one arm into the rock pool. The motion of her hand disturbed the waters, her view of the creature instantly dissolving into a thousand pieces. The water was cool to the touch, the sensation washing the final remnants of sleep from Sally's mind. And then a new sensation struck her: something making contact with her hand.

Sally slowly withdrew her arm from the water. As she did, she found she was clutching one of the creature's forelegs. The girl's touch was as cool as the water, cooler than life had any right to be. Its suckered limb caressed her skin with a thousand tiny kisses, hundreds of rubbery nubs ebbing and flowing across its flesh in an imitation of the tide.

As the girl raised her head from the pool, Sally fancied she could discern a flicker of recognition in its alien eyes. She pointed out to the sea and the creature gibbered in response, its gills flaring outward like a chorister's ruff. Still clutching Sally's arm, the creature ducked its head back beneath the water, pausing a while as it drank a fortifying draught of the life-giving liquid.

Temporarily sated, the creature re-emerged, and Sally began to pull with all of her might. Combining their strength, Sally half-lifted, half-pulled the alien girl aloft, finally dragging her free of the water's embrace.

At once she saw the problem. The girl had no legs. Beneath her swollen belly lay only a scaled appendage that beat at the rocks with a series of meaty slaps. When Sally saw the tail everything clicked into place. She had heard of mermaids, though she had thought the creatures of legend were supposed to be beautiful. Was that why this creature was an outcast? Was she simply too ugly?

Sally soon realised that the struggle to return the creature to the sea would be impossible for her to achieve on her own. The girl may have been slightly smaller than her, but the extra mass of its bulging stomach made it weigh all the more. The mermaid's tail was useless for movement on dry land, and after every few moments of struggle it needed to submerge its face in the pool for another breath of water. The cause was hopeless.

Sally and the mermaid seemed to come to the conclusion at the same time, and each relaxed their grip upon the other. The creature slowly sank back beneath the water, its body shuddering from the effort of its struggles.

Sally gazed at the surface of the rock pool bitterly, watching as the ripples flared and faded.

It was over.

She had failed.

Sally's parents had often told her the importance of telling the truth. She decided it was time to take them at their word.

"Mum, I found a mermaid on the beach today. It was caught in a rock pool, up by the Old Town."

Mrs. Wallace turned to face her daughter. "Really, dear? That's nice." She didn't sound very impressed. She was busy washing the dishes, her rubber-gloved hands immersed in soapy suds.

"It's true," Sally continued. "But I think it's stuck. I can't get it back to the sea on my own. Can you help?"

Her mother smiled. "Well, it sounds like a nice game, dear, but I'm a bit busy right now. These plates won't wash themselves! Why don't you ask your father?"

"I already did," Sally pouted. "And he told me to ask you."

"Hmm." Mrs. Wallace upended a milk bottle from the sink, foam gushing from its neck in a spumescent tail. "There is another option, dear," she said, after some consideration. "Why don't you ask your brother? I'm sure he'd be glad to help."

Sally decided to bite her tongue.

The answer came to her at school the next morning, during a particularly dull maths lesson. It was obvious, really. She may not have the strength to carry the mermaid herself, but there was another way to transport it.

Two years ago a cold snap had hit the country, and following a sustained downpour, the whole of the region had been blanketed in crisp, white snow. Eager to make the most of the weather and the closure of school, Sally had pestered her father for a sled. The purchased item was still stored in the garage: bright red, plastic, and with a handy loop of string attached. All she had to do was take the sled down to the beach, help the mermaid onto it, and drag her to the water.

Sally was so relieved she couldn't stop smiling for the rest of the school day.

As she walked home, it seemed to Sally that the world smiled with her. She felt the first faint stirrings of adulthood, an early taste of the freedoms to come. She may be fat, she may be ugly, but she wouldn't have to put up with her brother's taunts forever. One day, she would be free. When she was old enough, she could cut herself adrift from the ties of school, home, and family. She could leave this town and go anywhere she wished. Anywhere at all.

She only hoped that, like the strange mermaid on the beach, wherever she did find herself, she would also find a friend.

"What do you want with that old thing?" asked her father. He was on his knees before the family car, his overalls spattered with streaks of oil. The car was up on blocks and partially dissected, its mechanical organs arranged before him on a tarpaulin sheet.

"I'm taking it to the beach," Sally replied, deciding to leave the details vague. Her parents had made it quite clear that they didn't believe in mermaids, and she didn't see what good the truth would bring now. Sally pulled the plastic sled free from its hiding place and winced at the spindly spiders that emerged in its wake. They darted about the wooden shelves in a panic of legs, racing over each other in their desperate attempt to hide from the light.

"Oh, that's a good idea," said Sally's father. "Say hello to your brother if you see him."

"Michael's at the beach?"

"Of course. I told him all about your fishy friend. He seemed very keen to help. He said he'd meet you there."

Mr. Wallace smiled wryly at his daughter as she raced out of the garage.

Children. Why were they always running everywhere?

Sally should have known it would all end in tears.

She heard the boys before she saw them. The sound of their laughter washed across the beach, undercutting the cries of the seagulls above. There was nothing warm-hearted or pleasant in the sound of their laughter. Just the spiteful sound of one group of creatures asserting their dominance over another.

"Stop it! Stop it!" Sally shrieked, but the boys paid her no attention. They were too busy torturing the thing on the beach. Michael, 'Neezer, and Donald stood about the creature in a loose triangle, cutting off any means of escape. The dying thing flopped on the shingle before them, its mouth open in a desperate grimace. The boys took turns to kick at it, goading each other on with a series of bestial shouts.

"What are you doing? You're killing her!" Sally yelled, charging across the beach toward them.

"Easy, Sis," Michael laughed. "Don't get too close; you might get hurt!" He grabbed Sally roughly by one arm and dragged her away. She struggled against him but was easily overpowered.

Eventually Sally's knees buckled, and she dropped to the hard ground. The mermaid turned its blood-shot eyes in her direction and vomited a pale milky fluid onto the beach. She wondered if it recognised her. She wondered what was going through its mind.

"Hold her down, 'Neezer." Sally felt heavy hands upon her as Martin pinned her down. She could feel his soft blubber shaking violently and realised he was laughing.

Sally didn't say anything when her brother rolled the mermaid onto its back. She didn't say anything when he placed his boot upon the swollen expanse of the creature's midriff and began to press. What could she say? She felt powerless, weak. There was nothing she could do now that would not goad her brother onto even further extremes. All she could do was hope for was a swift end. For the creature's sake, and her own.

Michael stood there for a while, posing astride the creature like he was some Victorian hunter on safari. The mermaid whimpered beneath him pathetically, squirming futilely in her attempts to get free. Michael ground his boot down harder and the creature's cries increased.

As if the noise had spurred him into further action, Michael suddenly hoisted his other leg up until he was standing with both feet upon the mermaid's belly. It howled in response, drawing a fresh round of laughter from the boys. Below the creature's belly, at the point where hips met tail, a rubbery slit had begun to ooze, the crimson fluid staining the shingles below. Something wet suddenly slipped greasily from the hole, and Sally hurriedly turned her face away.

The sounds of adolescent mirth increased and suddenly the pressure on her shoulders was gone. Martin had left to join in the fun. Sally turned her head to look one last time at the mermaid, then immediately turned away.

Sally sprang to her feet and ran. She tried not to think about what was happening on the beach. She tried not to think about the boys taking turns to jump up and down upon the mermaid's swollen belly. Her heart couldn't take it anymore. The mocking sounds of the boys' laughter followed her as she fled along the beach, merging with the mermaid's painful cries.

Eventually, she could no longer tell which was which.

Later, when it was all over, she went back.

Sally stared at the scene of violence and felt a deep sadness welling within her. The mermaid's body had been pummelled into the ground. Jagged pebbles had torn through its hide, revealing glimpses of the beach below. In death, the body no longer looked remotely human. What remained of the mermaid's caved-in face looked more like a bloated dogfish, while her limbs were flattened fins. The swollen sack of the creature's belly was now hollow and slack, the rotund mass having given way beneath the booted heels of the boys.

When Sally had seen something slip from within the mermaid, she had presumed it to be some part of the creature's internal organs working loose; some tuber of gut forced through a wound under the intolerable pressure of weight. The reality was different, and, in its way, worse.

Three tiny bodies lay alongside that of the creature. Three wasted childhoods, broken against the beach. The shrunken corpses were a curious hybrid of human and fish. The mermaid must have been pregnant, Sally realised, must have come ashore to spawn, only to find itself caught in the rock pool. Trapped by the departing tide, and then by her brother.

Sally waited a while as the water crept up the beach. The sea's approach was hesitant, as though bashful of intruding upon her grief. The boys had dragged the creature from its rock pool and killed it within reach of the water's edge. It was ironic, really. So close, and yet so far.

Sally waited patiently as the sea took the creatures' remains back into its care. Within a few hours the outgoing tide had swept the beach clean. It was as if the violence had never occurred. Some unseen hand had been at work beneath the water, smoothing and erasing any sign of the disturbance. But what about her? What internal tide could sweep her emotions clean?

Sally sat upon the rocky perch, the cradle that had birthed such strangeness into her world, and wondered at her own feelings. She examined herself delicately, mindful of the damage already done.

No matter how horrible the events she had witnessed, they were over now. The mermaid and her offspring had suffered terribly, but they suffered no more. They were at peace, buried beneath the waves.

Sally's brother and his friends would be untouched by their actions, having taken nothing but amusement from inflicting pain upon another being. Within a few days they would have forgotten it altogether, having found a new target for their endless, mindless hate. Only Sally was left. Only she would bear the scars of this crime.

Sally pictured the scene of violence and knew she would never forget. For her, the wounds that had been inflicted this day would never fade. She would carry them forever, bearing the pain like an unwanted child, never to be birthed.

Feeling the mermaid stirring within her, Sally clutched at her stomach and wept.

Uncle Alec's Gargoyle
Rebecca Fraser

It winked at me once, Uncle Alec's gargoyle. I was only eight at the time, but I'm as certain as I'm talking to you now, it winked at me. A sly, deliberate closing of one stone eyelid, in broad daylight. The rest of it remained static, perched on a podium of stone, all bat-like wings and clawed talons and grotesquely carved countenance of gaping maw and knobbled horns.

My mother didn't see, and Uncle Alec didn't see. They were busy greeting each other with their usual polite restraint. A kiss was delivered to my mother's cheek, her head tilted to accept it. Mother patted Uncle Alec's arm, a gesture that evoked more matronly concern than sisterly affection. I was subjected to the usual vague stare from my uncle although, if I recall correctly, on this occasion I did have my hair ruffled in the manner that many adults consider an appropriate greeting for young boys. The gargoyle positioned on Uncle Alec's doorstep stared straight down the front path with unseeing eyes, a baleful expression permanently etched on its ugly visage. I gave it a wide berth as I stepped into the dimly lit cottage.

It was mid-term holidays, and I had been flown from Melbourne to Tasmania to spend the duration of the school break at Uncle Alec's little bungalow, off the Channel, just south of Hobart. My parents were taking a trip to Europe; hence my sojourn. After exhausting the more attractive custodial prospects, my father grudgingly agreed that "the old bugger could be trusted to at least feed the lad."

I had met Uncle Alec before, when I was about four years old. He had made the trip to the big smoke of Melbourne on one of his antique-hunting expeditions to satisfy his penchant for the curious, unusual, and moth-eaten. The meeting was apparently unremarkable; in fact, I barely remember it.

The time spent with Uncle Alec that holiday was a combination of awkward attempts at interaction on my part and well-meaning efforts on my uncle's behalf to make me feel, if not exactly welcome, at least endured. It must be said though, for a boy of my age, that I saw and participated in some wondrous activities. Uncle Alec had a love of the wilderness, and countless days were spent rambling through the wilds of Tasmania's south. The Hartz Mountains were his favourite, and I recall trotting at a fair pace to keep up with him as he strode with an alarming gait along various rock-hewn tracks, pointing out the sinuous tail of a tiger snake here or the diamond pattern of a devil's tracks there.

At the cottage, evenings were spent in the dusty and cluttered lounge room, Uncle Alec reading from one of the voluminous tomes that haphazardly lined his bookcase and me, stretched out by the hearth, writing to mother and father, or perhaps flicking through one of my beloved comic books. On occasion, Uncle Alec would engage me in a bizarre show-and-tell of a select piece of his antique collection. I enjoyed these sessions immensely. Each curio was accompanied by a recounting of its history, and Uncle Alec spared no detail when it came to bloodthirsty origins. His normally stilted tone became animated as he described tales of cruelty and convict times, of d'Entrecasteaux's landing at Recherche Bay, of foreign royals and bloody battles fought centuries ago in countries whose names have long since changed. I believe Uncle Alec enjoyed this interaction, too. I was an appreciative audience; my childish imagination was fueled, and I hung on every word.

Summer passed, and I kept a vigilant watch on the gargoyle. It remained unremarkable in its immobility. However, its cruel countenance and constant air of malevolence, whether felt or imagined, kept me from enjoying the pleasures that the front garden would normally have afforded. I felt uneasy and self-conscious under its lifeless stare whenever I came down the front path, the furtive wink it had tipped me on arrival never far from memory.

One particular day, however, I was spurred on by the gargoyle's inertia and a feeling of self-reproach at my own lack of valour. On returning from a lone exploration of the nearby woods, I walked down the front path as usual, but instead of skirting the grotesque statue as was my normal custom, in a moment of brazen audacity I bent down and placed a hand on its flank.

I recoiled in shock and revulsion. The gargoyle's hide, which I had assumed would feel cold and inflexible, was warm to the touch. It had a repulsive, leathery texture, and a throbbing sensation could be felt beneath my palm ... the faint but unmistakable beat of a pulse.

I'm not ashamed to admit that I fled in terror to my little box room and remained huddled there for the rest of the afternoon. Even the smell of Uncle Alec's freshly baked bread, which I normally couldn't get enough of, failed to coax me out. I ventured down later that evening for tea.

"Y'all right, boy? You look a little peaked." Uncle Alec looked up from the book he was examining from the depths of his armchair. I was surprised to see a touch of concern in his faded blue eyes as he peered over his half spectacles.

"Yes, Uncle Alec, I just feel ... a little off-colour." This wasn't far from the truth. I had caught sight of my appearance in the large gilt-framed mirror that adorned the hallway. Looking back at me from the dusty surface was an insipid apparition that appeared to be all eyes. I was reminded of Smeagol, of Tolkien fame.

"I've got just the thing to cheer you up, lad." Uncle Alec closed his book with a loud clap and began fossicking in the pockets of the shabby, well-patched coat that hardly ever left his back.

"Voila!" He produced with a flourish a bone spearhead. Beaming with obvious delight at the latest artifact in his collection, he continued. "Found it near Taroona Beach earlier this week. What do you say, eh, boy? Must've belonged to the Mouheneenner people..." I let Uncle Alec go on. The fervour in his voice as he spoke of hearth groups along the western banks of the Derwent River was strangely comforting, and presently I decided I would make enquiry as to the gargoyle.

"Uncle Alec," I ventured, taking advantage of one of the infrequent pauses in my uncle's lively interpretation of Mouheneenner customs. "What about the gargoyle? You know, the one by the front door."

I wished I hadn't said anything. Uncle Alec's words dried up as instantly as if a switch had been turned off. His enthusiastic narration was replaced by a sudden "Eh!" that was close to a shout.

"Eh!" he repeated. This time he was up and out of his chair and standing over me. I cringed into the floor. "Why d'ya ask, boy?"

Frightened by Uncle Alec's sudden and fierce outburst, I stammered, "I, that is, um, I ... just was curious, that's all. It's so, um ... unusual," I finished weakly, not wanting to give away anything that would alert my uncle to my true feelings toward the hideous statue.

Noting my obvious anxiety, Uncle Alec softened a little. He reseated himself in his arm chair and regarded me with a look that I couldn't read.

"It is unusual," he said finally. "Unusual and very old. I'll tell you about it if you like, lad. It does have a story. If you can't sleep tonight, though, I don't want to hear about it in the morning, mind."

And so Uncle Alec told me of how the gargoyle came to be seated at his front door. His voice was low and careful, though, not like when he was telling me about his other treasures, and I had the feeling that perhaps Uncle Alec would not sleep well that night, either.

It has been many years since I sat on the threadbare carpet of Uncle Alec's floor as he told the gargoyle's tale, but the story went something like this.

A young seaman by the name of Etienne Fournier volunteered his services on the frigate *L'Espérance,* with the sole agenda of making his way to the Friendly Islands to partake of the affections rumoured to be generously proffered by the resident dusky-skinned beauties. Such tales were legendary in maritime circles at that time, and it was Fournier's plan to desert ship immediately upon landing.

Setting sail from Brest, northwestern France, in the late seventeen hundreds, *L'Esperance* and *La Recherche*, under the command of Bruni d'Entrecasteaux, traversed the Pacific following the route of de La Perouse, who had not been heard of since leaving Botany Bay in 1788. It was in the hope of La Perouse's recovery that the expedition had been launched. Assuming it would be a lengthy voyage, in the spirit of harmonious communion, crew members had been permitted to bring aboard a keepsake or memento to placate the eventuation of melancholy for their homeland.

When Fournier lugged the ugly, stone gargoyle onto the deck of *L'Esperance*, it can be supposed that there was much astonishment and ribbing from officers and crew alike. Fournier passed off the statue as an important family heirloom presented to him by his mother as a talisman to promote good luck and smooth sailing.

Fournier was an insalubrious character through and through, however, and the truth of the matter was otherwise.

A bawdy night in a local tavern had seen Fournier down a large quantity of ale. Mixing with a sleazy collection of vagabonds in one of the grimy seaport holes that attracted his ilk, a combination of liquor and boastful talk of his pending adventure had emboldened him.

Whether it was premeditated theft or simply an act of spontaneous drunken tomfoolery is not known. What is known is that Fournier staggered sometime after midnight toward the mouth of the River Penfeld, presumably for the purpose of finding suitable shelter to sleep off his hangover before reporting for duty at dawn. When he passed the sweeping stone stairs that lead to Château de Brest, it is presumed that one of the stone gargoyles mounted there attracted Fournier's attention. With no one to bear witness, it must be left to the imagination as to how Fournier carried off his prize; suffice to say it was in his possession when *L'Esperance* departed France some hours later.

Uncle Alec paused briefly and tapped his stinking old pipe. "You want me to go on, boy? It all gets a bit mysterious from here."

"Yes, please, Uncle Alec," I whispered. I was transfixed by the story.

And so Uncle Alec continued. It would seem that Fournier's fate had been decided the night he stole the statue, for ill fortune befell him ever after. He was an unpopular crew member and often fell afoul of the officers, earning him punishments of increasing severity. Among his fellow seamen he earned a reputation for untrustworthiness and was deemed lazy and mean of spirit.

The gargoyle had not won any admirers, either. Its unattractive appearance and general air of insinuation made it most unpopular. All claw and maw and evil stone eyes, it was declared an abominable creature and caused much superstitious talk among the seamen. Furthermore, rumours had begun to circulate about its true heritage and where Fournier had actually acquired it.

Nothing was ever proven in this regard, however, for not two days later, Fournier was found dead in his cot. His throat had been slashed in a very untidy manner. The ship's doctor was baffled as to the murder weapon, the incision not being the customary clean cut of a sharpened blade. Rather, he determined, it was almost as though the claws of some savage and powerful animal had done the job.

No one was ever charged with Fournier's murder, and his body was consigned to the deep. The gargoyle, serving no useful purpose, was relegated to the hold on officer's orders.

The rest of the voyage proved uneventful insofar as the occurrence of comparable events; however, one curious incident was reported. The seaman who was charged with transferring the gargoyle to the cargo space was possessed by a bout of insanity shortly after fulfilling his duty. Records describe the seamen *'launching himself pell-mell onto the deck, in the fashion of a lunatic and gibbering incoherently.'* It is documented that the source of his terror derived from the gargoyle itself, and that, on placing it in the hold, it had licked him. The seaman was naturally confined solitarily for the remainder of the voyage for fear his madness should be contagious. The poor fellow babbled incessantly of a *'long, forked tongue that flickered forth from the beast's chops and licked me bloody 'and.'*

"And that's it, lad." Uncle Alec relit his pipe. "When d'Entrecasteaux anchored harbour in Van Diemen's Land in 1792, the gargoyle was unloaded from *L'Esperance* and dumped unceremoniously. I picked 'im up from an antique dealer in Richmond some years ago now—glad to be rid of it, he was. Said something about it unsettled him. Can't say I'm that fond of it meself; ugly bastard, aint he? Still, I've tried to trade it on since with no takers, so 'til then, he can stay on the doorstep."

Uncle Alec stood up as if the matter was closed. I stood up too and made noises about going to bed. The story had greatly disturbed me, and I could imagine how the gargoyle's horrid, elongated tongue would feel grazing my hand. I shuddered involuntarily.

As I left the lounge room to turn in for the night, Uncle Alec called me back.

"Why did you ask, boy? Eh?" he looked at me with his head to one side. "Has anything ever happened—you know—with the statue? Ever see anything strange?"

I didn't speak for a long time.

"No, Uncle Alec," I answered finally. "I was just curious, that's all." I don't know why I lied to my uncle that night. Perhaps it was the thought of the unfortunate seaman confined for months. Perhaps it was the childlike mind of an eight-year-old fearing that Uncle Alec would think I, too, was mad.

Uncle Alec gave me a very long, hard look that made me feel uncomfortable and self-conscious. There was something knowing in that look, and my own eyes dropped to my slippers.

"G'night then, boy," said Uncle Alec.

We never spoke of the gargoyle again after that.

The remainder of my holiday passed in a blur, and it was not long before I was ensconced back in my family home in Melbourne. The gargoyle committed no further salacious acts, although I do recall once seeing a strange rippling emanate from its stony hide, not unlike the undulations a horse makes when it is trying to rid a fly from its flank.

Years elapsed, and I left childhood reminiscences behind as I commenced university and discovered cars and girls. My thoughts seldom returned to Uncle Alec and my time spent in Tasmania as an eight-year-old boy. Obligatory Christmas cards were exchanged, of course, and my mother would occasionally impart news of his well-being and undertakings.

It was, therefore, with some surprise that I cleared my pigeonhole one day to find a letter from Uncle Alec nestled among my usual periodicals and occasional letter from Mother. I recognised his spidery hand. Intrigued by this singular communication, I tore the envelope open as soon as soon as I reached my dormitory. Inside was a letter: a single sheet of bonded loose-leaf that was covered on both sides with Uncle Alec's tight cursive script, punctuated here and there by the telltale watery blemish of a fountain pen.

I sat on the end of my bed and read it through. Then I read it through a second time, and a third. It began with a polite enough salutation; Uncle Alec enquired about my studies and health, and offered perfunctory details about the weather and other such trivialities. What I read after that caused goose flesh on my arms and an unwelcome tightness in my throat.

...I'm just going to cut to the chase, boy. I need to know if you recall anything peculiar about that summer you spent with me—you were just a sprog at the time. Remember, you asked me once about that damned gargoyle, and I told you its history? Told you that I bought it from an antique dealer in Richmond. Thing is, boy, I lied. I didn't purchase it at all. I stole it.

Many years ago, I met a fellow drinking at the Salamanca Inn. French, he was, and an antique enthusiast, too, so we were well met and drank and yarned well into the afternoon. By and by he told me of his latest acquisition—the gargoyle—and shared the story of Fournier's theft. Swore up and down he was a direct descendent of his. He showed me the statue; had it bundled in a wooden crate behind the Inn, ready for transportation to France, its rightful home, he said. I thought he had quite lost his senses; even back then it was a diabolical-looking thing, leering and malevolent.

We said our farewells and when he had safely retreated back inside the Inn, I lugged the bloody gargoyle—crate and all—back to my old jalopy and drove straight back down the Channel with it.

So that's the story, boy. Not my proudest moment, but I was young then, full of drink, and thought it a great joke. The next day, with remorse in my heart and a rage in my head, I did try to return it, but my Frenchman had already left.

The thing is, lad, just lately the confounded beast almost seems to be looking at me. And I don't like the look at all. Once I swear it appeared to move. Out of the corner of my eye, I saw it, and swung round to catch it "settling" itself back onto its haunches.

I've been doing some reading. Turns out a gargoyle can remain dormant for years; centuries, even. You know what awakens them? The presence of youth. Youth, boy. *Such as in that of a visiting young nephew perhaps... What's more, they bide their time, gargoyles do. They watch and wait until they feel the time is right for vengeance. Fournier stole the gargoyle. Look at his fate. I stole the gargoyle...*

The letter concluded with a heartfelt plea for communication on my part: *"... a letter, a phone call, I know you're busy, but please just get in touch."*

I sat on my bed looking at the letter for a very long time before folding it and burying it deep in my sock drawer. I didn't like the way it made me feel. The unease that I had buried for well over fifteen years flooded back, and I was once again that eight-year-old boy, scared and vulnerable in Uncle Alec's garden. Indeed, so shaken was I by the letter that I took myself off to the campus bar for a fortifying drink. After several restorative beverages and an uproarious game of darts, the letter was quite forgotten for the remainder of the evening.

I fully intended to reply to it, I truly did, but the days went by, and I never could quite find the words.

You can imagine that it was with great shock that I received a phone call from my father some weeks later with the news that Uncle Alec was dead. Murdered. He had been discovered in his bed with his throat literally torn out.

All of Tasmania was agog with the news. *The Mercury* reported that whoever had committed such a heinous crime was probably an opportunist in search of antique valuables. The murder itself had been a most unpleasant business. The cause of death was obvious; however, forensic experts were at a loss to determine the instrument that had inflicted the fatal wound. The wound, it was reported, was akin to the sort of injury associated with the talons or claws of a wild animal.

I accompanied my parents to Hobart to attend Uncle Alec's funeral. Thereafter I stayed on to assist my mother with the execution of Uncle Alec's estate and the sorting out of his affairs. The bite of guilt gnawed at me relentlessly as I went about the administration. Had my presence indeed been the trigger that had roused the gargoyle? Moreover, I had lied to Uncle Alec as a boy, and, unforgivably, had let him down as a man. Perhaps if I had not been such a coward, Uncle Alec would still be alive today.

Memories of a long-ago summer washed over me as I walked up the front path of my uncle's little cottage. My eyes were instinctively drawn to the front door step, seeking out the statue that had caused me such consternation.

The tatty old doormat was still there, and the stone plinth. But of Uncle Alec's gargoyle, there was no sign.

Carrington Cove
Davin Ireland

They only appear with the outgoing tide, like vampires arising after dark. This is what Alan Wanless thought as he watched a familiar batch of middle-aged men and women emerge onto the windswept sand of Monmouth Beach that Saturday morning in October. There were more of them than usual, he realized, possibly because of the recent storm. Extreme weather conditions accelerated the coastal erosion process, causing slippage on the ancient cliff faces, and this is what lured the members of that otherwise hidden community into view.

Alan hated them all. He hated their petty grievances and constant one-upmanship. He hated their secrets and their narrow-minded pursuit of wealth. He hated their lies. But most of all he hated their competition.

Dressed as he was the whole year round in salt-stained waterproofs and decaying Wellington boots, he retreated from his vantage point at the brow of the headland and resumed his journey. There was little love lost between the professional fossil hunters who scoured Dorset's Jurassic Coast. All were loners, all suspicious of strangers at the best of times. Alan had often heard them referred to as the current century's gold prospectors.

He assumed he was no different.

Ruthless, determined, ambitious to a fault, he hiked the extra mile to Carrington Cove in under ten minutes. He knew that his rivals lacked the conviction to brave the mudflows and landslides at what was easily the nation's most dangerous ammonite bed, and he relished the opportunity to work the rockface in solitude. Alan didn't care about the risk. In his career to date he had been swept out to sea, engulfed by avalanching shale, and upended by slippery algae more times than he cared to remember. But he wasn't to be deterred—especially on a day when excess rainfall and pounding surf had hammered the coastline since before sunrise. The treasures such intense bouts of erosion revealed could make careers. And sometimes fortunes.

Pitching a glance over his shoulder, Alan left the road and paused at the cove's treacherous summit. Surrounded on three sides by salt-silvered cliffs, the narrow spit of sand below was strewn with kelp, broken stones, and a scum of pulverised shells. But he wasn't here for the view. Let the tourists have Burton Bradstock and Lulworth Cove, he thought, let them have Durdle Door and the Kingbarrow fossil forest. Let them grub for the brachiopods and crinoids of this world to their hearts' content. What Alan had in mind was a much grander project. For years he had dreamed of uncovering a really big find, something like a complete ichthyosaur skeleton or a plesiosaur.

And now the conditions were just about perfect.

Initiating his descent, Alan forced himself not to think of the giant shelf of rock that had partially dislodged itself over the course of recent weeks. He had stumbled across it by chance mere hours after another typically violent storm had swept the coastline. Since then he had returned each day anew to monitor its progress. And with each fresh visit, the tiny glimmer of anticipation in the back of his mind had bloomed closer to certainty. One more good battering, he thought, and it'll give. Oh, how he would love to go at the precariously balanced deposit with a four-pound lump hammer or one of his new Chrome Vanadium steel chisels. But such infringements were forbidden by the National Trust. The Jurassic Coast was a World Heritage site now—much like the Grand Canyon or Australia's Great Barrier Reef—and he knew that if he broke the rules, he could be excluded from the area for life.

And so, for now, he bided his time.

The protruding shelf of rock had, indeed, moved. Standing at the base of the looming cliff, ankle-deep in fresh scree, Alan could just make out where the underlying shale had given way. It wouldn't be long now. Maybe not today. Maybe not tomorrow or the next day. But definitely sometime in the coming fortnight.

He unshouldered his pack and breathed the invigorating ocean air. At his back, the retreating tide gargled and hissed in tune with the breeze. Well, seeing as he was here anyway, he may as well make himself useful. There were bound to be worthwhile specimens lurking in the crevices and rock pools of the cove, and one didn't succeed by dreaming only of that one big score. Dedication was the key, Alan had learned—not to mention a lively imagination. Picturing the massive cypresses and monkey-puzzle trees that had once decorated the primeval coastline, he began kicking through the latest piles of shale deposited by the collapsed stratigraphic horizon. There was plenty of it. Drifts of blue lias littered the sand, as fragile and abundant as autumn leaves.

He was about to select a promising piece when a faint sound reached his ears. A mewling, he thought. A distressed whine. He allowed the delicate shale to drop from his fingers. Not again, he thought. No way this is happening again. But of course, it was. Breaking into a jog, Alan skipped over tide pools and the remains of shattered boulders, feet sinking into the mushy sands of the cove. He found the porpoise stranded beyond an outcropping spur of rock roughly the size of a single-decker bus. It twitched limply in a puddle of water stained with its own blood. The dying mammal's broken body lay tangled in the remains of a monofilament fishing net.

Kneeling beside it in the sand, Alan placed a reassuring hand on the animal's sleek hide. He had witnessed all too many strandings in his time on the Dorset coast. Repeated exposure to the phenomenon rendered it no easier to witness. The porpoise would die. That much was clear. Even if he could keep it wet until the tide returned, its injuries—the result of being hurled repeatedly against the rocks during its entanglement—would kill it as surely as a bullet through the blowhole.

Alan unsheathed his utility knife and sliced into the net with a feeling of utter hopelessness. The marine mammals that traversed these waters were clever and trusting of humans, but they were also blind to the incredibly fine nets employed by the modern fishing industry. When it came to commerce, these magnificent creatures were little more than accidents waiting to happen. He cut away the last of the net and sheathed his knife. Now came the worst part. It happened every time. The porpoise tilted its head to peer up at him, a fleeting spark of gratitude in its eye. Then it expired with an all-too-human sigh.

The porpoise was gone the next day. Swept out to sea by the restless, greedy current, it would inevitably feed the next generation of crabs and lobsters destined for the nation's restaurants. And so the cycle continued. Alan clambered down the cliffs once more, nearly dislodging a gull's nest with his boot in the process, and took fevered notes on the characteristics of the jutting rock shelf. He was exhausted by the time he returned to the village, yet content in the knowledge the moment was drawing ever nearer.

Unfortunately, a less salubrious moment was nearer still.

They were there as usual, importantly sipping their cream teas in the café opposite the Lyme Regis Fossil Shop. Diane Kitchin and her *Logbook of Extraordinary Finds*; Brian Bellinger with his collection of Whitehouse hickory hammers; Colin Redpath, who was so inept that he had to supplement his income doing guided tours. They were all saturated and exhausted, their waterproofs grimed with generations of salt.

"Alan, old mate, take the weight off," Redpath urged, pulling out a chair.

Alan accepted the invitation with good grace, exchanging nods with the others as he offloaded bags and equipment. None of those who returned here for elevenses each morning did so out of a liking for their colleagues. The daily gatherings were a product of a pathological curiosity, a burning desire to learn if you had outdone your competitors. Or they, you. Today it seemed that Diane was in the ascendancy.

"*And* I found a nice little cluster of brachiopods down at Chippel Bay," she beamed. "That's another two-hundred-and-fifty pounds saved for the Easter bank holiday." She beamed again and drained the last of her cup. "Teas all round, then. My treat. How about you, Alan?"

"I'll have a coffee, please, Diane. It's very kind of you to offer."

"Nonsense," she said, "I do so love celebrating success with friends."

The others nodded in agreement. Alan couldn't bring himself to join in. He knew Diane Kitchin for what she really was—a whingeing, scheming, two-faced little cow who'd sooner stab you in the liver than share news of a fertile location opening up along the coast. And she was jealous of anyone who succeeded at what she perceived to be *her* expense. As they gave their orders to the waitress, Alan gritted his teeth and seethed at the memory of how vindictive Diane had been these last weeks, when her own finds had been uncommonly thin on the ground. Not a day had gone by when she hadn't bitched and complained about how the dignified prospector kept one's personal victories to one's self out of deference to others. It made Alan puke. Now that the tables were turned, she couldn't resist rubbing their noses in it.

Well, he'd show her. Just as soon as Carrington Cove paid off, he'd hang a framed photograph of himself and his find on the wall for everyone to see. Then he wouldn't need to engage in this petty score-keeping ever again.

"Alan?"

"Hmm?"

It was Diane, peering triumphantly at him over the rim of her cup.

"I was asking how your day has been so far," she said. "I didn't see you in the shop."

"That's right," he mumbled, "I don't sell to, ah, retail any more. Getting my own website, you know? Dealing straight to the punters from now on."

"Is that so?"

"Cut out the middle-man, eh?" Colin Redpath's shaggy head bobbed up and down in a manner reminiscent of one of those awful nodding dog ornaments found in the backs of cars. That was him all over. Platitude upon cheerful platitude, like endless layers of paper shale, ultimately concealing nothing.

Brian Bellinger, on the other hand, merely sat in his chair and stared vacantly out to sea.

"But I thought you were about to be evicted?" Diane was asking. She appeared barely able to mask her glee at the oversight. "I mean, I don't wish to pry or anything, but a decent online shop costs serious money, doesn't it?

"Got to speculate to accumulate," Alan muttered, sensing the shameful glow in his cheeks. Everyone knew he was penniless.

"Well, just in case you encounter any difficulties, dear." Diane lifted a flat sheaf of rock from her lap and set it down on the table. "You know where to find me."

The three men at the table sat and gaped. A perfectly formed infant scelidosaurus, barely hatched by the look of it, lay curled upon the surface of the rock. The quality of the piece was beyond doubt—not only financially valuable, but significant in paleontological terms, too. Diane, who hadn't stopped beaming since Alan sat down, broke into a cascade of delighted giggles. This was it, he realized, her *eureka* moment. And he was there to take the full brunt of it.

The other men whistled in astonishment, patted Diane on the shoulder, and looked on in bewilderment. Alan could certainly manage the last. His greatest rival leered at him across the table, invidiously stroking the gorgeous relief map of the fossil's ancient surface with her salt-raw hands.

"What's the matter, deary?" she taunted, "aren't you going to congratulate me?"

The following days and weeks passed in a haze of self-loathing and depression.

I'm fifty-six years old, Alan kept telling himself, *and I've been at this lark as long as anybody around here, so why is it always someone* else *who lands the big scores? I'm dedicated, I'm knowledgeable, there's nobody willing to take risks like me.*

This interior monologue continued morning, noon, and night, growing more savage and increasingly spiteful the longer the rock shelf failed to collapse. And all the while, Diane Kitchin revelled in the continuing plaudits. Even the local media were getting in on the act. They awarded her front pages and on-site interviews almost daily, with a growing rumour—unconfirmed as of yet—that the nationals were about to take an interest in the plucky housewife. Alan had to do something. If Carrington Cove didn't break for him soon, he would give up, move away, do whatever it took to relieve the unbearable pressure of his ignominy.

And then came the night of the storm. It arrived like a scene from a romance novel. Alan lay awake in his dingy bed-sit after an unsatisfactory nap, the useful part of the day already spent, a feeling of yawning unfullfilment settling into his bones. But something was different. The air had grown cold while he slept, and now it rippled the net curtain at the window, calling to him, beckoning him to rise.

He obeyed.

The skyline beyond the window was crowded with seething charcoals and menacing blacks—a maritime storm of the kind not seen in these parts since the previous century. And it was barrelling straight for the coast.

Still fully dressed, Alan donned his tool belt, his hammer holster, his photographic equipment, and—most important of all—a copy of today's newspaper sealed in a large Ziploc envelope. It was crucial he stake his claim at the earliest possible opportunity, and if that meant mailing a snapshot of his miraculous find to the *Times*, *National Geographic*, hell, the *Daily Mail*, if necessary, he'd do it.

The competition looked as if it were getting ready to do the same. From a grubby corner bathroom on the third floor of his building, Alan could just make out Brian Bellinger's ancient Lancia standing on its own in a car park the one-time accountant favoured because the attendant let him doze behind the wheel between tides. Alan could picture him now, gawping through the windshield at the approaching tempest, binoculars at the ready, empty thermos grown cold in his lap. He'd never met such a despicably dull man in all his life, but he couldn't fault the old boy's tenacity. Bellinger really lived for the hunt.

Well, so do I, Alan told himself, and returned to his room to await the inevitable.

He wasn't disappointed.

The storm raged from dusk till the last hour before sunrise, thirty-foot waves battering the little resort town in an unbroken assault that sent the tourists scuttling inland and the residents scrambling for their attics. Close to midnight, radio reports started coming in of whole areas of the coastline collapsing into the sea. Charmouth, Black Ven, Chippel Bay; the names read like a litany of Dorset's greatest fossil hotbeds. But Alan ignored them all.

Carrington Cove was his destination, and as the first rips

appeared in the grey blanket overhead, he hauled on his waterproofs and headed for the door.

The local devastation was considerable, certainly worse than anything he had experienced during his time in the area. Overturned kiosks, toppled lamp-posts, marquees swept into the waves. Talking of waves, the tide was coming in fast. Alan jogged the last hundred yards to the battered cliffs and started down without so much as a second glance. He knew beyond a shadow of a doubt what he'd find upon reaching his destination, and he wanted to avoid being overwhelmed before his feet touched the ground.

It took him six minutes and a grazed palm to reach the cove's sandy bottom. The collapse was everything he had hoped for. His mind reeling, Alan shrugged off his pack and lurched forward. It was wondrous, incredible. The giant shelf of rock he had so dreamed of had detached in its entirety, breaking into a trio of couch-sized slabs at the cliff base. He estimated there was an hour left before the tide engulfed it, and every minute of that hour was going to be valuable. Like nature itself, he told himself, fame and fortune waited for no man. He retrieved the lump hammer from the holster at his belt, and hefted it in his hand, luxuriating in the weight of it. An item like this would make short work of the friable Dorset rock. And if there was anything lurking in—

The sound was a cross between a screech and a subterranean groan, and it pierced the air like a faulty klaxon. Instantly Alan knew he was dealing with something far greater in size than a porpoise or stranded dolphin. Basking sharks and Minke whales were not uncommon in these waters. Given the right combination of severe weather and abandoned nets, the sea could toss anything ashore.

Not this time, declared a voice in the back of Alan's mind. *Too much riding on this one. The clock is ticking.*

Heeding his own advice, he swung the heavy lump hammer. Delicate beef shale exploded beneath the force of the impact. Thirty minutes later and the first section of rock, the largest—the one that had carried the bulk of his expectation—was so much rubble at his feet. He hadn't pulverised every square centimetre of it or been as scrupulous in his examination of the various pieces as he would have liked, but then he wasn't grubbing for ammonites at Durdle Door, was he? What Alan wanted, what he *needed*, would swing its magnificent tail out of the rock and just about knock him off his feet. It was that simple.

Only there was nothing there.

Breathing hard, he put the distressed grunts of the whale out of his mind and moved onto the next biggest deposit. The waves were lapping closer now; another half hour and he'd be shin-deep in sea water. He made a decision. He kept the sledge hammer hidden in a narrow crevice just a few feet from where he stood. Much too large and unwieldy for the job at hand, Alan nevertheless retrieved it and set to work with renewed vigour, busting the great boulder into manageable chunks. He ruthlessly pounded its heart to smithereens in search of concealed treasure.

Again, nothing.

It was as empty and barren as the daily conversation at the tea shop, and about as useful. Alan sobbed, released the sledge's handle, and rubbed his aching arms. The mental image of Diane Kitchin—or, God forbid, those other two morons—yanking prize specimens from Monmouth Beach by the barrowful drove him to redouble his efforts. But his progress was slowing. The adrenalin rush of anticipation was running down as naked desperation took hold.

Icy water slopped over his boots. Alan yelped and launched himself into a full frontal assault on the last remaining boulder. He knew from the diminishing cries of the whale that the tide would arrive in time to prolong its agonies. But only he could release it from the net. He only hoped they would both return home with their just rewards. Either way, he didn't yet have time to help or even comfort the ailing creature.

And then, as if scripted, the rock cleaved in two to reveal a shape—an angular knob jutting from the rock—that might have been a bone the size of his fist. A vertebrae, perhaps? Could this be it? With the rhythmic ebb and flow of waves swallowing first his ankles, then the lower portion of his calves, Alan erupted in a final frenzy of violence, his mind frantic with dreams of an ichthyosaur specimen to rival the one found by the great Tony Gill on this very stretch of coastline. He stopped only once, to wind and focus his old Nikon in anticipation of the great moment. Then, switching back to the lump hammer, he continued his assault.

The regular thud and crack of tempered steel on rock began to fade. The echoes reverberated around the isolated, rain-swept cove with ever-diminishing frequency. There could be no doubt about it now. Alan was looking at nothing grander than the fossilised remains of a giant cycad fern. It was useless to him, the final insult in a series of disappointments and lost opportunities that had dogged him these last months. Almost knee-deep in water now, his ankles sinking fast in sticky, mud-like sand, he flailed for the cliffs. Alan wept uncontrollably as he went, roundly cursing his non-existent luck and those who had conspired against him. The time that passed between starting his ascent and reaching the cove's summit was a blank. All he remembered was how badly damaged the cliffs had been by the storm and how little regard he'd had for his own safety.

It didn't matter. What was there to live for anyway? The wind still fresh in his face, Alan Wanless surveyed the endless seascape now that it was done. The incandescent glow of the post-dawn horizon stretched out before him, as did the shattered remains of his life. His tools, his specimen bag, even his camera were still down there, perched on a boulder the tide was doing its level best to consume. And beyond a familiar outcropping spur of rock, a prehistoric mosasaurus writhed and struggled against the confines of the monofilament net.

Alan's mouth fell open, and an astonished cry escaped his lips.

Tail thrashing in the shallow waters, the great beast—supposedly extinct these last 65 million years—rolled from side to side, a legendary forty-foot monster fighting to wriggle back among the waves.

Alan sank to his knees. Tears of joy and disbelief blurred his vision. *Holy mother of God*, his mind screamed at him, *am I dreaming?* As impossible as it seemed, he was looking at a creature that had ruled the oceans for the final twenty millions years of the Cretaceous period. Its reign had only ended with the same asteroid that had bludgeoned the dinosaurs into the darkest depths of pre-history. And yet here it was, right before him. Surely this couldn't be happening?

But it was, it so definitely was. Not a basking shark, whale, or giant lobster, this was the real thing—ejected from the murky depths by extreme weather conditions, stranded by modern fishing techniques, recorded by he and he alone. To unearth the bones of such a creature would be tantamount to a miracle, but to behold one in the flesh was, quite simply, the scientific discovery of the millennium. And it was worth *millions*.

Instinctively, Alan reached for his camera. It was gone, of course—swallowed whole by the incoming tide. His outraged screams echoed back and forth across the amphitheatre of the cove. Deprived of his recording equipment, it was all he could do to gaze on in despair. Hope gradually deserted him as the first of several large waves engulfed the writhing beast, dragging it back to the depths by slow increments. But its movements were constricted by the giant nets.

Sensing it might be permanently maimed and therefore likely to be driven back ashore by cross-currents and the next incoming tide, Alan began laying his plans in haste. For if fortune were to smile on him a second time, he'd be ready. Ready with pickaxe and sledgehammer to finish the job. Ready with digital camera and harpoon. Greed had denied him the ultimate prize once. That wouldn't happen again.

More waves followed. The weakly flapping mosasaurus was dragged ever deeper. Dislodged from the narrow spit, it turned and flicked its mighty tail. The gesture lacked power, and for several minutes the creature remained stranded. But soon the waters swelled enough to achieve flotation, and the ocean finally engulfed its prize.

Alan closed his aching eyes and felt the warmth of the morning sun on his face. He willed the coastal fleet to cast forth its indiscriminate nets, implored the gods of the sea to ferment the perfect storm. The pale relics pedalled by the souvenir shops were old hat now. Before long, his dedication and resolve would be immortalised in a way no slab of rock or dusty text book could ever match. Let them bicker about *that* in the tea shops on the shorefront. Who'd be the object of ridicule *then*?

Alan Wanless's insanely triumphant cackle rose in the post-dawn quite, and all along the coast—from Monmouth Beach to Lulworth Cove and beyond—people stopped and shivered and pulled their coats tighter about them without knowing why.

Companion
Rob E. Boley

It's dawn when I pull off the highway and smash a dog's ribcage with my Toyota Corolla. The thin edge of the night is sliding sluggishly into the western sky, and the thickening mass of day rolls out of the east. That's the direction I've been driving all night—east.

It's a wet Ohio morning and snow is falling in a speckled curtain. I exit the highway at the rest area just past mile marker 71 on I-70, and I have another 500 miles to go to reach New York. There's a mess all over the exit ramp that might have once been a deer—looks like bruised hamburger plastered with fur. I look away, rubbing my eyes.

At that moment, what looks like a German Shepherd runs right in front of my car. Its eyes glow in my headlights, wide as half-dollar coins. A leash hangs from its neck like a noose.

The impact sounds like a shovelful of dirt tossed onto a tin roof. I brake, and the Toyota slides and grinds to a halt. I look back in the rearview mirror, but there's no sign of the dog. So I keep driving to the rest area.

The rest area's long parking lot is bordered to the south by a patch of woods and to the north by rest rooms, vending machines, and a picnic grove. I park at one of the first desolate spaces in the lot—right at the entrance. Nearby sits a VW bug. Further down the lot, another half a dozen cars are parked directly in front of the main building.

I jog back up the entrance road, looking for any sign of the dog. I have no idea what I'll do if I find it, of course, but I feel obligated to look for the poor pooch. I find nothing—just frozen pieces of deer and bloody paw prints leading into the forest. Damn it. What if that dog had been a person? Clearly, I'm in no shape to drive.

Shrugging to myself, I walk back toward the rest area to take a piss.

A few minutes later, I'm back in the car. And I think I'm in love.

That cute little VW Bug parked nearby, it has a bumper sticker with a pink ribbon on it that says *Save the Ta-Tas*. A gorgeous girl is sleeping in the front seat, all scrunched up under a thick blanket. She has a dainty nose like an elf, and a tiny nose ring.

Try as I might, I can't get her image out of my head.

According to the clock on my dashboard, it's seven thirty-three in the morning. No, wait. I think I'm in Eastern Standard time now. So, it's eight thirty-three—about the same time that I left Denver yesterday.

Based on the weather report posted at the rest area, it's supposed to snow all day. If I keep driving, I might be able to reach New York before sunset, but I'll be driving the whole way through a snowstorm.

This might be crazy, but I'm thinking of hanging out here for a while. If I wait out the storm, I'll have an easier drive home. I'm not due back at work for three more days, and it's not like I have anyone special to come home to. The girl is bound to wake up pretty soon. I mean, the sun's coming out. It's daytime. I've gotta see this girl. It's just ... I don't know. Every trip I've ever taken, I think I'm going to meet someone, find a companion who sees all I have to offer, but it never seems to happen. I'm thinking this time it could.

I'm going to get a cup of coffee. If she's not awake by the time I finish the cup, then I'll keep driving. If she wakes up, I'll see if I can accidentally bump into her on the way into the rest area.

Is that creepy?

I consider calling my mom back in Denver to let her know that I may not be home until tomorrow and to see how she's doing since Uncle Leo's funeral. That's why I was in Denver, for my uncle's funeral. But then I picture my mom sitting in her family room, talking to and playing with Carl the rottweiler. She bought Carl soon after I graduated from college, as a distraction from her own empty nest. He has since become her favorite thing in the world.

Even at Uncle Leo's funeral, she seemed more interested in the dog than her own dead brother. During the eulogy, she leaned over to me, tears in her eyes.

"I hope Carl is going to be okay," she said. "He really loved your Uncle Leo."

Okay, new plan. I am now on my second cup of coffee. If she hasn't woken up by the time I finish this cup, I'm definitely leaving.

I spent my first cup of coffee trying to write poetry. It'd been a while since I'd written, maybe years, and everything I wrote seemed unfocused, untamed. The words were wild animals roaming the countryside—desperate notions of love and death. Some dim metaphor about the girl's nose ring and a constellation. The words needed to be fenced in. Leashed. Bound by a form or pattern—like a haiku.

Or a couplet.

I once had a professor in college, Dr. Loranger, who called couplets "the lonely stanza." For some reason, that really made me laugh at the time. It still does, in fact. I'm laughing right now.

"The couplet is the lonely stanza," she said. "Like a pair of shuffling footsteps trudging across a vast plane of white space." To illustrate her point, Dr. Loranger shuffled back and forth across the room.

It is now nine o'clock a.m. No, wait. It's ten a.m. The snow keeps coming down, though in no discernible hurry. The VW bug sits nearby, and the two of us are surrounded by ever-thickening white space.

After my second cup of coffee, I check the VW's plates. Turns out she's from Franklin County, Ohio. I trudge into the rest area and check the large state map pinned to the wall under a thin pane of glass.

Franklin County is essentially Columbus, just a few minutes away. So, our mystery girl is not a weary traveler taking a few minutes to snooze. She's local, so why is she sleeping here?

I imagine she's an actress. She just landed a role in a movie about homeless people. So she's sleeping in a rest area, trying to find her motivation. I bet she's driven by her work, often immersing her real personality into the characters she portrays.

I imagine she's an addict, doing her best to recover from a crushing addiction. She has lost her job, her friends, but not her dignity. Not the passion for living that makes her such an amazing lover. She just needs someone like me who has so much to give.

Maybe she'll want to come back with me to New York and start a new life. We can open a little deli together and sell bagel sandwiches and coffee. We'll call it Rest Stop 71, and folks will just have to guess why. We'll close at ten o'clock each morning so that we can get set up for lunch, eat brunch, and make love. It'll be a beautiful life.

It's almost noon, and definitely getting colder. I use some of my toll road change to raid the vending machines. A Snickers bar dipped in hot coffee: not so bad.

Passing back by her car, I consider knocking on her window and asking for a jump. I could tell her that my car has died and I just need a bit of juice. The problem is, I'd look like a tool if I came knocking on her window when someone else, someone awake, was here. So I walk back to my car and bide my time, waiting for the lot to empty out.

Know what? Rest areas are busy places. Busy, busy places.

Late morning through early afternoon, the rest area played host to a steady stream of travelers. A surprising number of them had dogs. Those people spent long moments wandering with their dogs through the park's snow-filled picnic area. It made me wish that I had a puppy of my own; that'd be a great way to introduce myself to her. Women love puppies.

It's now almost two o'clock. Finally, there is a lull in the traffic. The rest area is desolate, covered in snow. Some men came a few hours ago to shovel and salt the lot and sidewalks. But the snow just keeps coming.

I get out of my car and stand outside her snow-covered window. I brush a little bit of snow away, just enough to peek inside and see the glint of her nose ring. I decide her name's Victoria Wheeler.

But I call her Vic.

I imagine she's abandoned. Vic spent the night partying because she broke up with her boyfriend, a worthless, ungrateful bastard who couldn't appreciate her taste in music, which I'm sure is awesome, by the way. I'm thinking probably very diverse tastes with a lean toward dark industrial. Not moody, depressing stuff, and certainly not techno. Vic has a lot of energy. A zest for living. Anyhow, this guy changed the locks on her apartment. So she drove all the way out here to sleep. Only flaw I see in this story is that this is the eastbound side of the highway, and we're west of Columbus. Maybe she made a U-turn on the highway?

I am about to tap on her window, but I can't find the nerve. A pickup truck exits the highway, so I retreat to my car and snuggle under a blanket.

It is very cold. Very, very cold.

I pull the blanket up to my nose and pull my wool hat down to my eyes. Memories from last night blossom like muddy flowers behind my eyes. No, strike that. Memories from two nights ago. My friends and I hit the bars after the funeral. The girls kept feeding me candy-flavored shots. Chocolate this. Caramel that. Buttery something. I drank as much as I could, hoping the sticky medicine would help cure me of my loneliness. Hoping one of the girls would see all that I have to offer.

Sometime close to last call, I remember announcing, "This feels more like a wedding than a funeral."

Someone replied, "I'm glad I didn't catch the bouquet."

I can't imagine I slept more than four hours before waking up to drive home. By that point, the medicine I'd consumed the night before had turned to poison. My head was stuffed with gauze. My skin was thick with used vegetable oil, my eyes dry and numb, and the miles ahead were a weight on the tip of my nose...

The first thing I did after crossing the Colorado state line? I threw up and promised myself, "Never again."

I wipe my eyes and sit up. Interstate traffic roars past. The snowstorm has passed. The sun, now low in the sky and free from the clouds, casts an eerie glow on the snow. I must have fallen asleep.

Taking a moment to orient myself, I scramble out of my Toyota, sure that the VW will be gone. But it's not. It's now covered in several inches of snow, except for the driver's door that has recently been opened. I jog over to the car, peering inside.

She's gone.

A station wagon glides past as I run back to my car and grab a stick of gum to tame my horrid breath. The spearmint gum combined with the icy air puts a chill down my throat into my lungs.

I loiter in the rest area's main building, assuming that Vic's in the ladies' room. I really, really have to piss, but I don't risk missing her. I read the entire state map of Ohio twice before I realize she's not here. I even poke my head inside the women's restroom, just to be sure. It's just like the men's room, only a little brighter. No urinals.

Back outside, I shuffle across the lot, pondering what could have happened to her. Who sleeps all day at a rest area and then abandons her car? As I walk, my footsteps crunch on the salty sidewalk, splashing grey slush into the air.

I pause and stare at my feet. Of course. Footprints.

Jogging back to her car, I scan the ground. Sure enough, a set of footprints, preciously small, leads across the asphalt toward the woods. I follow the footprints, careful not to step in her indentations—as if her steps are hallowed ground.

At the edge of the woods, I stop. Maybe I've taken this far enough. Turning around, I stare at my car, imagine it urging me to return. To get back on the highway and continue my journey east.

As I make my way into the forest, I pause to pee, steam billowing upward from the melting snow. A few paces later, a set of large paw prints coming from the west falls in step with Vic's tracks.

The two sets of tracks merge into a couplet and head deeper into the woods. The animal's tracks are erratic, a weaving path with alternately shuffling and staggering steps. The beast must be wearing a leash, because a long, wavy line snakes between its blood-speckled tracks. I think of the dog that I'd hit earlier this morning. A wounded animal can be deadly. Vic might be in real danger.

I move quicker now, slipping and running over the uneven ground. Ahead, I can hear the snuffling and grunting of an animal, the swish of limbs sweeping over snow and dead leaves, the sound of a woman straining and grunting. Now I'm running.

Finally, I come to them, a hairy beast straddling Vic, its jaws snapping at her face. She holds the beast back with a forearm pressed into its neck and a hand clamped around one furry ear. I don't think; I just react. On the ground is a thick chunk of wood, big around as my thigh. I grab it and run forward, swinging with all my might.

Right before I connect with the side of the beast's head, it cocks its head to one side, probably sensing danger. Then wood collides with skull, and the beast whimpers as I knock it over.

I bend over to examine Vic, to make sure she's okay, and the beast bites my shin. Its teeth feel as sharp as razors. Imagining bite marks on my shinbones, I swat at the beast's muzzle with the wood. When that doesn't work, I jab the wood like a spear onto the beast's skull. Finally, it falls unconscious.

"You saved me," says Vic, her voice full of gratitude.

I turn around, gasping for air. My muscles are shaking, my body flooded with adrenaline. She approaches me, kneels down. For a second, I think that she's going to go down on me, and I wonder if I'm still in my car, dreaming. But no, she's examining the bite on my shin.

"This is a nasty bite. That was very brave." She pats my leg, just about the knee, gripping the muscle in a warm, familiar way.

"It wasn't any big deal, Vic."

"Vic?" she asks, now on her feet, an eyebrow arched. But then she nods, as if she understands. "Okay."

She leans in close, kisses my cheek and whispers into my ear. "What about you, Hero? You got a name?"

But before I can reply, my legs give out on me and I hit the ground ass-first. The beast is right in front of me, sprawled on the ground. Its ribcage goes up and down, and I see that a couple of its ribs are bruised. One jagged bone even protrudes from the beast's thick hide. This is the dog that I hit this morning, except it's not a dog.

The beast is covered in patches of fur as thick as attic insulation. Between the patches of fur, the beast's skin resembles a bad sunburn—blistered grey leather speckled with stubby wiry hairs. Its claws are bone—sharpened extensions of its skeleton. Its snotty nose is a chewed-up wad of steak.

"What is it?" I ask.

She ignores my question, kneels, and pulls a thick chain out of her purse. She takes off the dog's leash, clamps the chain onto the dog's collar, and attaches the chain to a nearby tree.

"How are you feeling?" she asks.

"I'm very tired."

I realize that my muscles have stopped shaking. In fact, I'm not moving much at all. I'm perfectly still, except for my eyes and mouth. I fall backward against a fallen log, my head partially propped upward.

"Do you feel a tingle in your chest? Like a butterfly fluttering in your lungs?"

I try to nod, can't. So, instead I whisper, "Yes."

"This little shit's saliva is poisonous." She nudges the sleeping beast with one foot. "The toxin leaves you paralyzed for several hours." She pulls back one sleeve, revealing a shallow bite mark. "It nipped me good this morning. The poison paralyzes its prey, so that the beast can eat you alive. Terrible, huh?"

"Yeah," I say. Except I don't. The word can't make it past my throat.

Suddenly, my chest tightens. There's a wet, raspy noise in the back of the throat as I try—and fail—to breathe. I'm choking on my gum.

"Whoa," she says. "You having some kind of allergic reaction to the poison?"

She bends over me, opens my mouth, and peers inside. If I wasn't paralyzed, I could sit up and kiss her. Despite the situation, that's all I can think about. How she might taste. She scoops the gum out with her finger, and suddenly I can breathe again.

"You scared me," she says, holding both my cheeks.

And suddenly everything's right with the world. She's my

savior. She's going to see me through this thing. I blink at her in gratitude.

"He bit me this morning, the little shit, on the other side of the highway. Fortunately, I was able to escape and find shelter inside that car until the poison wore off. I saw you there, all those times you stood outside the car. You probably thought I was asleep, but I wasn't. I figured you were some kind of stalker. That you were going to rape me. But no, you're what? Some random stranger?"

She pats my cheek gently.

Next, she pulls out a nylon case filled with assorted sharp objects—everything from razors to kitchen knives to scalpels. She holds up a stainless steel chef's knife, one continuous piece of metal from tip to handle glowing golden red in the late day sun. Next she holds up an old-fashioned bone-handle straight razor.

That's when I notice the slight movement beside her. It's the beast. First one of its paws twitches, then its dull yellow eyes blink. Slowly, it begins to roll upright. I try to make some movement, to warn her, but now I can't even blink. I can only watch helplessly as the beast sits up. Its snout is covered in prickly hairs so thick they might as well be thorns. Its eyes are the color of hardened mustard. Worst of all are its fangs: a mouthful of ivory blades covered in my blood. Vic is focused on her knives and has no clue of the impending danger.

"Hey, buddy," she says. "You want a treat?"

What the hell is she talking about? Oh, please. Please, Vic. Turn around.

But she doesn't. Instead, she shuffles over to me and unbuckles my pants. Is this the treat she was talking about? She's going to pleasure me right here? Now the beast is on its feet, staring first at me, then at her.

Turn around now before it's too late.

Thankfully, she does.

She turns around and pats the beast on the head. Then, humming to herself, she scoots over to me and begins scraping the razor along the length of my thigh. She swats the shaved hairs away like gnats.

"If I don't shave you," she says, "he'll get hairballs. Have you ever tried scrubbing bloody hairballs out of upholstery? Of course you haven't. It's murder, I tell you."

The beast lumbers over and lies down at my feet. Its eyes flicker over the motions of Vic's hands as she shaves my legs. A line of drool, as thick as gravy, slides out of its open mouth.

She leans over and spreads the beast's back legs. It growls—a noise like a rusty saw dragged over a dead tree—but tolerates her intrusion. Its belly and crotch are one continuous stretch of gnarled skin. It has no genitalia, no nipples.

"It's sexless, birthless, deathless. No one really knows where it came from. Some of the others—there's only a handful of us, looking after these beasts, you know—they think it's a hell hound that escaped from the devil.

"Normally, it's such a good boy, unless it gets hungry. It was my fault that it bit me. The others warned me about playing so rough with it. They said I'd get bitten sooner or later." She laughs under her breath. "So you thought I was in danger. Funny! I don't need a hero. I need food for the beast. It's just … it only eats people, and you can't exactly buy a can of people at Wal-Mart, you know?"

She's done shaving me now, and she puts the razor down. Now she lifts up the chef's knife, studying the blade.

"The thing everybody agrees on is that the poison not only paralyzes the victims, but also leaves them incapable of feeling pain. It's a mercy."

When she digs the blade into the flesh of my leg, it's as if a flaming tongue licks across my flesh. Inside, I scream. On the outside, I do nothing. I can't even cry.

"But we both know that's bullshit now, don't we?" she asks.

"Imagine my surprise when I lay in that little Volkswagen all day, expecting to be numb but instead feeling the day's cold in my limbs. My hand was stuck under one of my legs, and it ached something fierce all day long. It was ... hell, it was agony."

She cuts again, tearing away a square of skin the size of a piece of bread. The cold air bites into my exposed flesh, slurping its icy tongue along the jagged window of my body. I want so much to scream.

The first piece of me she tosses to the beast who swallows it nearly whole.

What follows is agony. Vic cuts coaster-sized squares of flesh out of my legs, turning me into a bloody checkerboard. She hums as she butchers and seals me into Ziploc bags. And I, I can only watch, my eyes pleading for her to stop.

She dips her finger into the pool of drool that has gathered at my feet. As she slides the drool-covered finger between her lips, her eyes close and she trembles, licks her lips. Her eyelids flutter open.

"Oh, that's right. I haven't told you yet about the medicine. You see, your poison is my medicine. It cures all illness, heals most any wound. Hell, it even adds years to your life. Plus, it gives you the most amazing feeling. Better than drugs. Better than sex." She leans in close, almost whispering. "And I've had plenty of both, so I speak with authority."

She's close enough that I good a close-up look at the bite mark on her wrist. I see the wounds fading to just a scar.

She must see something in me because her eyes soften.

"I'm sorry about this, really I am."

She leans in and kisses me. Softly at first, but then with greater depth and intensity. She tastes like strawberries and wine and something else ... Like warm broth, only—

Drool.

She tastes like drool. My stomach muscles are paralyzed,

otherwise I know I'd lose my coffee and candy right now. Pulling away, she wipes her mouth, smiles. She picks up her blade and returns to my thighs. But then she stops.

Maybe...

Maybe the kiss meant something. Maybe we've bonded, connected somehow. She stares at my leg, then at my face, then at my leg. She dips her finger again in the drool and licks it clean. Rushing forward, she kisses me again, her tongue licking at my teeth. I don't know what she's thinking, just that I'm not going to die. For whatever reason, she feels it, too. She feels the connection between us.

When she pulls away, the beast begins to whine. She ignores it.

"It's working," she says.

What is she talking about?

She holds up my leg for me to see. The checkerboard of skin that she's cut away, it's growing back. The saliva from the beast is working on me, even though I'm paralyzed. Already, I can feel the pain fading, replaced by an itching tickle.

"You're healing," she says, holding my cheeks with her hands. "Do you know what this means?"

It means I'm not going to die. Sweet relief blossoms in my brain. I'm going to be okay. She kisses me again. My cheeks. My mouth. My eyelids.

She hugs me tight, her breasts pressing against my chest. When she pulls away, my wrists are bound by handcuffs that I didn't even know she had. She's holding the chef's knife again, jabbing it into my thighs. A thousand needles of pain weave themselves inside my muscles and skin.

"It means that I can just keep butchering you again and again," she says, looking at me with eyes overflowing with affection. "And no matter how much I cut away, it'll eventually grow back."

She throws another chunk of me to the beast and wipes her

blade on the pants crumpled around my ankles. She shrugs and then throws another.

Why not? I have so much to give.

Lollipop
Jason Sizemore

The pale-faced little boy appeared while Mark sipped a beer during his nightly hot bath. The child poked his tiny, wounded head over a tower of soap bubbles and smiled.

"Hello."

Mark jumped up, sending a considerable mess of water and soap bubbles to the floor. This boy ... his head was sliced open; a jagged gash ran from the top of his left ear over the middle of his skull to the base of his neck, leaving a flap of skin that hung like a butcher's wrap over a raw cut of steak. Brain matter oozed through a small crack in the bone. A piece of brain dropped and made a sickening 'plop' sound when it landed on the white tile floor.

Yet the boy kept right on smiling.

Mark felt a warm release in the water.

"Oh man, you just pissed yourself, didn't you?" the boy asked. He leaned over and peered into the tub. "I used to do that when I was a little kid."

"I ... I ... what do you want?"

"Do you have any candy?"

Mark eyed the folded towel resting on top of the hamper next to the clawfoot tub. He measured his odds of safely hopping out of the tub, grabbing the towel to cover his shyness, and dashing like mad out the door of his apartment.

"No ... no candy, sorry."

"Want your dry hankie, do you?" the kid asked.

Mark nodded.

"Good, 'cuz you might want to get out of there, mister. You've got goose pimples all over your body. Next time, try some hot water."

Mark stood, shakily, leaning against the cold, moldy yellow tile that decorated the interior walls of his ancient brownstone. The ghost and the man stared at each other. They remained like that for several seconds, water dripping from one, brains from the other.

Around the urge to scream, call the cops, pray to God for forgiveness, and simply pass out, a twinge of remembrance poked through the mess of emotions.

"I ... I ... know ... knew ... you, didn't I?" Mark asked.

The kid nodded vigorously, spattering more speckles of blood and brains over the tile. "That you do, Mister."

Keeping his eye on the boy and his back to the wall, Mark gingerly slipped his left leg out of the tub and placed his foot on the floor, using a hand to protect his modesty. He eased the rest of his body out of the water and began inching around the visitor toward the folded towel, just out of reach of his water-pruned fingertips. With impeccable manners, the boy stepped over, picked up the towel, and offered it to the shivering, naked man.

"You're welcome," the boy said.

Mark wrapped the threadbare towel tightly around his waist. His legs wobbled, betraying his fear of the ghoulish apparition. *You don't mess with spooks.* His grandmother's advice, given to him thirty-something years ago, echoed in his head. *Because spooks always meanin' something bad.*

She'd been a practicing granny witch during his younger days, when he lived in eastern Kentucky. And ever since his granny's death from colon cancer, he'd seen spirits off and on, though it had never turned into a comfortable experience.

The bathroom air, once warm, humid, and redolent with a clean, soapy fragrance, now reeked of rotted brain matter and rank graveyard dirt. Frost began forming on the vanity mirror over the sink. The word "Lollipop" appeared as though someone, perhaps the boy, had written it with an index finger.

Mark's skin steamed like those tough professional football players who played during the bitter December afternoons on television. He folded his arms over his chest, feeling his cold, erect nipples brush against his skin.

"I know you. Do you know me?"

The kid nodded.

"You're Horace Taylor, right?"

Horace nodded, again sending blood and brain matter flying around the room.

Mark swallowed. Despite the steamy room, he had cotton mouth.

"Are you here to hurt me?"

Horace laughed. Not a spooky, ghostly laugh you'd hear in Halloween music, but the laugh of a gleeful child hearing something funny.

"No way. I'm here to help. But first I want some candy."

Mark looked at the word marked on the mirror. "A lollipop?"

Horace smiled.

Mark slipped on his night sandals and robe, mostly for the warmth. The visitor kid was refrigerating the house quicker than a giant bag of ice inside a cooler filled with beer. He walked from the bathroom to the bedroom, with Horace trailing along like a happy puppy.

Mark pushed down his fright to reach through his memories. Horace Taylor. Third-grader at Big Branch Elementary School. They hadn't been neighbors, hadn't even been friends, really, but they had shared the same circle of playmates. And to the annoyance of everyone, Horace had *always* wanted to be Luke Duke when they role-played *The Dukes of Hazzard* during recess. Never mind that Horace hadn't looked anything like John Schneider—he hadn't been blond or cute, even in that little-kid way. But Mark never minded because he had *always* pretended to be Roscoe P. Coltrane, and *he* didn't have a basset hound, so he figured that had made them even.

Slipping on his glasses, he glanced at Horace and shuddered. It suddenly came back to him—the horrible way that Horace had died. An 18-wheeler had run over Horace when the kid had chosen, for some insane reason, to ride his rusty ol' dirt bike down U.S. 421-80. U.S. 421-80, a half-paved, narrow and curvy road that served as the main thoroughfare for coal trucks traveling home to Hyden and Hazard after dropping their loads in Manchester. The heavy-lidded drivers drove fast, hopped up on caffeine and uppers, eager to get home after a sixteen-hour workday.

The collision had sent Horace spinning like a top, sending him flying forty feet through the air. His flight had abruptly ended when the left side of his head, just above the ear, had struck an electric pole, killing him instantly.

The coroner had remarked on the local news that it was a wonder the boy's head hadn't exploded on impact.

It was a major event back then for a small community such as Big Branch. The accident had even made the big-city Lexington papers. Mark remembered being interviewed by a female reporter about Horace. *Did you know that Horace had stopped at your house for lemonade just before his accident? How often do you ride across U.S. four-twenty-one-eighty?*

Granny'd told him that spirits didn't just show up without a reason, and most of the times that reason was malicious. His stomach ached with fear, but he faced the dead kid and willed himself to confront him. He even crouched on one knee, coming face-to-face with Horace, like he'd seen parents do when talking with small children.

"Why are you here?"

"Do you have a lollipop?"

Mark's left eyebrow lifted toward his receding hairline.

"You came back from the dead for a lollipop?" He mentally rummaged through the pantry for candy, but he'd given his last bit of sweets to his bratty nephew last week. Mark frowned in annoyance. He hoped it wouldn't upset the dead kid.

"You don't have a lollipop, do you?"

"I'm afraid not."

"Then I can't tell you."

"Tell me what?"

The cold intensified, causing the room temperature to drop below freezing in a matter of seconds. Frost coated the bed, walls, and floor. When Mark spoke again, fog came out of his mouth. He felt the moisture from the bath freezing on his body and hair.

"Jesus, Horace, please stop, you're hurting me." Mark put his arms around his chest and shoulders and shivered. "Look, I'll run out to the store and buy you a bag of lollipops. Then you can tell me your secret and be on your way."

He checked the clock: 7:42 p.m. Ignoring the staccato chattering of his teeth, he slipped on a pair of dirty jeans, a T-shirt, socks, and shoes. He didn't bother brushing his hair; it was frozen into short, crystalline spikes.

Sporting numb hands and a purple nose, Mark slipped on a jacket and went to the door. Horace stood on the sidewalk, waiting. With hands in pockets, he stepped outside the brownstone and entered the cool autumn evening. They began walking and together they turned left toward Vine Street, where Mark knew of a 24-hour pharmacy. The place would have plenty of candy for his crazy ghost visitor.

"When was the last time you played *The Dukes of Hazzard*?"

Mark grunted and told the kid he no longer played such childish games.

"I don't understand. You liked it the last time we played."

"We last played thirty years ago," Mark said.

"Oh."

"I remember when it happened. Your ... accident."

"Hey, do you remember that time when I was Luke Duke?" Horace asked.

"You were *always* Luke Duke."

"And you were Boss Hogg because you were fat." Kiddy laughter echoed throughout the neighborhood. Pedestrians turned to stare at Mark.

"Buddy, I was Sheriff Roscoe P. Coltrane," Mark retorted. "Besides, I might have been fat, but at least I knew better than to ride my dirt bike on the highway."

"I guess so."

A cold wind howled across the sidewalk, sending tiny tornados of fallen maple leaves scurrying across the street.

"Sorry, Horace. Just—you knew I was sensitive about my weight back then. I guess I still am."

"Hey, Mark. Bet you don't know that Abby has a crush on you."

Mark's brain traveled backwards on a highway of memories, grasping for a face to place with the name. Abby ... Abby? Abby Maguire? Ah, he remembered her now. She always wore a long, braided ponytail, ashamed of her curly golden hair because of the attention it received from all the old ladies at church.

"That's her," Horace said.

Mark frowned. "You're reading my mind?"

I'm not mind reading. That's her right over there.

Mark looked around and then down at Horace. Horace pointed silently to a bloodied girl of twelve at the corner of Vine and First.

She waved and hopped over on one leg to where they stood. Her other leg hung limply, mangled, broken at excruciating angles, with shards of bone sticking through torn bits of flesh.

"Hi, Mark," the little ghost said, a blush affecting her bluish, pale cheeks. She wore a powder-blue summer dress and frilly socks that matched.

"Hello?" Mark began to feel queasy as he recalled how Abby Maguire's life had come to an end. It was during their sixth grade year. She, too, had been struck down by a semi while crossing U.S. 421-80 after visiting his house. The parking lot for Big Branch Baptist Church was on the other side of the highway, three houses down from granny's. Abby had liked to walk to church with his older brother. Somebody, perhaps her mother, or perhaps a friend, had called out "Hello," not knowing they were calling Abby to a sudden, gruesome, and truly terrible death. Her attention distracted from the road, she didn't have a chance to see what hit her.

Had she even felt the impact? Mark shook his head to clear out such dreadful thoughts.

I did. It hurt so bad, Mark. The last thing I remember thinking was how sad Mommy would be.

"Okay, you two have to stay out of my head!" Mark yelled, pressing his hands to his ears. More people began watching him. A few others pointed, while a street cop began to take notice.

"Why are you here?" Mark asked Abby, calmer.

"I want a candy bar," she said.

Mark rolled his eyes. "I'm going mad."

"I told him," Horace whispered to Abby.

Abby's eyes bulged as she gave Horace a playful light swat. "He knows? Already?"

"Not that. Not yet."

Mark stopped. "Not what? Tell me, now."

"Not until we get our sweets," Abby chided.

They turned the corner at the intersection. The pharmacy's bright storefront beckoned them like the witch's candy house.

The wind gusted, and again Mark shivered, the addition of a second ghost child chilling the autumn to unseemly cold temperatures. His hair, once thawing, began to freeze again.

"I have a crush on you," Abby said.

Mark regarded Abby with abject horror. As she skipped along beside them, her stomach split open and her bowels began sliding out through the hole. He thought his brain might explode as it worked overtime to reconcile the sickening appearance of these two dead children. How do you respond to such a statement from an entity? Were these two even real, or was this only some nightmare expelling the darker memories of his childhood?

"I always ... I mean, I like you, too, Abby."

"Like? That's not the same as a crush, is it, Horace?" Abby asked.

"Nope," Horace said.

A homeless man leaned against the pharmacy's front wall. He sipped at something from a bag. He looked at Mark.

"Mister, perhaps a drink. You look like you're having a hell of a day."

Mark motioned the man away. "Go away. I don't have a dollar to give."

Abby's intestines unraveled as they approached the pharmacy. Five feet, ten feet, fifty feet of intestines had spooled from her belly after a piece hooked on a tree root jutting from of the sidewalk. A sharp angle on the root had ripped open the organ, and viscous brown fluid oozed from the puncture.

A golden retriever appeared and started gnawing on the rope of entrails. The threesome stopped and watched. Grimacing, Mark told Horace and Abby to stay put and he jogged toward the animal.

"Get on out of here, stinking mutt!" Mark kicked at the dog

but missed.

"I wouldn't do that," Horace called out. "Remember what Granny always said about upsetting the spirits."

"Christ, no, not another one," he cried.

Then a heartbreaking twinge of recognition hit him. He started laughing. Tears of happiness formed in the corner of his eyes.

"Baxter, is that you?"

The dog dropped the intestines and looked up.

It is *Baxter*, Mark thought.

"Hey buddy, how you doing?"

The dog jumped up and licked Mark in the face, replacing tears with slobber. Mark rubbed the dog's belly and back. He embraced his old pet in his arms.

Then he remembered. It was the day he left for college. *We'll take good care of him, son*, his mom had said. When he had returned home three months later for Thanksgiving holiday, Baxter was dead—run over and killed by a semi on the highway.

I fed him, and then he ran off to eat Granny's dinner scraps she leaves out for him. I'm so sorry, Mark. Mom had been so remorseful.

"Come on, boy, let's get you a treat."

Mark led the dog back to the other waiting ghosts. Horace and Abby giggled like the children they still were, playfully ruffling Baxter's back and belly. The sound was joyous and innocent in the way only children could be. Mark herded the strange group inside the pharmacy as fast as he could and found the promised sweets in aisle three and doggy snacks in aisle five.

He stepped up to the counter and cleared his throat. He needed to hurry. A weary pharmacist came forward to assist him, bifocals hanging precariously from the man's nose.

"What can I do you for?"

Mark dropped the items he'd picked up from the aisles—

lollipops for Horace, a box of chocolates for Abby, and a doggy treat for Baxter—to the countertop.

"That'll be eleven-forty-three."

He handed the pharmacist twelve dollars. "They're for my friends," Mark said, motioning behind him to Horace, Abby, and Baxter.

"Oh, yeah?" The pharmacist scanned the store, looking left, then right. "Hey friend, like a fifth of Bald Knob bourbon with that?"

"No, thanks."

The pharmacist gave Mark his change and went back to organizing his shelves of drugs.

The group rushed outside, and Mark handed out the goodies. Horace jumped for joy, flicking blood and brains over everybody. Abby nearly cried when she received her box of candy, ripping it open and swallowing down two chocolate bourbon balls at once. Baxter yelped in excitement as he tore into a doggy treat. For a moment, the world was no longer surreal, but somehow—well—normal, and Mark felt happy.

Speeding down Main Street, a city bus roared past, obliterating all sound, sending a dusty, hot gush of air over Mark's body. His eyes closed, as usual, just a fraction too late, and he tried to rub the sandy grit from them, just like he had as a child whenever a vehicle went past on U.S. 421-80. Mark opened his eyes to find that his three ghost companions had vanished and that he'd wandered into the street.

I'm sorry, Mark, Horace said in Mark's mind. *I meant to tell you to not to go near the road tonight ... but I really wanted a lollipop, and then I forgot..."*

"What?"

For a brief moment he was airborne. He landed. The road scraped all the flesh from the right side of his face as his body slid to a stop. Mark's left arm rolled into a storm drain. The right had popped out of its socket and was twisted behind him.

Mark's gaze fixed on the bright headlights of a semi. His consciousness ebbed away.

Sands of Time
E. C. Seaman

It was my eldest daughter May who first saw The Grey Lady, on the very day we moved, while we were still a mess of packing boxes and sticky tape and crumpled newspaper. Baby Tessa was bouncing in my belly just waiting to be born, the reason we were moving to this larger house.

"There's an old lady in our new house," little May announced importantly. "She was knitting something and smiling at me."

Well, of course I instantly waddled off to check and found the sitting room completely empty except for our carelessly dumped furniture. The sofa was still swathed in plastic sheeting, and there was no sign that anyone, other than the removal men, had ever been in there.

I laughed and tried to downplay my disquiet, and then I distracted May by sending her out into the huge new garden to explore. Funny little May; she was always such a serious child. For several weeks before we moved she had been grumpy and contrary and quite unlike her usual sunny self, so I didn't want to question her further; to keep pressing the issue.

But it niggled at me; May was far too young to make up a story like that for attention, and anyway, she was never that kind of child. Tessa, when she got to that age, was airier, more fanciful— she would leave acorns as tiny cups for the fairies in the rockery and could easily have become caught up in her own stories. But not May. Thankfully though, May seemed calmer after that day, reassured perhaps that all her beloved teddies and precious possessions had moved with her, and she revelled in the acres of garden and our new house's proximity to the seashore.

It didn't end there though, and though Bryn privately christened our visitor 'The Grey Lady' and made a big joke of it, as if she were a dubious ancestress haunting a stately home, well, what on earth else could she be? At least if she were a spirit, we soon came to realise that she was a benign one, a silent, hazy yet reassuring presence who would appear at precisely those times when we needed her most.

Today I'm in a reminiscing, nostalgic sort of mood and can almost feel the years slipping through my fingers, like the sand on the beach sliding between my toes, silky and elusive. It's funny, when I look back at my life; having children didn't turn out at all how I expected it would be. When the girls were small, I used to gaze at them in bewilderment and wonder—how had I created these little spitfires? I don't mean that to sound as if I'm not proud of my girls. It's just that they have always been so astonishing; so instantly themselves and not merely the tiny versions of me I had dreamily anticipated while pregnant. They were not placid little curly blonde moppets but as dark-haired and passionate and fiercely Welsh as my Bryn, and though I adore them, it wasn't always easy, living with their rows and tears and tantrums. I used to lie awake worrying about every new step of their lives, fretting about each new hazard to be negotiated, and I would love to be able to go back and reassure my younger self that despite it all, my daughters would turn out just fine.

The Grey Lady saw it all. Every argument, every drama; from childishly scraped knees to first boyfriends and broken hearts. She even came to witness my shame, possibly the only one who knew. Today is the first time I've let myself dwell on that much-regretted episode for oh, so many years; certainly the first time I've thought about it since the dark days after Bryn died. The whole sordid little affair was such a dreadful cliché, after all. I had started an art class to stave off my boredom, and before I knew it, a few intimate moments with the sympathetic tutor escalated into furtive kisses and lunchtime assignations. We were all having troubles then, there is no doubt of that—Bryn had been working too long and too hard and the girls were growing up so fast that I was questioning myself. I no longer knew my role, my place in their world, and I felt the sands shift beneath my feet.

The Grey Lady came to me in the kitchen one evening as I was preparing the girls' lunchboxes and concocting a hasty alibi for visiting my lover. The Lady said nothing; she just looked at me, and her expression was so knowing, so sad. She reminded me of my mother then, just a hint around the eyes, though unlike me, my mother had never grown old enough to acquire grey hair. But something about the Lady, perhaps that reminder of what Mother would have thought of my behaviour, gave me a warning; made me pause. Bryn, very sensibly, never asked why I suddenly gave up my much-loved watercolour classes, and the storm passed over us, in time.

Now that I really picture her, I remember the Lady wore something very like the dress I've got on today; a jaunty, rainbow-striped number that for once I bought myself without needing persuasion from the girls. The moment I saw it in the shop it felt familiar, though it's taken these memories to make me realise why. I've been wearing it today to cheer myself up, and I've been thinking about Tessa, dreaming of her baby and longing to be with her when it is born. She hasn't yet decided whether to have it at home or hospital—I must ask her when she gets here.

All these recollections—so many things I haven't let myself think about until today. I generally keep myself too busy to brood, but this unaccustomed spell of inactivity is making me relive it all so vividly, and the room spins before my eyes. Lying here, I can just glimpse the old-fashioned kitchen timer the girls always found so intriguing. It was the one I used to time my contractions when I went into labour, the measure for soft-boiling their teatime eggs, the tool to teach them what 'wait a minute' really felt like, as the pale pink sand slid inexorably from one teardrop to the next. Curious May, ever the scientific one, always wanted to see the sand run uphill again.

"The sands of time can't flow backward," I said, but it took Bryn several weeks of patient explanation and many careful diagrams to convince her of that.

The last time I saw the Grey Lady was when Bryn died. That was a bad time; the very worst. His death was so sudden, so unexpected, so damned unfair. He was barely six months into the retirement he'd craved, so he didn't live to see May graduate or Tessa pregnant at last. Awful. Oh God, I can feel the tears start to my eyes as I remember. Oh Bryn, my dear love ... I didn't know how to go on without him, after all those years together. But then one night I woke and sensed the Lady sitting in the darkness, in the shadows beside my bed, and she reached out her hand with such understanding, such compassion, such devastation ... I'm sure there were tears in her eyes, too. It shocked me, but it also helped, a little.

Time doesn't heal all wounds. I couldn't stand the sound of the clock ticking in the hall after Bryn went; it seemed to be counting out the days, and not gently, like the sand slipping away. Some days still drag, it is true, and then other days it seems a mere moment since we moved here. But we've all come so far. Dear May is a junior doctor already, so busy and tired, yet always trying to make time for her poor old mum. And my Tessa now has time on her hands; she's counting down the precious days until she becomes a mother herself.

The Grey Lady was always there for us. I look back at all her visits and can see every one as clearly as if they were happening here and now. I was sitting on the sofa this afternoon, just before I fell, knitting a tiny jacket for Tessa's soon-to-be baby, and I swear that I could see little May walking into the room, just the age she was on that very first day we moved here. But I shouldn't have been able to see her, should I? I'm confused; I wasn't there. No, it's not me sitting there; it's Her, The Grey Lady. But still, here is little May, and she's talking to me, or to *Her*. Bless May, all wide-eyed and curious; she's much too young to be afraid.

"Is this your house?" she says to me inquisitively. "Because we'll leave if you want us to go. I don't want to live here anyway; I want to go back to my old home."

"This is a nice place," I say. "You'll find it's a very happy house."

"But I don't want to leave all my friends behind," she says plaintively.

I never knew that. I didn't understand until now quite how vulnerable she was; how scared of moving on. Her lip quivers, but she juts out her chin; my brave little girl doesn't want to cry in front of this old lady, this stranger.

"But there's a beautiful garden here, and you'll enjoy being so close to the sea," I say gently.

She looks at me suspiciously and whispers, "That's exactly what my mummy says."

And then I know. I realise that the Grey Lady has been *me* all along; that I have been reaching back through the years. I smile and stretch out my hand to May, knowing that the love I feel will carry me back to my tiny girl and give her the reassurance she so needed on that day.

That love for your children is so unlike anything else; it is so strong that you would walk into fire, punch through glass with your bare hands, do anything, absolutely anything, to keep them from feeling the slightest pain. You'd rather bleed yourself than see your children cry. And yet sometimes there is nothing you can do but watch and wait and be there for them. And sometimes, like today, you have to wait for them to come for you.

I do hope the ambulance comes soon; it's getting very cold here, lying on the kitchen floor. My hip must have shattered when I fell, for every movement, even breathing, sends spears of pain through me, and my head! Oh, how my head hurts.... But I know I can hold on, if I will myself to. I can hold on until Tessa and May come to me, until help arrives. It's that yearning, the need to see my girls again, to see my first grandchild born. Oh, yes, that love will carry me through the years as if they were yesterday, and stretch these minutes into a lifetime.

There's a knock at the door. And the sands of time shiver...

About the Authors

Rob E. Boley earned his B.A. and M.A. from the English Department at Wright State University. He lives in Dayton, Ohio, with his wife, daughter, and three cats. His short fiction has appeared in *Leaf Garden* and *A capella Zoo*. He is currently working on a novel. For more information, visit him online at www.facebook.com/rob.boley.

Jack Bowdren is a working writer living in Manchester, UK.

Scott Brendel is the author of "The Seventh Green at Lost Lakes," which appeared in *Read by Dawn, Volume 1*. Ramsey Campbell called the story "…satisfyingly grisly… the kind of fun in the sun Sam Raimi might have had in his less respectable days." Scott also wrote "The House Beneath Delgany Street," which appeared in *Subtle Edens*, an anthology nominated for a 2009 British Fantasy Award. Scott lives along the Front Range of the Colorado Rocky Mountains, where he is at work on a novel.

Lawrence Conquest is a British author who has sold stories to various magazines (including *Black Static, Crossed Genres, A Thousand Faces*), anthologies (*Sick Things, Night Terrors, Pellucid Lunacy*), comicbooks (*FutureQuake, Something Wicked*) and audiobooks (*Doctor Who Short Trips, Big Finish Productions*). Full bibliography at www.lawrence-conquest.blogspot.com. He is also a member of three bands, is studying for two degrees, and attempting to hold down a full time job. "A Day at the Beach" is based on a true story.

Rebecca Fraser is an Australian author based on the Gold Coast in Queensland. She has a keen interest in horror, dark and speculative fiction...and anything that goes bump in the night. Her short stories and poems have appeared in various genre publications and she is currently working on a novel-length manuscript. To provide her muse with life's essentials, Rebecca supplements by freelance writing for the corporate/professional world...however, her true passion lies in disturbia!

J. M. Heluk is an affiliate member of The Horror Writers Association (HWA) and has been published alongside Jack Ketchum, Poppy Z. Brite, Joe R. Lansdale, Robert Weinberg, Owl Goingback and other great authors.
And this tale, as every tale born before it, is dedicated to Monty. Rest in piece, my dearest friend.

Harper Hull. An Englishman by luck, Harper now lives in the Southern US (with his Dixie wife) penning horror, sci-fi, existential drama and other writings whenever he can. Inspired by his dad's 'scary bookshelf' as a kid and later by an education in the classics, Harper reads like a demon and gets his own ideas from the strange and surreal things that happen in everyday life. His stories have appeared in N. America and Europe with fine publishing houses such as Comet Press, The Penny Dreadful Company and Northern Frights Publishing.

Davin Ireland was born and bred in the south of England but currently resides in the Netherlands. His fiction credits include stories published in over fifty print magazines and anthologies on both sides of the Atlantic, including *Aeon, Underworlds, The*

Horror Express, Zahir, Neo-Opsis, Rogue Worlds, Storyteller Magazine and Albedo One. You can visit his site at http://members.ziggo.nl/d.ireland

Lorna D. Keach is a horror writer and humorist from Manhattan, Kansas. Her stories have appeared in several publications, including *The Willows, Dog Oil Press, Theatre of Decay, AlienSkin, and Necrotic Tissue;* she's also a staff contributor for DarkMarkets.com. She lives in Lawrence, KS with her husband and one irritable cat.

Scott Lininger is a dad, entrepreneur, and mystery enthusiast who lives near Boulder, Colorado. When not programming 3D software for Google he occasionally uses the computer as a typewriter. His fiction has been sold to the likes of *The Battered Suitcase, Flash Fiction Online, Everyday Weirdness, Powderburn, Resident Aliens, Wretched Moments Anthology, and Short Story Me.* More info available at www.scottlininger.com.

Chad McKee is a biologist by day and author of short stories and poetry by night. His contributions have been published in the anthologies *2012 AD, The Best of House of Horror (2009), and The Garden of Life.* He has also published scientific articles in a variety of medical journals. He is an American Southerner who currently lives in Oxford, England.

Gregory Miller's stories have appeared in a number of national publications over the last few years. His first collection, *Scaring the Crows: 21 Tales for Noon or Midnight,* was published in 2009 by StoneGarden.net Publishing, and has garnered positive attention from such luminary authors as Piers Anthony, Brad Strickland, and Ray Bradbury, who recently wrote, "Gregory Miller is a fresh new talent with a great future." A high school English teacher in addition to a writer, Miller lives in Pittsburgh with his wife and two young sons.

John Jasper Owens lives in the South and was not named after the painter, although thank you for your concern. When not fending off satire groupies, he shamelessly attempts to raise enough money to get married by offering unpublished fiction and humor at low, low prices.

Aaron Polson was born on the Ides of March: a good day for him, unlucky for Julius Caesar. He currently lives in Lawrence, Kansas with his wife, two sons, and a tattooed rabbit. To pay the bills, Aaron attempts to teach high school students the difference between irony and coincidence. His stories have featured magic goldfish, monstrous beetles, a book of lullabies for baby vampires, and other oddities. *The House Eaters*, a YA Dark Fantasy, is due from Virtual Tales in 2011. You can visit Aaron on the web at www.aaronpolson.com.

Mark Rigney is the author of the play *Acts of God* (Playscripts, Inc., 2008) and the non-fiction book *Deaf Side Story: Deaf Sharks, Hearing Jets and a Classic American Musical* (Gallaudet University Press, 2003). His short fiction has been nominated for a Pushcart Prize and appears in *The Best of the Bellevue Literary Review, Talebones,* and *Lady Churchill's Rosebud Wristlet*, among many others. An upcoming trilogy is slated to begin in *Black Gate* #17. His website, with links to many of his original stories, is www.markrigney.net.

Daniel R. Robichaud lives and writes in southern Texas. A few blue bonnets populate his wife's garden, and he keeps a wary eye on them. He is a featured scribe for *Dark Scribes Magazine* and keeps a semi-regular blog at http://dark-towhead.livejournal.com

Trent Roman is a writer from Montréal with an interest in all types of fiction strange and unusual in addition to academic interests in archaeology, anthropology, history and a number of other fields. He is fascinated by what makes people tick at both the intimately personal level and the sweeping societal level, and enjoys every opportunity to pursue such questions through the means of fiction.

Emma Seaman lives between the moors and the sea in South West England and is intrigued and inspired by that wild and beautiful scenery. An award-winning short story writer, she is currently editing a 'modern gothic' thriller novel, set in the world of celebrity lookalikes. She apologises for the absence of terror in her tale, but fervently hopes that any spirits she may encounter prove to be equally benign... To discover more, please visit www.emmaseaman.co.uk

Jason Sizemore is an editor, publisher, and writer from Lexington, KY. He owns and operates Apex Publications. His most recent work can be found in *Dark Discoveries* and the Stoker-winning *Writers Workshop of Horror*.

Adam Walter is a native of the Pacific Northwest and lives with his wife and daughter in Washington state's Puget Sound region. His fiction has appeared previously in *Supernatural Tales*, and more will surface soon in the Paroxysm Press flash anthology *100 Lightnings* and in *Fungi* #20.

Lee Clark Zumpe, a proofreader and entertainment columnist for Tampa Bay Newspapers, earned a bachelor's degree in English at the University of South Florida. He lives a few miles from the Gulf of Mexico with his wife and daughter.

Lee's inclination toward horror manifested itself early in his childhood when he began flipping through the pages of Forrest J. Ackerman's *Famous Monsters of Filmland* and reading Gold Key Comic classics like *Boris Karloff Tales of Mystery* and *Grimm's Ghost Stories*. His short stories and poetry have appeared in a variety of publications such as *Weird Tales, Space and Time* and *Dark Wisdom* and in the anthologies *Horrors Beyond, Corpse Blossoms* and *Cthulhu Unbound, Vol. 1*.

Visit http://muted-mutterings-of-a-mad-poet.blogspot.com.